The Wolves of Fireborn Pack

Fated Bonds

USA TODAY BESTSELLING AUTHOR

GENEVIEVE JACK

Fated Bonds: The Wolves of Fireborn Pack Book 1
Copyright © 2023 Carpe Luna Publishing
Published by Carpe Luna, Ltd., Bloomington, IL 61704

**Portions of this story were previously published under the title VICE.*

First EDITION: July 2023

eISBN: 978-1-940675-89-3
PAPERBACK: 978-1-940675-90-9

V1.1

ABOUT THIS BOOK

No one comes between a wolf and their fated mate.

Werewolf Laina Flynn has been dodging pressure to mate for years. The successful veterinarian may be Fireborn pack royalty, but she's happy to leave raising pups to her alpha brother Silas. So when a human triggers her mating instinct, no one is more surprised than her.

As the face of Hunt Club, Kyle Kingsley is no stranger to doing things out of obligation and responsibility. The public demands that he uphold the lifestyle the club has come to embody, even if his playboy persona is all a lie. No surprise then that Kyle volunteers to care for his recently deceased father's dog, even if the mutt is roughly the size of a barn. But when he lands in the clinic of Dr. Laina Flynn, her presence draws out something wild and untamed within him that has nothing to do with his new pet.

An act of violence on Fireborn shifting grounds drives Laina into hiding... and into Kyle's arms. Instant attraction develops into something more when fated bonds challenge everything.

ONE

D r. Laina Flynn navigated to the examination room on autopilot, her stomach rumbling. Who had time to stop for lunch when you were running Carlton City's busiest and most trusted veterinary clinic? Four Paws Animal Hospital was the type of state-of-the-art facility you'd expect to find associated with a university veterinary program, not a rural town in New Hampshire. But Laina had the resources and know-how to bring the best in veterinary medicine to the area, and she had the passion to ensure her patients' unsurpassed care.

"What's going on with Milo?" she asked, shouldering open the door with her eyes fixed on the chart of the one-year-old English Mastiff her assistant, Becca, had wedged into the schedule at the last minute. Milo was not a regular patient, but it was obvious the dog needed her help. He barely raised his head to greet her as she approached the examination table where Becca easily held the 160-pound canine in place. The mastiff was clinically lethargic.

"He's been sick since Tuesday afternoon," a deep male voice said.

"Tuesday? This has been going on for three days?" Laina positioned her stethoscope to listen to the dog's heart and lungs. Typical. Too many owners let their animals suffer in hopes of avoiding veterinary bills. For Milo's sake, she prayed to the goddess it was nothing serious. She palpated his abdomen. The organs were normal, but the skin of his belly was covered in an itchy-looking rash. When she moved the assessment to Milo's head, she found dry eyes and nose, and the capillary refill rate in his gums was much too slow. "He's dehydrated. Has he been vomiting?"

"Once or twice."

"Is he eating and drinking?"

"I think so."

"What are you feeding him?"

"ButcherBits."

"Ah. Has he been scratching a lot?"

"Constantly. How did you know?"

"I think Milo has a corn allergy. Switch to something grain free. No peas or lentils, though. Avoid anything generic. Will that be a problem? I might have some samples to get you started." She scribbled some notes to herself on Milo's chart. When the man didn't say anything, Laina raised her head and looked directly at Milo's owner for the very first time.

For a second, her mind blanked, her synapses shouting in unison, *all power to the visual cortex!* The eye candy standing in her examination room was best described as sin covered in chocolate sauce, poured into a pair of blue jeans and a trendy dress shirt. Polished, she thought. More polished than the usual pet owner who graced her halls. Groomed dark brown hair, physique developed enough to pass as a professional athlete, and eyes the golden color of ripe wheat—hazel, she supposed, with uneven chocolate-

and-evergreen pigment dispersion that made her wonder if he suffered from a mild case of sectoral heterochromia. She caught herself leaning across Milo for a closer observation.

Rarely, if ever, did looks alone stir something inside Laina. As a werewolf, she was no stranger to attractive men. Her kind enjoyed genetically fast metabolisms and above-average muscle mass. Even an out-of-shape werewolf carried the appearance of a fit human. Besides, Laina was the type of woman to be attracted to brains over brawn. She'd once enjoyed a passionate affair with a height-challenged professor of archaeology during her university days. Still, one look at Milo's owner and the wolf inside her got to her paws and panted like she was in heat.

Curious, Laina took a deep breath through her nose, theorizing that perhaps he *was* a shifter, wolf or otherwise. Could the stirring in her lower abdomen simply be her inner animal sensing a playmate? But after sorting through the odors of dog and disinfectant, all her hypersensitive nose detected was the scent of human with a hint of cedar and pine needles. Had he been on a long walk through the deep forest recently?

"Are you okay?" Becca whispered, nudging her arm.

"Hmm?" Laina blinked rapidly, breaking the spell. "Oh, oh yes, of course." She cleared her throat, but her gaze snapped back to Milo's owner as if he carried a Laina-charged magnet in his chest.

He reached for her face with one knuckle in an oddly intimate way, and her breath caught. "I think you have something in your hair."

"Excuse me?" Her lashes fluttered again.

Becca ripped a paper towel from the roll they always kept on the desk and handed it to her. "Looks like you might have a leftover from your surgery this morning, Doctor," she murmured.

Laina took the paper towel and turned toward the small mirror above the hand-washing station. There, in her untamed mahogany waves, was a blob of congealed blood. How it got there, she wasn't sure. She'd worn a cap during the surgery itself. Maybe when she was cleaning up her operating room? Frantically, she wiped it out as best she could, then turned back to the owner, face blazing. Her ears had to be the color of ripe tomatoes by now.

"Had to operate on an intestinal blockage in a Rottweiler this morning." She tittered nervously. "I carry a little bit of each of my patients with me always." She laughed harder, mortified when her inhale morphed into a snort. *Crap. This is a veterinary hospital not a sports bar. Pull yourself together!* With another rapid blink, she tucked her hair behind her ear and refocused on Milo. "So...corn-free food. Will that be a problem?"

"Cost is no object," he said in a gruff voice. Oh good lord, he was sexy. *Don't look, Flynn. He'll burn your retinas like the sun.*

She exchanged glances with Becca, whose expression promised she'd position Laina on the table next to Milo if she didn't snap out of it. Why wasn't her assistant swooning at the knees over this guy?

Clearing her throat, Laina said in her most professional tone, "I want to run some blood tests to rule out other, more serious conditions. Is Milo up-to-date on his immunizations?"

"I'm not sure," the man murmured. "His last owner... had an emergency, and I agreed to take him in."

"Wait, this isn't your dog?"

"He is now. I adopted him...Tuesday. We're on our way

home. I was just worried about him and didn't think this could wait."

"Smart. It can't. How far is home?"

"A day's drive."

She rubbed the mastiff's ears and looked long and hard into the dog's big brown eyes. As a werewolf, Laina could communicate dog-to-dog through smell, sound, and body position, but those things weren't as specific as human words. For example, by the vacant emptiness behind Milo's pupils, she could tell that he'd been through a distressing experience recently. But she couldn't read his mind and had no idea what that experience was. Whatever his last owner's emergency, it had left its mark on Milo in more ways than simply adjusting to a new owner.

"Can you give him twenty-four hours here? I'll administer some IV fluids and run a few blood tests. If all goes well, he should be good to go tomorrow."

The man retrieved his phone from his back pocket and stared at his calendar app for the better part of a minute. Even from across the examination table, Laina could see he was booked solid. Would he clear that mess of a schedule for a dog he'd owned a couple days?

"If you think that's what he needs, I'll plan to spend the night in Carlton City."

"I do," she said softly, her heart warming. Attractive and an animal lover.

He stroked a hand over Milo's side. "Okay. Do what you need to do."

"Perfect. We'll get started." She helped Becca get Milo off the table and through the door to the procedure room. "If you'd like to wait out front, Becca will check you out and take your number so we can contact you when he's ready."

"Actually..." The man scratched the back of his head, the deep forest scent filling her nostrils once again.

That was definitely pine and cedar. An outdoorsy type, just like her. Well, not just like her. He didn't sprout a nose and tail during the full moon. Had he been hiking? Fishing?

"I was hoping I could take you to dinner," he blurted, shifting from foot to foot. "I don't know anyone in Carlton City, and since I'll be here tonight waiting on Milo, I thought... It would be nice to have some company if you're interested." The man tucked a hand into a back pocket in a way that was both casual and endearing. Was it possible to be jealous of someone else's hand?

It took her a second to process what he was asking. "Sorry, what?"

"Dinner. Would you like to eat with me?" He cocked an unbelievably sexy eyebrow.

"Are you asking me out?" The question erupted from her mouth with an unpleasant aftertaste. She'd blurted out the words as though his invitation had annoyed her. She wasn't annoyed; she was flabbergasted.

"I'd love to hear what you know about raising a mastiff." He gave a breathy laugh, rubbing his slightly stubbled chin.

Ah, that was it. He needed advice on the new dog. Made sense and explained his interest in her. "Sure. Why not?"

"Around seven?"

"Seven it is!" She bobbed her head awkwardly.

"I saw a place called Valentine's driving into town. Is it good?"

"The best. I'll meet you there. We can stop back here to check on Milo afterward."

"It's a date," he said, opening the door that led to the waiting room.

Her heart jumped slightly at the word *date*, and she quickly reminded herself he was just passing through town. This wasn't a *real* date. "I didn't even catch your first name," she said before he could leave. "It's not on the chart."

"Kyle." His hazel eyes crinkled slightly at the corners when he smiled. "Nice to meet you, Dr. Flynn."

"Laina." She scratched the side of her cheek, catching a glimpse of fingernails badly in need of a manicure. She stuffed her hand into her pocket.

He nodded. "See you at seven, Laina."

TWO

Three days earlier...

Kyle Kingsley stared at his brother Nate across their father's failing body and tried to deal with all the awkward and uncomfortable going on inside his chest. Holed up in a cabin in the middle of nowhere, Kyle had more questions than answers about the man who'd brought him into this world but had spent so little effort seeing him through it. Only, the time for questions was long gone.

"The lawyers are meeting on the Tanaka deal tomorrow. They'll want to revise the paperwork. Dad's name will be replaced by mine unless you have a problem with that." Nate's dress shirt and tie clashed with the general rustic appeal of the cabin but perfectly matched the brash ambition in his eyes.

"You mean, will I contest your claim to the throne?" Kyle shifted forward in his chair, his eyes falling on the dog who'd stayed curled by his father's side for two days now.

Fuck, the thing was gigantic. *What the hell were they going to do with the dog?*

"Play to your strengths, Kyle. You're the face of Hunt Club. Do you think for a second that if I had the clock-stopper you wear every day, I'd want to do what I do? Hell no. You've always been the beauty. I've always been the brains. Do you think the public wants to see this ugly mug when they think of an adult lifestyle brand?" He pointed to his own face. "We need your billion-dollar abs. Leave the desk-jockeying to me and enjoy the good life as nature intended."

"The good life? Hmm. Funny, it didn't seem so great when that redhead—what's her name?"

"Kate? From the New York agency."

"She tried to set me on fire."

Nate followed up his breathy snort with a shrug. "Red-heads." He ran a finger inside the neck of his tie, loosening it a few inches. "Kyle...the deal."

"The position is yours."

Nate smiled in that lippy, gaping way he did that always reminded Kyle of a filter-feeding whale shark, only instead of krill, his gaping maw collected entrepreneurial opportunities. He had to hand it to his brother—what Nate lacked in attractiveness, he made up for in cunning. Could premature hair loss be triggered by a hot-running brain?

"I'll call the transition team and have them prepare the necessary documents for overnight delivery."

"Two things. One, Dad's still alive. Two, we are in the middle of nowhere. Unless you plan to go medieval and have the lawyer send the papers by carrier pigeon, it's going to have to wait. Relax. There's no hurry." Hell, the tiny town of Red Grove had one grocery store, and it doubled as a bait and tackle shop.

"It won't be long, though. The doctor said any minute now." Nate's brown eyes shifted, fixing on their father's lumbering chest. "We should get the paperwork started."

Although the lip-smacking and carcass-circling didn't exactly surprise Kyle, his patience with his brother waned. Unrestrained ambition made for hasty decisions in the heat of the moment. Kyle preferred a more deliberate approach. Estranged or not, the man between them shared their DNA —one of the few things Kyle had in common with his brother. He deserved respect.

"I'd like to experience these last moments with our father minus the paperwork. It. Can. Wait." After everything, he couldn't exactly muster true grief for the loss of this man, but he did feel…something, if only regret that they'd never been a real family. He would have liked that. He wanted that.

Nate shifted in his chair. "Why do you think he chose to come out here to die anyway? I didn't even know this town was on the map. What's it called again?"

"Red Grove. I didn't know it existed either, but I think that was the point. He didn't want the public to see him like this."

"His will says no funeral. Nothing public. Does Red Grove even have a crematorium? What do we do with the body?"

Kyle nudged back his chair, the legs protesting with a rumbling screech against the wood floor. The dog lifted its massive head, brown eyes tracking Kyle as he circled to Nate's side of the bed. Despite his brother's considerable size, Kyle fisted Nate's collar and lifted him from his seat.

"I'm not going to say this again," he said in a low voice laced with menace. "Dad is still alive. As far as we know, he can still hear us. We'll handle the arrangements when the time comes. Until then, unless you want to talk about what few personal memories we have of him, shut the fuck up." He released his brother, who dropped into his chair as if his knees had gone out. Kyle returned to his own chair, his eyes shifting back to his father.

Nate spread his hands and shrugged. "Sorry." He did not sound sorry. Annoyed, but not sorry. Still, he hushed. The cabin grew quiet, aside from the deep, wet rattle of their father's breathing and the occasional whine of the four-legged beast lying at his side.

"Am I allowed to ask what we should do about the dog?" Nate tugged at his pant leg, clearly perturbed by Kyle's restrictions on the conversation.

Kyle reached out and stroked the dog's head. "His name is Milo."

"I can't have a dog. I'm allergic," Nate said. "We'll have to take him to the humane society."

"He's a 160-pound mastiff. No one is going to adopt this dog. Three-quarters of the population doesn't have a house big enough for this dog. Frankly, one fart and he could knock down the walls of this cabin."

Nate snorted. "*You* can't keep him. You're barely home. And I don't need to tell you the staff is not going to want to deal with a dog like this."

"Dad loved Milo."

"More than he loved either of us." Nate's nostrils flared. "Just another way for the old man to deliver one last jab to the balls."

"I'm keeping him," Kyle said definitively. The decision came as a surprise even to him, but it seemed right somehow.

"Don't be ridiculous. They'll never let you on the plane with that thing."

"I'll drive him back in my rental."

Nate scowled. "This is a bad idea, Kyle. You don't adopt a dog to fill the absentee-father-shaped hole in your heart."

Kyle let his eyes drift over his brother's stocky frame. "Better than filling it with peanut butter."

Nate flipped him the middle finger.

Silence settled between them again, interrupted only by their father's labored breaths. For once, even Nate had nothing to say. He crossed his arms and stared blankly at their father.

An unsettling scrape came from the direction of the front door, causing Milo to raise his head again. The canine gave one low *woof* but didn't find the noise concerning enough to leave the bed to investigate it. Kyle rubbed the tightening skin at the back of his neck. "What was that? Sounded like claws."

"Who knows? We're in the middle of the woods. Probably raccoons." Nate stood and stretched. "I'm going to grab a cup of coffee." He waddled toward the kitchen.

With a whimper, Milo laid his head back on the bed, staring at the old man with the single-minded intensity only man's best friend was capable of. Kyle scratched the dog behind the ears. "It'll be okay, Milo. I'll take care of you."

The quiet morphed into something even quieter, a silence that only came at the end of things when man and beast became equals and the last stroke on the portrait of a life was cast upon the canvas. No rattling breath filled the space between them. Kyle waited. His father's chest did not rise. It did not fall.

Kyle stood and, with two fingers, searched for a pulse.

And then he said good-bye.

THREE

"Becca, can you turn up the music?" Laina spread the incision she'd made in the belly of the spaniel on her operating table and skimmed the spay hook along the inside of the pup's abdominal wall. On her first two attempts, she'd caught the intestine instead of the uterus. She swore this dog was hiding its reproductive organs on purpose. Thankfully, as her assistant upped the volume on the Doja Cat tune blaring into the operating room, she found her surgical mojo. "Ah, there she is." She clamped the ovarian vessel and proceeded with the spay.

If she didn't hurry, she'd be late for her date with the mysterious Kyle. She'd never experienced anything like the moment she'd laid eyes on Kyle Kingsley. Her wolf had pressed against the inside of her skin the way it did when the full moon was about to rise, fur rubbing her inner flesh, bones stretching in his direction.

A werewolf's inner wolf was a second soul, a personality separate and distinct from her human mind, one that usually got its way only three days per month. It was common for wolves to have relationships with other wolves during the full moon, when their human counterparts were asleep. Those relationships didn't remain when the wolves were in human form. Likewise, human relationships rarely translated to wolf world. As far as Laina was aware, it was unheard of for an inner wolf to wake up and show attraction to a human. Laina had no idea what it meant, but she was bound and determined to find out.

"You seem distracted, Laina. Are you still thinking about Mr. Sexy Dog Owner?" Becca teased over the speaker. Laina caught her assistant's eye through the observation window and watched her curly brown hair bounce with her off-speaker giggles.

"Aren't you?" Laina asked incredulously, keeping her hands steady as she tied off the blood vessels to the ovaries and uterus before removing the lot. It was careful, delicate work. She prided herself on her execution of the procedure, one she'd perfected for ease of recovery.

"He was sexy if you like that chiseled, underwear-model, superhero look, but I got a whiff of stiff and pretentious. Did you see his watch? That thing cost more than my entire net worth. I bet he's warped. Rich guys are always warped."

"Maybe."

"Anyway, too clean-cut for my tastes. A man without a tattoo is like a hot dog without mustard."

"I don't want to hear about the way you like your wieners, Becca." Laina grinned. Becca's laughing face broke eye contact to answer the phone on the desk behind her. After a few heated words, she pressed the hold button before returning to the loudspeaker.

"Your older brother is on the phone. He says it's an emergency."

"Tell Silas I have a patient open on the table. I'll call him back in forty-five minutes."

"That's what I told him. He said it was a family emergency and if I didn't ask for your immediate attention, he'd see that I was fired."

Laina rolled her eyes as she continued the procedure. "You're not going to be fired. Tell my brother, if it's such an emergency, he can come to the clinic and talk to me in person. By the time he gets here, I'll be done."

"You got it." Becca turned back to the phone.

Laina continued her work. "You know," she whispered to the anesthetized spaniel, "you don't realize how lucky you are that puppies aren't in your future. Being part of a pack isn't all it's cracked up to be." She checked for bleeding, then began the arduous process of stitching the incision.

"Why the hell didn't you answer my call?" Silas said from the door to her surgical suite. *Fuck*, he must have been in the neighborhood.

"So help me God, Silas, if my patient gets an infection because you dragged your flea-ridden ass into my OR, you'll be next on my table. I'll have you neutered before you can say sepsis."

"I'm the alpha, sister. When I call, you answer." It was true that her older brother was alpha of Fireborn pack, and as such, she was obligated to obey his direct command. To be honest, it was why she regularly refused to answer the phone, instead leaving that task to Becca, whose humanity made her blissfully immune to pack hierarchy.

Until recently, despite his machismo, Silas had housed a soft heart for her and her younger brother, Jason. But Alex Ravien Bloodright changed all that. Three years ago, the rogue pack member had murdered their parents in cold blood, forcing Silas to become alpha of Fireborn pack before his time. As head of the largest pack in North America, the Fireborn alpha automatically became first alpha, the leader of the Lycanthropic Society, the council that led all werewolf packs. Grieving and orphaned, Silas was thrown into both roles overnight. He wasn't ready for either.

Alex was cruel and exceptionally deadly. Thanks to a dragon-scale amulet he'd stolen from a family of Siberian dragon fae, he'd wielded elemental magic similar to a warlock. He used it to slaughter pack leaders and force their packs to follow him. If Silas hadn't used his position as a detective to hunt Alex down and stop him last summer, all the members of the Lycanthropic Society would likely be dead, and every werewolf in North America would be forced to bow to a madman.

Technically, the threat wasn't even over. It had been more than two months since Silas had recovered Alex's body, and they still hadn't confirmed it was him and not Jonah, his Zafka—a doppelgänger used as a security detail for werewolf royalty.

Werewolves, as shifters, could change small things about their appearance at will, but with the help of the type of dark magic Alex had access to when he possessed the amulet, complete transformation was not only possible but could be permanent. After taking down Alex, Silas had wanted a DNA test to prove the body they thought was Alex's was actually his, which meant he'd needed a family member's cooperation. Alex's sister, a society member herself, was more than happy to oblige, but supernatural DNA testing took time.

Even Laina had to admit that was a good enough reason for her brother to adopt a more totalitarian leadership style. To keep the pack safe, Silas had to lead with an iron fist. It was understandable. She simply wanted no part of it. She envied the freedom of the human woman sitting at the front desk, blissfully unattached and unencumbered. Laina wanted a life free of both pack politics and Silas's over-reaching protection.

She wanted to be her own alpha.

Laina lifted her gaze to meet her brother's. "Seriously, Silas, I know you wouldn't risk the life of this sweet pup on my table unnecessarily. What is so important that it can't wait?"

"We confirmed the body we recovered from Silver Sparrow Mountain was Alex's."

Laina paused midstitch and released a relieved breath. "Alex is dead, then, without a doubt?"

A smile spread across Silas's scruffy face. "Sister was a match. It's him. He's dead."

She finished her last stitch, shaking her head. "You did it, Silas. If Mom and Dad were alive, they'd be so proud of you." She gave him a genuine smile.

"The society seems happy about it." He pushed his hands into the pockets of his blazer. "They're throwing a party in our honor tonight at Rivergate Manor, formal attire."

She groaned. "I can't go. I have a date."

"A date? With whom?"

"A guy."

"What guy? All the society members are going to be at the ball."

"Not a wolf."

"A human?" he scoffed. "Come on, Laina. Be serious. You can reschedule your playdate. This is part of your royal duty."

"You know how I feel about these things."

"Yes, I do. You hate being a princess. You think that because I'm the alpha, your involvement in the society isn't necessary. And you would prefer to simply live your life in the human world, only joining us for an obligatory run on Rivergate Manor's protected property three days a month."

"Exactly." She cleaned Ginger's stitches and applied a sterile dressing. "You're the heir. And frankly, even if something happened to you, Jason would get the crown—not me. I'm completely dispensable, and that's okay. I prefer it that way. I didn't spend eight years in school to leave veterinary medicine behind and raise a litter of werewolf pups."

Silas frowned. He opened his mouth as if to say something and closed it again. She backed off the anesthesia and removed the intubation. Ginger whined softly. Laina whispered, "You're going to be fine, sweet girl."

"It's not all about you, you know," Silas said.

She straightened, gritting her teeth. "If my life isn't about me, who is it about?"

"The pack. Whether you like it or not, you are Fireborn royalty, which means the largest pack in North America looks to you for leadership. They also look to you to provide the future of the pack."

"You mean children."

"Royal children. You are a descendant of a primary family, a pureblood. The society is going to expect you to choose a suitor from within its ranks."

A drop of werewolf blood was enough to technically make someone a werewolf, but such a person might never shift. The greater the concentration of primary werewolf blood, the greater the chance of displaying werewolf qualities: strength, speed, ease of shifting, enhanced senses. Pureblood babies kept the pack strong and preserved the werewolf way of life. It was why mating with humans was discouraged.

"They expect the same of you, Silas, but I don't see you picking out your wedding tux. Hell, the last woman you dated wasn't even a werewolf." Her brother had dated a celestial fae for ages. Although the relationship was casual, he'd enjoyed her company regularly enough.

Silas scowled at being called out. "I can father children into my senior years. Your biological clock is ticking."

She scooped Ginger into her arms and carried her through the doors to the kennels they used for recovery. Silas followed, parking himself against the wall while she made the spaniel comfortable.

"I'm not marrying someone simply to appease society elders," she said. "I will marry who I please, and I will marry for love or not at all."

Silas drew a hand through his wild brown hair, his bushy eyebrows giving him an unquestionably wolfish appearance. "Listen, Laina, you know how this works. You can have something on the side. Marriage among werewolf royalty has often been more contractual in nature than anything else."

"No," she said.

"I could make you."

"You could, but you won't."

"I will if I have to."

"You won't because you know I'll hate you for the rest of my life. Don't risk losing one of the few people who loved you before you were alpha."

He stared at her, unblinking. "You don't realize how important you are to the pack. An alliance by marriage with another primary pack member would strengthen our numbers and our position in the society."

"Oh, I understand that."

"If you did, you'd never be this difficult."

She shrugged. "I understand. I just don't care. It has nothing to do with me. You don't need me. You are all the leader Fireborn will ever need. Alex's dead body proves that. *You* can marry to unite the packs. *You* can sire pups to fill our ranks. You don't need me."

He placed his hands on his hips, looking defeated. "You will attend the ball tonight. Seven o'clock. Formal dress. That is a direct order from your alpha."

She raised two fingers to her forehead and saluted him, ending the motion by flipping him her middle finger.

"And you will act like the princess you are." He gave her a smug grin before turning on his heel and leaving the room.

"Ooh! You asshole!" She stomped her foot. With a glance at her watch, she headed for the sink to wash up. She'd have to ask Becca to call Kyle and cancel their date. If she was going to make it to Rivergate Manor tonight, properly attired, she'd have to leave now to prepare. She couldn't be late, and she couldn't say no. Silas's direct alpha command meant she had no choice. If she tried to disobey, life would get extremely uncomfortable.

FOUR

The dress Laina wore to the ball was a style she'd never have chosen for herself. Stephanie, her Zafka, had picked it out for her. One of the benefits of having an employee who resembled you well enough to be your twin was that they could shop for your clothes. Laina was thankful Stephanie had made the time to obtain the dress on short notice, even if the midnight-blue strapless gown was more revealing than she preferred. Still, she understood the cut of the dress served a greater purpose than flattering her figure; it revealed the phoenix tattoo on her upper-right shoulder, the sacred emblem of Fireborn pack. Tonight, everyone at this party would proudly display their pack ties.

"Princess Laina? Is that you?" Evelyn, the matriarch of Crescent Star pack, adjusted her bifocals and reached out to grip Laina's right hand. "I expected to see a ring on this finger by now, dear. After the horrors of the last year, nothing would cheer this old soul like a royal wedding." Crescent Star had lost seven males to Alex before Silas had taken him down. Laina's heart ached for Evelyn's loss.

"I guess I just haven't met the right male," she said softly.

"Since when did that ever stop anyone?" Evelyn whispered. "Look around. Anyone in a tie would jump at the chance to have a beauty like you on his arm." She winked before crossing the veranda to enter the ballroom, passing Silas as he walked out to meet Laina.

"What did Evelyn want?" he asked.

"Nothing more than to dig for gossip."

"As if she doesn't have enough tales of her own to tell."

"What she wants is to have happy stories to talk about —something other than the tragedies that have been all too common among her pack. I can empathize, but she'd have better luck reading a romance novel than looking to my life for inspiration." Laina sighed.

"You look beautiful, by the way." Silas leaned against the open archway of Rivergate Manor's ballroom. "I love the hair."

"Stephanie did it." Laina shrugged. Her mahogany hair had been smoothed into a glamorous pomp with a high ponytail. Along with the mani-pedi and salt scrub she'd endured at Spa Stephanie, the hairstyle was enough to make her appear a proper princess.

"It suits you."

"Don't bother buttering me up. You're on my shit list, brother. How dare you alpha me here."

"Would you have come otherwise?"

"Of course not."

Silas stared into his glass, swirling his vodka and tonic. "Then, I did the right thing. It would look ungrateful if you didn't show. Like it or not, you're a princess. You have a duty to your race."

She groaned. "Silas..."

The tension between them was broken when Cameron James, her childhood friend turned alpha of Rivergate pack, tapped the side of his glass with a spoon. "If I could have your attention, please," he called from inside. "If everyone would join us in the ballroom, we'd like to toast our guests of honor."

"Where's Jason?" Laina asked.

"Already inside sniffing butts," Silas whispered.

"Crude."

"That's Jason." Their little brother was obsessed with the female of the species. Not one female. All females. The man bedded any woman, wolf or human, who would have him. The copulation was quick, and the relationships rarely lasted longer than the act itself. Still, she had to hand it to him; her little brother was always brutally up-front about his intentions, and thanks to a pretty face and his career as a highly successful venture capitalist, there was rarely a shortage of females interested in what he had to offer.

The ballroom of Rivergate Manor had been decked out in pale flowers and bright twinkle lights that perfectly complemented the stucco and ivory marble of the Italian palazzo-style mansion. Against this monochromatic backdrop, the colorful attire of the guests became like works of art: ruby, emerald, and sapphire swirling against heavenly white. Laina accepted a glass of champagne from a passing server and took her place beside Jason, slightly behind and to the left of Cameron. Silas stepped to Cameron's right side, in the true place of honor.

"Should we kneel before our brother-savior?" she groused to Jason.

"Hmm?" Her brother wasn't listening. He was staring across the ballroom at a blonde in a tight green dress.

"Stop staring," Laina said.

"Why? She's been catching my eye all evening."

"She's only seventeen," she singsonged in a whisper. "That's Cameron's little sister, Allie."

"How seventeen? Seventeen-almost-eighteen or…"

"Sixteen, just turned seventeen. Allie has only shifted once before. Just got her Rivergate tattoo. The last thing she needs is the complication of your stow-and-go dick. Plus, it's against the law."

"The human law."

"Your brother and alpha is a cop. Don't make me ask him to order you to leave her alone."

He drained his glass, the smell of bourbon filling her nostrils when he spoke again. "Relax, big sister. I'll leave her be. Plenty of other bitches in the doghouse."

"Gross."

"It's my responsibility as a royal male to sow my noble DNA. There isn't a woman in this place who'd turn me down."

"And that doesn't bother you?" She raised an eyebrow. "Spare me the DNA business. You'd have several litters of pups by now if you weren't being careful."

He straightened his bow tie. "Just keeping my equipment in good working order for when it *is* needed."

She rolled her eyes. Cameron raised his glass again, and the room went silent.

"We've come here tonight to honor Silas Flynn and the royal family of Fireborn pack. Just weeks ago, our common enemy threatened every wolf in this ballroom. Because of Silas, Alex Ravien Bloodright is dead and the amulet he used to gain power has been returned to the Siberian fae, restoring amicable relations between our communities. Please raise your glasses, and help me toast leader, alpha, and all-around hero, Silas Flynn."

Applause broke out in the expansive room, and Laina caught Jason wrinkling his nose as if he'd stepped in dog shit. *All-around hero?* He mouthed to her, left eyebrow raised. She stifled a giggle.

It wasn't easy living in Silas's shadow. No wonder her little brother was such a manwhore and she was a workaholic with no discernable personal life. At times like this, it was impossible not to feel like a pawn in a game she couldn't win.

"How long do you think we have to stay?" she whispered to Jason.

He chuckled. "Just long enough for Silas to have his ego properly stroked. And for me to find a woman who will properly stroke me."

She snorted despite herself.

"And now," Cameron continued, "Silas has given me the honor of kicking off the evening by joining his stunning sister, Laina, in a traditional folk dance."

Laina almost fell out of her shoes. In fact, she wobbled so violently that Jason had to steady her. Her glass tipped, spilling champagne.

Cameron approached and took what was left of the drink from her hand, passing it to one of the servants for safekeeping. "Are you okay?" he whispered. "You look like you might be ill."

"I'm fine. Silas neglected to tell me we were opening the show. You caught me off guard."

"Don't tell me you're nervous. We've been doing this dance since we were children."

"I remember."

"Please, Laina. You're the only partner I'm comfortable with." He lowered his lips to the back of her hand. They were warm and soft, too soft. Cameron was attractive. He had the long, lean physique that was typical of a werewolf and a face that belonged in a Hollywood blockbuster. But he was also gay. Blazingly gay with shooting rainbow stars that followed him everywhere. Gay enough that even his wolf had gay tendencies. He'd come out to her when they were both seventeen, trusting that their tight friendship could endure the shared secret. Of course, she'd accepted him fully and supported him throughout their young adulthood. Still, now that he was one of the society's most eligible bachelors, the steward of Rivergate Manor, and alpha of Rivergate pack, it was harder than ever for him to avoid suspicion. She was the only partner he could dance with because she was safe, a genuine and true pillar of support.

"I'd never turn down a dance with you. Lead the way." She collected herself, raising her chin and straightening her back. She hated Silas for forcing this on her, but she wouldn't take it out on her friend.

Cameron grasped her hand and led her to the center of the dance floor, where he pulled her against his body, free hand landing in the groove of her back. A string quartet in the corner of the room broke into a traditional folk song called "The Rose and Her Thorn." The dance they would perform was unique to their kind, similar to a tango but more violent. The movements told the story of star-crossed lovers entangled in a volatile affair, constantly teetering between the heat of passion and the fire of rage.

Cameron bent over her, dragging his teeth up the skin of her neck. Laina snaked her leg around his and shoved against his chest, following his big, dramatic steps backward across the floor. They'd practiced this dance hundreds of times as teens; she could do it in her sleep. Still, Cameron caught her twice when the height of her new heels caused her to miss a step. Despite the errors, when they ended with her dramatically sagging into his chest, a move that represented her death in the arms of her lover, the room erupted in applause.

"I'm glad you came tonight, Laina. You don't come to Rivergate Manor often enough," Cameron whispered in her ear as he helped her to her feet again.

"I was just here a few days ago for the shift. I'm here once a month for the full moon."

"But I miss your nonfurry friendship."

"I'm only as far as my animal hospital in Carlton City. Come in any time. I'll stick a thermometer up your ass and check you for fleas."

He chuckled. "It's nice to have you around. You don't know how dark things have been here because of Alex."

"You're too close to the politics. You need to find a vocation outside the pack. It's important to self-protect."

"Hard to do when you're the alpha responsible for maintaining safe shifting grounds." When she paused to think about it, Cameron's position was more limiting than her own. As owner of Rivergate Manor, he was ultimately responsible for the mansion and its surrounding acres of protected woods—the perfect place to exercise their monthly curse without interfering with humans. Cameron had become alpha the same way Silas had; his parents had been murdered at the same time and place, shot to death in a crowded theater by a madman they would later learn was Alex Ravien Bloodright. And, just like Silas, he'd been thrust into the position far too young.

"Your parents would be proud of you," Laina said.

He smiled weakly. "Come on. I'll show you what I've done in the garden." He led her, arm in arm, through the halls and out the glass doors to the grounds behind the manse. They strolled along a stone walkway that snaked between newly planted flowering trees and shrubs.

"It smells amazing," she said.

"I did that on purpose. Once we've shifted, we'll always know where home is by the scent."

"It's brilliant, Cameron." She ran her fingers over the plate-sized bloom of a potted hibiscus.

"Are you cold?" He offered her his jacket.

The early evening held a late-September chill, but she wasn't uncomfortable. She shook her head.

"I have a confession to make. I didn't bring you out here to show you the flowers."

"No?"

"I want to ask you something, and I hope you will take my question in the spirit in which it is offered." He placed a hand on her elbow, and she stopped to give him her full attention.

"What are you asking?"

"Will you marry me?"

She almost swallowed her tongue. A fit of coughing overtook her, and she held her chest as she tried to catch her breath. He thumped her back until she regained her composure.

"Are you joking?"

"I know it sounds crazy, but it would solve both our problems. You could do whatever you wanted to do, whenever you wanted to do it. You could run your veterinary hospital. If you didn't want children, I'd lie and say we were trying. No one would know the difference. If you wanted kids, we could make that happen too. It wouldn't be easy for me." He glanced away from her and pointed his fingers at his lower torso. "I've never been with a woman. But I hear there are ways. Medical ways."

"And, I take it, part of your plan is pursuing your personal desires on the side as well?"

He nodded. "His name is Byron. He's an accountant. Human. I can't help myself."

"I... Cameron, this is so unexpected."

"I know. There was no easy way for me to broach the subject, but we're both twenty-nine. The society isn't going to be patient much longer."

"The society has never pressured males to marry. You can sire pups into your senior years."

"Maybe. But if they marry off my best girl, there will be no female left I'd ever share my life with."

No female who understood his secret. Eyes burning, Laina took an interest in the half-moon above her. Empathy was one thing, but martyrdom was another. "Cameron... I..."

Cameron rested his hands on her shoulders. "It's a beautiful night. I'm sorry to ruin it for you."

"No," she said, shaking her head. "You haven't. What you propose isn't crazy or unheard of. It's an amicable solution."

"But..."

"But..." She narrowed her eyes at the moon. "Since the day I was born, my life has been dictated by my curse. My brother has the power to control my every move. Thank God he doesn't exercise it often, but the fact is that he can sometimes make me feel like I want to chew off my own arm to escape his hold over me. When it comes to this one thing—deciding who I will marry—I want my freedom. I want to find someone or not find someone of my own voli-tion." She faced him, begging for his understanding. "Isn't determining who we love the most basic, intimate, and personal choice? Why should either of us have to pretend anything?"

He frowned. "The pack is made up of human animals. Maybe it's in their nature to be cruel."

"Last I checked, the human part of me was in control." She smoothed her hair and wiped under her eyes. "You were kind and brave to propose to me."

He snorted. "Not bravery but desperation. You'd be an answer to my prayers."

"Does your proposal come with a time limit? Can I think about it?"

He smirked. "Fifty years. If you don't decide before we're eighty, all bets are off."

"Come here." She embraced her friend, kissing his cheek. Now would be an excellent time to change the subject and put her friend at ease. But she never got the chance.

An ear-piercing scream cut through the darkness and chilled her to the bone.

FIVE

Breaking from Cameron's embrace, Laina rushed inside toward the shouts coming from the ballroom. She cursed her stilettos as she skidded on the marble floor and had to steady herself on the wall. A ring of pack members had assembled on the dance floor. Once she'd excuse-me'd through the crowd, she stopped short, hand over her mouth when she saw their cause for alarm. The space where she'd performed with Cameron only moments before had become the stage for a bloody murder. A white wolf lay butchered, the white-on-white décor now marred by grisly streaks of crimson.

A grunt of disgust came from Laina's throat. Her stomach turned. Strong hands gripped her shoulders from behind. *Silas.* "Don't get any closer. There's nothing you can do, and you could contaminate the scene."

He edged past her, shouting instructions to the others to stand back. He'd call for help, Laina knew. The supernatural department of the Carlton City PD would be on this in a heartbeat.

Laina turned back toward the scene, intellectual

curiosity warring with sheer revulsion at what she was witnessing. She tallied the number of bones in the pelvis and quickly determined the victim was an animal, not a shifted werewolf. That gave her a modicum of relief. Still, whoever did this meant it as a personal threat. Wolves were considered family by her kind.

The snowy fur of the abdomen had been split open. *Dissected,* Laina thought, wiping away a tear. The white wolf was positioned on her back, limbs stretched unnaturally as if drawn by invisible cords, bones and muscles locked in a painfully strained position. Whatever atrocity had been inflicted on the poor creature, the murder must have occurred before transporting her here, enough time for rigor mortis to set in. Nothing secured the limbs now, but they were frozen in the horrid position, a morbid memento of the torture she'd endured. Still, the abdomen appeared soft, and Laina could only make out the smell of blood, not decay. She'd seen joints stiffen within ten minutes of death in certain animals, although one to three hours was more common. The color of the blood suggested a recent death. She'd have to tell Silas she estimated the murder anywhere between an hour and two hours ago.

Laina pressed her knuckles to her lips, her chest aching for the ill-fated wolf.

"What does that say?" Cameron asked from behind her. He was peeking around her side as if he were using her body as a shield against the horror and squinting at the smudges of blood on the floor.

"I can't make it out from this angle," Laina said.

"Maybe we should go to my room and sit down. Let Silas do his job. It might not be safe here." He tugged her elbow.

She shook her head. "If you think I'm running and hiding, you don't know me."

"And if you think I can stand to look at this a moment longer, you don't know me." Cameron grimaced. "Fuck, I need a drink."

"Go," she whispered, giving him a little push. "There's nothing you can do here."

He did as she suggested.

She rounded the scene and stood at the tail end of the tortured animal. "By blood, we rightfully ascend," she read aloud.

"Looks like someone isn't happy about Alex's death," Silas said. He'd arrived beside her, snapping pictures with his phone.

"You think a remnant of Bloodright pack is out for revenge? I thought they all submitted to you as their new alpha?"

"Me too. Except we never found Alex's Zafka, Jonah. He's missing. I assumed he had gone into hiding. Looks like he chose another path."

Normally, when one alpha killed another, the dominated pack would be bound to the victor. Submission was almost inevitable. Almost. It was possible under the right circumstances—extreme emotional stress or suppressed alpha tendencies—for a wolf to go rogue, break off, and form its own pack. Any Zafka eventually took on characteristics of the wolf they protected. Clearly, Jonah didn't just serve as Alex's doppelgänger; he was cut from the same power-hungry cloth.

"The heart is missing," Laina said.

"How can you tell?"

"The way the corpse is mutilated makes it difficult, but what you are seeing behind the rib cage is actually the liver.

It looks like they took out all the organs and shoved them back in wherever they would fit. It doesn't make any sense."

Silas growled. "I don't like this, Laina. Something like this appears in a crowded room, and no one saw a thing? Whoever did this has friends in the magical community."

"You think a witch is helping Jonah?"

"Or a fairy. Go home and lock your doors."

"Silas—"

"That's an order." He took her hands in his large, rough ones. "I'm sorry to pull alpha on you again, but if Jonah did this, he isn't going to stop at terrorizing us. I'm responsible for Alex's death, and like it or not, we are royalty. He'll want to hurt me. He'll want me dead. He'll come for you or Jason to get to me. Or he'll come for me, and you'll end up getting hurt."

"I could help you. The state of the body suggests the death occurred around an hour or more ago. If I could do a necropsy, I might find more clues."

"No, Laina. It's too dangerous. Home. Locked door. Go."

It was an alpha command. She tried to stand her ground, eye to eye with her brother. "Silas…" She grabbed his wrists and held on, determined not to obey. Every moment she fought it grew more uncomfortable. Her head buzzed, and the inside of her skin prickled as if her veins were filled with acid. The muscles in her legs began to tremble.

"Don't fight it, Laina. You'll be sore tomorrow."

In a huff, she gave in and yanked her sweating hands from his wrists, striding toward the exit.

Her Zafka met her on the veranda. Stephanie wasn't her exact twin, but she was close enough that someone who didn't know her intimately would easily presume she was Laina. Same face, same coloring, same height and weight. A convincing doppelgänger. Most importantly, she was deadly, trained in mixed martial arts and never without the gun she kept holstered to her thigh.

"Please take the back roads, Princess. I'll take the highway," Stephanie said, bowing at the waist. "That will give me time to sweep your apartment before you get there."

With a deep breath, Laina nodded reluctantly. "You don't need to bow. And please be careful. I'll see you at home."

Stephanie bowed again, ignoring Laina's request, and jogged toward her car. Laina tried to take a shortcut across the lawn to the place her car was parked, only to have her heels sink through the grass and into the mud. She kicked them off and continued barefoot to her silver Audi R8, tossing her muddy shoes and purse onto the floor of the passenger's side. She slid behind the wheel and fired up the engine.

"Fucking Silas." If she didn't feel like an egg being hard-boiled every time she disobeyed an alpha command, she'd enjoy kicking his ass.

Halfway home, she paused at a stop sign. No one behind her. Nothing but road ahead. If she turned right, she'd be on course for her condo. Left was Four Paws Animal Hospital. Silas said to go home. He never said to go *straight* home. With a smug grin, she sped in the direction of her veterinary hospital. She'd check on Milo before heading home, maybe call and give Kyle an update and an apology.

As she pulled into her usual parking space, she noticed the light above the front door was still lit. Her assistant should have gone home hours ago, although it wasn't completely unheard of for Becca to forget to turn the light off. Still, given the night's events, Laina glanced over her shoulder as she slid her key into the lock. She was defiant but not stupid. If any of the Bloodright supporters wanted to challenge her, she'd be ready.

The scent of blood filled her nostrils as she slipped inside, and a chorus of barking came from the kennels. *What the fuck?* All the file cabinets behind the front desk were hanging open. Papers littered the floor around the toppled chair. Quickly, she rounded the desk and grabbed a pair of scissors from the drawer.

The tile floor felt cold under her bare feet as she hiked up her dress and crept deeper into the room, scissors squeezed in her fist and poised to strike over her right shoulder. She swung open the door to the kennels.

She'd designed the room to be accessible from both the front office and the surgical suite, each dog with its own climate-controlled den connected to an accessible, private outdoor run. Reinforced glass doors and mounted cameras allowed her and her staff to easily monitor patients indoors or out. The setup was ideal and unique to her practice.

But as she passed through the door, the hair on the back of her neck stood at attention. The monitors mounted behind the workstation were turned off, and a cursory inspection found the computer was unplugged. She plugged it back in, continuing around the corner to the kennels while the system came online. Milo was fine, as was the spaniel she'd operated on that morning. But what she found in the third kennel made her drop the scissors and race to its locked gate.

"Becca!" Her assistant was sprawled facedown, blood staining her light brown curls and smudged across the back of her lab coat. The barking grew louder. Laina woofed in response, the deepest part of her inner wolf coming to the surface. All the dogs, including Milo, froze, eerily silent and intently waiting for her next command.

Unlocking the cage, she rushed to Becca's side and placed two fingers against her assistant's neck. A strong pulse thumped against her touch. "Thank the goddess." She rolled her human friend onto her back and assessed her further. "Becca? Becca?"

Her assistant roused, pressing a hand to the back of her head with a wince. "Laina?"

"I'm here. What happened?"

Her eyes widened. "A man asked for you. When I said you were gone for the day, he wanted your address. I wouldn't give it to him. He got angry." Her eyes darted wildly, and she struggled to get to her feet. "How long have I been out?"

Laina stood. "What did the man look like?" She helped her friend out of the kennel and settled her into the chair near the workstation.

"Tall but skinny. Wavy dark-blond hair. Rough around the edges, you know? I thought he was looking for the soup kitchen up the street when he first walked in."

Could be Jonah, Laina thought.

Becca raised a shaking hand and pointed over her shoulder toward the observation window to the surgical suite. Laina's gaze followed. The over-table surgical light was on. "Still here," Becca murmured, eyes widening.

Placing a finger over her lips, Laina retrieved the scissors she'd dropped and tiptoed to the stainless-steel door that led to her operating room. The surgical light only illuminated the table, leaving the corners of the room dark enough to hide an assailant. Something was on the operating table, a box of some sort, but she couldn't make out any details.

She slipped inside the door and fumbled for the light switch, scissors raised and back pressed against the wall. The floor was sticky under her bare feet, and the stench she'd smelled from the office was overbearing now, a mixture of blood and antiseptic. Her fingertips caught on the plastic nub. When the lights clicked on, she gasped into the back of her hand.

No one was inside, but she'd found where the white wolf had been murdered. Her operating room was coated in blood. The floor, the walls, the bindings used to torture the creature still secured to the operating table. But her eyes had not deceived her. At the center of all that blood was a...gift.

She approached the table, shaking. The box was wrapped in newsprint, the headline *Random Act of Terror Kills Eight* centered along the top. She carefully unfolded the article, her fingers cold and numb as all her blood seemed to rush toward her pounding heart. She already knew what it said—the newspaper story about the night her parents and Cameron's parents were murdered. She tossed it aside, eyes burning with unshed tears. Tears wouldn't solve anything. But resistance was futile once she opened the box. Inside, the white wolf's heart lay in a pool of congealed blood. A gift card rested on top —*You're next.*

CHAPTER
SIX

This was a first. Kyle could honestly say he'd never been stood up before. Not like this. Sure, one time in high school, Juliette Freeman had said no when he'd asked her to make out behind the bleachers, but never before had a woman so enthusiastically agreed to a date and then ghosted him.

Laina *had* been enthusiastic, hadn't she? He thought back to the way she'd leaned forward, licked the bottom lip of her nervous smile, and toyed with her hair. If that hadn't been flirting, Kyle was way off his game.

A waitress, not his, slid up to his table and handed him a folded paper napkin. Her phone number. She winked at him over her shoulder as she headed toward the kitchen. *Fuck that.* He wasn't off his game.

He needed an explanation.

The only phone number he had for Laina was Four Paws, and the line had been consistently busy for the last two hours. He'd waited for her at Valentine's Restaurant well past the time they'd agreed to meet. So long that the owner, a guy named Logan who seemed to sense he was having a bad night, talked him into a burger and some chocolate cake. The good eats barely numbed his annoyance. Once his plate was empty, he should have paid the bill and headed back to his hotel.

But he hadn't. After losing his dad and gaining a dog the size of a small truck, he needed closure on this. Had she figured out who he was and ghosted because she was turned off by his public persona? That would be understandable. Although plenty of women were members of Hunt Club, if that was the problem, he could accept it. He'd go on his merry way.

Only, he'd felt a connection with Laina almost immediately. She set off bells and whistles inside him he hadn't known he was packing. One look at her and something in his chest...moved? Loosened? He couldn't even describe it. What he knew for sure was what it wasn't. This was no simple lust or sexual attraction. Something else. Something more.

He had to know for sure. What was the worst that could happen? Maybe she'd tell him she wasn't interested. Big deal. He'd take Milo and leave for home. Resolved, he tore out of Valentine's like his ass was on fire and headed straight for Four Paws.

All speculation came to a chilling halt when Kyle pulled his rented SUV into the parking lot of the veterinary clinic and slid into a space next to a silver Audi he suspected was the doctor's. The door to the building was hanging open, and inside, the place looked like it had been hit by a hurricane—papers strewn across the floor, file cabinets ransacked. His heart broke into a gallop.

"Laina?" he called.

When there was no answer, he strode toward the back, then saw her through a window to the surgical suite.

"Jesus Christ." He shoved his way through the door and into the blood-splattered room. Laina looked like she was catatonic. Her face was stark white, and she was clutching the blades of a pair of scissors in her hand, tight enough to hurt, the steel biting into the edge of her palm. "Laina?"

She didn't seem to hear him. He took a few more steps toward her.

"Dr. Flynn, are you all right?" he asked more forcefully.

That seemed to shake her out of whatever shock she was in, and her eyes met his. "Kyle?"

She wavered on her feet, and he rushed forward to pull her into his arms. *Fuck*, in the back of his mind, a tiny voice said he should call the police. But no way was he doing anything until he knew for sure that none of this blood was hers. He ran his hands over her head, her back, her arms. "Are you hurt?"

She blinked up at him. Was it wrong that even in this blood-soaked horror of a room, he couldn't miss the way she fit against him, or the way that thing in his chest happened again. What the hell was that anyway?

"Kyle? What are you doing here?" Eyes widening, she planted her hands on his chest and made room between them.

"When you didn't show up for our date, I came looking for you," he said. "What happened?" He gestured vaguely at the blood and the box on the operating table. "Is that a heart?"

Laina nudged him toward the door, away from what was likely the grossest thing he'd ever seen. "You need to leave. It's not safe."

"No kidding. Who did this? We should call the police." He reached for his phone, but she caught his wrist in a surprisingly firm grip.

"No. Kyle, listen to me. I'll do that eventually, but the person responsible is dangerous, and he could come back. You have to take Milo and go."

"I'm not going anywhere without you. If it's dangerous for me, it's dangerous for you. Let me help you. We'll go together."

She frowned. "I'm sorry about our date, but—" Her eyes darted to the window in the door behind them. "Oh my God, Becca!"

Kyle started when the face of Laina's assistant appeared in the window, blood dripping down her ghostly white temple. Laina rushed through the door to her, wrapping one of the older woman's arms around her shoulders. Kyle rushed forward to help support her from the other side.

"Help me get her to my car," Laina said. "I need to drive her to the hospital."

"Let me drive. You can call the police on the way," he insisted.

Becca mumbled something between them, but it was incoherent. Together, they staggered out the door. "My car." Laina tilted her head toward the Audi.

He helped her lower the bleeding woman into the passenger's seat. "I'll follow you to the hospital."

Laina stopped to face him, her spine going ramrod straight. She pointed at his chest. "Kyle, I'm sorry I missed our date, but frankly, any relationship with me was doomed from the start. I'm going to walk into that building, and I'm going to come out with Milo. You're going to take him and go home, and you're not going to say a thing about this to anyone. Do you understand me?"

Damn. The tone in her voice finally registered, and Kyle backed up a step. What exactly had he walked in on? Running the type of business he did, he was no stranger to backroom deals, although he'd tried his best to avoid mob activity. He hadn't expected that type of thing in a veterinary clinic in New Hampshire, but now that he thought about it, the level of opposition she had to calling the police indicated something illegal was happening here.

She ran inside and, a moment later, appeared in the doorway with Milo. At least the dog was unharmed. Actually, the mutt looked one hundred times better than when Kyle had left him. She thrust the leash into his hands.

"I'm sorry, okay," she said. "It's...complicated." Her phone rang, and she tore it from her pocket. "Silas... There's been... Something awful has happened. I'm at Four Paws."

Who was Silas?

"Becca's hurt. I have to take her to the hospital. Can you meet me there? What...? Why?" She inhaled sharply. "I'll be there in five minutes."

She slid the phone back into her pocket, her gaze meeting his. "I've got to go. Milo will be fine. Just give him lots of water and watch his diet." She opened her car door.

"Right. Thanks for your help." Kyle couldn't keep the stiffness from his voice. "And good luck with...whatever this is."

A quick nod later, she sped from the parking lot, leaving him and Milo staring after her.

SEVEN

"I can't believe he did this to her." Laina stroked her thumb over the back of Stephanie's hand, the whoosh of air in and out of her Zafka's ventilator a constant reminder of the seriousness of her condition. At least Becca was all right. Her assistant, although rattled, had been released after an MRI showed no signs of concussion. Jason volunteered to escort her home. Stephanie was a different story. She'd been attacked in Laina's apartment by someone who must have thought she was Laina, and they'd shown her no mercy.

"Whoever did this to Stephanie left her for dead. We're hoping they were convinced it was you," Silas said.

"The note in my surgical suite said, *You're next.* Becca described a man who fit Jonah's description."

Silas ran both hands through his wild brown hair and paced the room. "It has to be Jonah, but who's helping him?"

Laina sighed. "I don't know, but blood was *everywhere*, Silas. You were right about him having help from another magical creature. I've never seen anything like it. It was as if he blew that poor wolf apart."

"I talked to every fairy and witch contact I have in the city. No one's heard anything."

"If Jonah's been out there all this time, why now? Alex was killed months ago. Why wait until today to strike?" Laina shook her head.

"I don't know."

Drawing a deep breath, Laina shoved the grim and panicky feelings she was experiencing into a box at the back of her brain. She'd always excelled at compartmentalizing. It was what gave her an edge in surgery. "What are our next steps? How do we find Jonah? Did he leave any clues in my condo?"

The apologetic glance Silas darted in her direction told her to brace herself. "You may not want to hear this, Laina, but you have to go into hiding. Our best hope is to send the message it's you in this bed."

Oh hell no! "Hiding?" She shook her head. "I have a business to run, Silas. I can't just up and leave."

Silas winced. "This threat is real, Laina. That card said you're next. *You.* I can't let you return to your daily routine like Jonah's not out there gunning for you."

She buried her face in her hands, knowing he was right but hating it with every fiber of her being. "What do you have in mind?"

"There's a safe house for our kind in rural Wisconsin run by a very powerful ogre called Uncle Monty. He's offered a place for you and Jason to stay in exchange for your help working in his bar."

"Wisconsin?" It was too far. She'd have to completely close the clinic. "No, Silas... No." She stood and slashed her hand through the air between them. "Nonnegotiable. I'm a veterinarian! I have a business, Silas. Patients! I can disguise myself. Pose as another vet temporarily treating my patients while I'm in the hospital."

Silas frowned, and when he spoke again, his voice was gentle but firm. "With the kind of magic Jonah is packing, he'd sniff you out in no time." He sighed heavily. "I know this sucks, but it isn't just about you. Rivergate Manor has been compromised. The pack is in danger. Uncle Monty owns protected acreage enchanted with ancient fairy magic. In exchange for your help with his business, he's agreed to allow Fireborn *and* Rivergate packs to shift there. Cameron and the others will join you during the full moon. We've found alternate arrangements for the other packs."

At that, all she could do was gape. "You want Jason and me to act as servants to an ogre in a...in a tavern in Wisconsin...in exchange for shifting grounds? Can't someone else sling drinks for the ogre? Where will *you* be?"

Silas leaned against the wall and crossed his arms over his chest. "I'm going undercover to track down Jonah and bring him to justice. I have the skills and the resources."

As practiced as she was at controlling her emotions, she couldn't stop her hands from breaking into a sweat at the implications. "Who will lead the pack in your absence?"

"You're the next eldest. Technically, it should be Jason because he's the next male heir, but frankly, I trust you more. He hasn't been...reliable lately. The biggest need will be during the shift. The rest of the time, the pack will be in hiding but will know how to reach me. By working for Monty, you'll be in a prime position to lead. You'll already know the layout of the grounds."

"Silas..."

"Fireborn pack is counting on you, Laina, to keep them safe."

She rubbed her face. "You're making *me* temporary alpha?"

He nodded slowly. "I've already given the order."

Fuck, she never thought she'd see the day. Silas must truly find the situation serious to take this step. She squeezed her eyes shut and fought back her urge to agree to his demands.

"What about Cameron? If his pack is shifting there too, why isn't *he* working for the ogre?"

"I need someone to lead the Lycanthropic Society in my absence. Everyone in both packs is going into hiding until the shift. Cameron will be the one person who knows where everyone is in case of an emergency."

"Why can't I do that?"

"Because that position needs to stay here, at Rivergate. Not only is it Cameron's home, but you're supposed to be in a coma. There's too much of a risk that you'd be identified. This isn't forever, Laina. I've asked a friend to cast a protection spell around his place and Four Paws, but because of the size of the property and the complexity of the spell I've requested, she says it could take a few months. But once it's safe, you can come home."

"Months?" She rubbed circles over her temples.

"Until and unless we capture or kill Jonah, we'll have to take precautions."

The walls pressed in around her, the air thick and hot with her rising panic. She released Stephanie's hand and rose from her chair, wrapping her arms around her middle and facing her brother head on. "Is there any other option?"

Silas's answer was quick and concise. "I'm sorry, Laina. No. The decision is made. As soon as Jason finishes securing Becca's place, he's meeting us back here to pick you up. You two leave for Wisconsin tonight. I don't think she'll be in any danger as a human, but we'll have a security detail watching her."

Laina doubted Jonah would waste energy on Becca now that he'd gotten what he wanted from Four Paws and thought Laina was incapacitated. "What about my things?"

With a sigh, Silas shook his head. "You're supposed to be here, remember?" He gestured toward Stephanie. "Leave it all. I've asked Jason to bring cash and a burner phone so you can reach me if you need to. Buy what you need. Uncle Monty will give both of you new identities when you reach Sable Creek."

"I don't want to do this," she murmured.

Silas blinked slowly, his expression grave. "This is how it has to be."

She saw it then, the deep lines of worry in her brother's face. He wasn't enjoying this, and he'd be risking his life while she was away. With a deep sigh, she nodded her agreement. She'd do this...for the good of the pack. He opened his arms, and she accepted his embrace.

Two weeks later, Laina didn't have time to waste worrying about her role as princess or temporary alpha. As a bartender at Monty's, an ancient, wood-paneled lodge that reeked of ogres and human sweat, she didn't have the luxury of thinking about much more than the next drink or the next customer. Although occasionally, like now, her mind drifted back to her old life and her days seeing patients at Four Paws, it never lasted long.

"Anna! Earth to Anna!" Jeff waved a hand in front of her

face. Who was Anna? *Oh*, Laina thought, *I'm Anna*. Anna Whitehall. Her new identity.

The memory of her old life faded slowly like air from a pinpricked balloon. Jeff, a sun-weathered construction worker who spent too much time on a barstool, waved his hand again. "Can I get another?"

Laina tightened her ponytail and forced a smile. "Sorry. Guess I didn't get enough sleep last night."

He grinned. "Someone keeping you up, babe? Who's the lucky guy?"

"No. Nothing like that," she said bitterly. It was impossible for her to talk about her current situation without sounding bitchy and resentful. "You want another amber ale?"

"Must not be worthy. If you're going to spend the day asleep on your feet, there should be a damn good reason, a reason to brag about." He lowered his chin and bobbed his eyebrows twice.

Laina dug his beer from the refrigerated bin and popped off the cap, skimming it across the bar into Jeff's waiting hands. The scrape of glass against polished wood reminded her she'd forgotten to turn the music on when she opened that afternoon. It was too quiet.

"You should try me on for size." Jeff shot her a flirty smirk. He was nothing if not persistent.

"I wouldn't be able to handle your mad skills," she said flatly.

He erupted into laughter and raised the bottle. "Damn straight!"

Laina added the drink to his tab, then turned her back on him, fussing with the bottles lined up along the shelves for longer than necessary in an effort to kill any chance he might try to reengage in conversation. Eventually, Jeff became bored and wandered to his preferred seat near the window, where he made a habit of watching the Sable Creek Savings and Loan in hopes of catching a glimpse of the young teller he fancied. She slid back into the groove when a biker at the end of the bar cleared his throat and raised two fingers to order a rum and Coke and a slice of apple pie.

Uncle Monty's lodge was the only restaurant and bar in Sable Creek, which wasn't surprising. The town was barely large enough to support a grocery store, let alone a restaurant. But Laina had learned the town's traffic far exceeded its population for a few key reasons. It was conveniently located off a major thoroughfare between Chicago and Minneapolis. Truckers flocked to Monty's like flies to honey, mostly for the pie, which was enchanted by a local fairy to be mildly addictive. The place was legendary among biker gangs for the same reason.

Monty's also bordered some of the best private hunting grounds in Wisconsin. As an ogre, Uncle Monty was unconcerned with licenses, endangered species, or hunting seasons. Hunters came from far and wide and frequented the area year-round, for a price. There were rumors he'd stocked big game on his grounds—buffalo and mountain lion.

And then there was the enchanted safe zone and lodge for supernaturals. Laina was as likely to see a vampire lying low after a particularly messy feed as she was to see a human construction worker like Jeff, one of the rare townies who frequented the place.

Laina sniffed the air as the stench of ogre grew stronger, not surprised at all when Monty's head appeared in the service window to the kitchen.

"Where's your brother?" The ogre's gritty baritone had

the sandpaper feel of plunging her ear into a litter box. Ogres could pass as humans—hulking, unhygienic humans with bad teeth. Monty was no exception. At six foot four and over 300 pounds of portly flesh, he dwarfed Laina. So did his smell, which was as overpowering as his presence. Still, there was nothing overtly supernatural about him, and if she hadn't known better, she'd have assumed he was an ordinary man. His heavily hooded eyes gave her the impression he was perpetually skeptical, and perhaps he was. Ogres were the loan sharks of the supernatural world. Thanks to notoriously harsh business dealings, they were hated by many and wished dead by more than a few.

"Late," Laina answered. No point in lying. Jason, new identity Jay Whitehall, was hardly discreet about his escapades. "He didn't come home last night." The word *home* stuck in her throat like a dry piece of gristle. The apartment above the bar that Monty had loaned them was an ancient relic that could barely be called shelter, let alone home. She'd spent all of her free time cleaning the place, and still, walking through the front door was the most depressing part of her day.

"Your brother has a penchant for the ladies."

"You could say that."

"That place you're stayin' in ain't free. One of you will have to make up his hours, or I'm going to need more cash."

Cash was one thing Laina had plenty of. The society had made sure of that. But anyone with half a brain knew it was folly to admit to an ogre you had money. She'd locked the cash in a fireproof case and secured it to the underside of her bed, intending to use it to pay off any unforeseen expenses that might crop up. Monty was notorious for accruing undisclosed charges in the amount he thought his victims were capable of repaying. Until she moved on from this purgatory, her apparent poverty was her best weapon for limiting her liability.

"I'll work a double," she said. She made herself busy, hoping he'd drop the subject and leave. Instead, he hovered as she filled the bar sink with scalding hot water and poured in the sanitizing chemical necessary to wash the barware.

Monty growled. "That's too much, Anna! What am I made of? Money?"

It wasn't too much. She'd used exactly the amount prescribed on the back of the bottle. Any less and it was impossible to get the lip prints off the glasses. Monty knew that but didn't care. He'd never met a germ he didn't like. "Bottle got away from me."

Out of the corner of her eye, she saw Monty scribble himself a note, no doubt charging her for the extra cleaning product. "Don't let it happen again."

EIGHT

"You can't keep missing work, Jason. I'm not covering your shift next time." Laina kneed her sleeping brother in the ribs, knocking the sofa bed he was lying on hard enough to give his body a creaking, spring-loaded bounce.

He groaned and rolled onto his side. "Just pay Monty the difference, La. Stop acting like this is a real job. We paid him to hide us. What's he going to do? Kick us out?"

She dropped into a dreadful olive-green armchair and worked her shoes off her feet, rubbing the arch of her right foot with both thumbs. "Ogres are ruthless. Not only will Monty evict us, he'll wait to do it until both packs are here and ready to shift. Besides, we can't let on that we have money. He'll figure out a way to weasel every last penny out of us. Trust me, you don't want Monty as an enemy. He's too powerful."

"I'm not saying you should piss him off. I'm saying you should pay him off." Jason scrubbed his face with his hands. "We're rich and we're royalty. We shouldn't have to do manual labor."

"I hate to break it to you, but the money we paid Monty was for the privilege of his protection and silence. He expects us to work to pay for this apartment. Even if I gave him more, he'd find a way to expect more. We need his cooperation, and the pack is relying on access to his land. You can't jeopardize that, Jason. We're responsible for keeping Monty happy for as long as we need him, and I can't do it myself."

He rubbed his eye with his knuckle. "I hate this. Silas is a shit."

Laina stopped massaging her foot long enough to agree. "Who was the girl anyway? I know all the women in this town, and, no offense, you've already blown through every one of appropriate age."

"No offense taken. She wasn't from here. Just passing through. A model from Chicago interviewing for a job at a new place they're opening across town."

"What kind of place hires models in Sable Creek?"

"I think it's some sort of club."

"You mean like a strip club?" What other type of club would hire models in a small town in Wisconsin?

He shrugged. "I assume. She didn't tell me the name of the place, just that they were offering top dollar for models with experience modeling nude. She was planning to leave town this afternoon if they didn't make an offer."

With a disapproving scowl, Laina stood. "Good. You should get plenty of rest tonight, then. You can open for me in the morning."

He growled.

"Don't force me to alpha you into submission, brother. I'll make it so you can't even look at a woman."

"Ugh. I can't believe Silas made you temporary alpha."

Jason rolled onto his back, dragged a pillow over his head, and huffed. "Fine. You can be a real bitch sometimes."

"I certainly hope so. Bitches make the world go round."

She stormed toward the tiny bedroom at the back of the apartment and stripped out of her clothes, climbing between the dollar store sheets. They were rough as sandpaper against her skin, but she was too tired to care.

As she spiraled toward sleep, she was surprised when her last thoughts were of Kyle. The way he'd come looking for her at Four Paws when she'd so rudely stood him up. It was silly to think about. Hopeless. Kyle represented something that had never been and would never be.

But the man had ignited a passion in her she hadn't thought possible. Even her wolf had been interested. And that tiny spark had made her wonder about the thing she wanted but could never have. Love. Real love. The type that couldn't be forced or manipulated. A love that wasn't arranged for the purposes of bearing children or pack politics. It was a silly thing to think about so late at night. Forcing it from her mind, she spilled into unconsciousness, thankful for the respite of sleep.

"SON OF HADES!" MONTY BELLOWED, TOSSING THE MAIL DOWN on the bar. "This will be the end of me."

Anyone who worked for Monty became accustomed to his frequent temper tantrums, but this one was different. The ogre paced behind the bar in the early afternoon light, gripping a flyer in his meathooks. A vein in his temple pulsed like the steam valve on a pressure cooker.

Even Jason showed concern. He stopped bussing tables

and sidled up next to her with his bin of dirty dishes, tapping his elbow against hers. "What's going on?"

Laina shrugged.

"I'll tell you what's going on," Monty said. Laina made a mental note that the ogre had exceptional hearing. "They're opening up a Hunt Club in Sable Creek."

"Another hunting lodge?" Laina asked.

"Not a hunting club." The ogre looked at her like she was stupid. "A Hunt Club."

Laina shook her head.

"It's a lifestyle club," Jason said. "There's an e-mag and a calendar...an online membership. Hunt Club is like an in-person Tinder on steroids. Men and women join to, uh... hunt one another, you might say." He grinned broadly and smiled up at the ceiling as if he had fond memories of his time at Hunt Club.

"Is this the strip club you were talking about?" Laina asked.

Jason's eyes darted to Monty, who was bright red with anger, before scratching a spot on his neck as he explained more. "Not a strip club. I think I was, uh, wrong about that. Actually, this makes more sense for a model from Chicago. See, Hunt Club's tagline is 'Enjoy the Thrill of the Chase.' The servers wear nothing but body paint, and they're painted to look like animals."

"The members are considered the predators, I suppose?" Laina landed her hands on her hips. "Crude."

"Predator, prey. Whatever floats your boat. Each Hunt Club has a kick-ass dance floor that's open to the public, but they also have private VIP lounge areas for members only. The membership is expensive and exclusive. The clientele value discretion."

Her brow shot up, wondering what went on in the VIP

areas. She'd never been much of a clubgoer. "If it's so exclusive, why here? Shouldn't it be in LA rather than rural Wisconsin?"

"They build these places in rural areas where there's a lot of hunting and fishing, that sort of thing. Gives the members an excuse to be there and privacy to do what they came to do. No one to recognize them." Hmm. The same reason she and Jason were there. "*Forbes* ranked it the fastest-growing business of the year," Jason added. "I offered to invest in it when they started expanding, but it's family owned and independently financed."

Monty pointed a meaty finger toward Jason's face. "Shut the fuck up. This place's gotta go, Jay. This could put me outta business, and if I'm outta business, your pack ain't gonna be safe nowhere. Nowhere."

At the early hour, only two people were in the bar, Jeff, who'd stopped eating his pie midbite, and a trucker, who took one look at Monty's pointing sausage of a finger and left without ordering.

"Can I get you another beer, Jeff?" Laina asked.

"No, I'm okay." His gaze drifted back toward the bank across the street.

Laina glanced between Jason and Monty. "How can we help? Maybe we could coordinate some live entertainment of our own to compete. Jay's an above-average singer."

Jason gaped at her like she'd grown a second head.

Monty flattened the flyer on the bar and rubbed his lumpy chin. "Their grand opening is Friday." He hummed a low, thoughtful note before narrowing his dark, beady eyes on Laina. "You're a pretty little thing, aren't you?"

"Why are you looking at me like that?"

"A girl like you could easily pose as a model."

"To what end?" Laina's voice was shrill. Over her dead

body was she going to traipse around in nothing but a layer of paint. She had boundaries.

Monty looked at Jeff, then stepped in close, close enough for the reek of his breath to turn Laina's stomach. "The right magic left in the right spot—say an ever-growing mold or a stench blossom—and a place like that might be closed down by the health department."

"Good idea. Have Jay do it," she countered.

Jason cleared his throat. "Uh, sorry, but I'm already a member. I could be recognized. Actually, there would be a very good chance someone would recognize me."

Laina glared at her brother.

"You, with the body paint and the mask, are the perfect weapon," Monty said, voice edging with excitement as his plan took shape. "You discreetly drop the package, Hunt Club gets the boot, and you and your family have a safe place to spend a couple months. Win-win."

"No," she said firmly. "I won't do it."

Monty narrowed his eyes. "You won't need my land, then?"

"We already paid for the use of your land," Jason said.

"Have Silas call me. I'm not sure this is going to work out."

"You don't understand. I *can't* do this." Laina lowered her voice to a whisper she knew only Monty and Jason could hear. "The grand opening of Hunt Club is the night before the full moon."

"So?"

"So, it's a bad idea. I'll be moody. Volatile. Prone to intense emotion." Monty's scowl made it clear he didn't give a shit. Ogres were like that all the time. Maybe the direct approach? She crossed her arms. "I'm not comfortable doing this. I think you should find someone else."

"No one else fits the part." He scanned her from head to toe. "You'll do this, or you can tell your pack to find a new place to shift by the end of the week."

She bit the inside of her cheek, determined not to cry or piss off the ogre. "Fine," she said through her teeth. "But I can't just walk in there and say *paint me*."

Monty grinned wickedly. "Don't worry 'bout that. I know a guy."

CHAPTER

NINE

The road to Hunt Club meandered to the point Laina worried she'd misread Monty's directions. But when the narrow drive ended at a row of picketers blocking a twelve-foot wrought-iron gate, she was concerned for an entirely different reason.

"Not in our town!" a woman yelled. She shook her fist at Laina on the other side of the window.

"Preaching to the choir," Laina murmured under her breath. The picketers were from a place called Eternal Light Ministries. A dozen or more men and women pressed around her car, chanting and waving freshly Sharpie-d signs.

"God hates porn!" a darkly dressed man screamed through her windshield.

A black woman in a uniform exited the gatehouse with one hand on her gun. *Damn!* Security here was packing heat. "You can't block the gate! Move aside." The picketers parted, still chanting, and Laina pulled up to the window.

"I'm the temp," Laina said, handing the guard the fake ID Monty had given her.

65

"Sorry about this. They come for every opening." She rolled her dark eyes and sighed heavily. "We can't call the police or take action as long as they remain peaceful and don't block the entrance."

The guard glanced from the fake ID to Laina's face, then checked a list of names on a yellow clipboard. The ebony skin of her forehead furrowed.

The seconds ticked by, causing Laina's stomach to clench. "I was added at the last minute"—she glanced at the woman's name tag—"Taneesha."

Taneesha frowned in her direction and flipped the page. "Ah, here you are. Anita Woody." She handed the ID back to Laina through the window without the hint of a giggle at Monty's attempt at humor. Professional. "Follow the drive around and to the left. You want to take the service drive to the back entrance. The staging area is in Studio 2."

The massive wrought-iron gate in front of her opened, a scrollwork *H C* parting to allow her through. She couldn't see much beyond the gate due to a row of thick hedges that obscured anything beyond the next bend in the drive.

"Staging area?" Laina grumbled. As if she were a thing requiring assembly prior to use. She gently pressed the accelerator, cruising at the posted fifteen miles per hour down the smaller, less decorative service drive. At the end of the densely forested route, she tapped the brakes and looked up. Way up.

Hunt Club was a castle. An honest-to-goodness, belonged-on-a-mountain-in-Germany castle. It was bigger than Rivergate Manor and absolutely dwarfed Monty's.

"What are you getting yourself into?" she asked herself. She coasted into a parking space at the back of a small lot near a relatively plain-looking door labeled *Studio 2*.

If the building resembled a fairy-tale castle, the man

who opened the door for her could have passed for Geppetto, with a shock of white hair and thin, wire-rimmed glasses typical of clockmakers of times past. The man rubbed his rounded belly through his Tommy Bahama shirt and raised two approving eyebrows.

"They just keep makin' 'em prettier and prettier," he said through a wily grin. Extending his hand, he introduced himself. "I'm Wesley. I'll be painting you today."

"Nice to meet you." She slipped past him and joined a small crowd of men and women waiting inside. At five foot eleven inches, Laina was used to being the tallest woman in the room, but the people inside dwarfed her. Each woman was more beautiful than the last: long-limbed, graceful perfection on high heels. She wondered fleetingly whether Jason's fling was among them. The men didn't disappoint either. Tall and stunningly handsome, their collective good looks made her head spin. She hadn't seen so many muscles since the last time her pack shifted. *A room filled with underwear models.* She smirked. What she would give to take a picture and send it to Becca.

"You can leave your clothes in the lockers," Wesley announced to the crowd, pointing at a bank of cubbies. "If your hair is longer than ear length, please tie it back for the painting process." Before Wesley had finished speaking, the people around her started shedding clothing as though they were on fire.

Laina was no stranger to nudity. Being a werewolf meant that, by necessity, she stripped in front of her pack-mates once a month. Aside from preserving her wardrobe, stripping avoided any potential complications for her wolf. The difference between that and this was she knew her pack intimately. These people were strangers. Would they judge her? Would they laugh at her paunchy stomach or the scar on her hip where she'd been bitten as a young wolf? Would anyone question the tribal phoenix tattoo on her upper-right shoulder?

Her hands trembled as she drifted closer to the lockers. *Fucking Monty.* She chose a cubby and placed her purse inside, followed by her jacket, black T-shirt, and bra. When all her clothing was perfectly folded and the cubby was closed, she took a deep breath and turned to face the crowd. The women were completely naked. The men were wearing thongs that left nothing to the imagination. All of them looked totally at ease, already in line behind a cart laden with spray-painting equipment.

Wesley's gaze locked on her first, his smile fading as he focused on the apex of her thighs. A red-hot blush crept onto her cheeks as, one by one, the others turned, lips part-ing. A breathy giggle escaped from behind someone's raised hand.

What? She thought. *Do I have some kind of rare vaginal deformity?* She glanced down at herself and at the other women. One thing *was* vastly different from her body and theirs down there—*hair.*

"I have a razor. I'll help her." A woman with a sleek platinum-blond bob jogged to her side and pulled a small vanity kit from her locker as the others resumed their conversations behind her. "You must be new."

"First time," Laina said.

"The latex doesn't lay right over hair, and even if it did, believe me when I say removing it afterward would be a time-consuming and painful experience. Most of us go as far as to shave or wax our arms before a performance." She ran a finger along the silky smooth skin of her forearm. "Although, a hot soapy bath will eventually soak it off."

Laina glanced at the light dusting of dark hair over her arm. "I'll take it all off."

"Good idea." The woman handed her a razor and a small can of shaving cream. "There's a bathroom through that door."

"Thank you," Laina said genuinely.

"You're welcome. Us girls have to stick together. If you need anything else, you know where to find me." She gestured toward the line. "I'm Nickie, by the way."

"Anna." Laina nodded. She instantly regretted using that name. Her fake ID said Anita Woody, and although she supposed Anna might be short for Anita, the less chance someone might trace her back to Monty's, the better. This was ridiculous. Who could keep all of her aliases straight? She entered the bathroom, cursing her ineptitude, and emerged twenty minutes later, hairless and just as embarrassed as ever.

But as she fell into the queue behind Nickie, Wesley's assembly line of artists completed work on the first model, and Laina's embarrassment morphed into pure awe. Wesley had transformed the woman into a peacock, her entire body coated in teal latex, then airbrushed with detailed feathers down the backs of her legs and subtle shading up her torso. Her previously Indian features were now an intricate series of ridges and lines to give her nose and cheekbones a beak-like appearance, while somehow enhancing her feminine characteristics. She was gorgeous and completely covered. A work of art. Laina had to remind herself the woman was naked under the thick layer of color.

"Once it dries, it feels like you're wearing a wet suit," Nickie said. "You'll forget you're naked. The latex is waterproof, but try not to spill alcohol on it. Not only will it remove the airbrushing, but it could also break down the latex if there's friction involved." She chuckled and winked.

Laina wondered how often "friction" happened in a club like this. From what Jason said, that was a major draw of the place. God, how did she get herself into these things.

She slid her attention back to Wesley, who'd transformed a man with sandy blond hair into a stunning interpretation of a cheetah. The meticulously drawn spots gathered along his sides and accented his already impressive physique. Laina had to stop from fanning herself.

Now she understood why the position required her to be on location more than three hours before opening. It took over two and a half to reach the front of the line. By that time, she stood among a herd of human animals—a bear, two tigers, several birds, rabbits, and gazelles, and wondered what was in store for her. What would Wesley transform her into?

In answer to her unasked question, he picked up the white spray gun and went to work. She closed her eyes as the cool spray tingled against her skin like a spritz of water, becoming heavier as it dried. Avoiding eye contact with Wesley, she held her arms out to her sides and stood with her feet shoulder-width apart. The paint caressed the outside of her leg, up her inner thigh, and over her most sensitive area.

Wesley seemed completely unaffected, almost bored. "Something got you here," he said as he painted over the scar on her hip. "Dog bite?"

"Yeah." If you counted a werewolf as a dog...

"Not a problem. I'll cover it up, along with the tattoo." He finished with the white and reached for the black airbrush. "The moment I saw your hair, I knew what I would make you." Interesting. She'd dyed her normally mahogany hair jet black the night before in an effort to disguise herself. Along with using some shifter magic to change her green eyes to blue, she'd hoped it was enough to limit her exposure.

Wesley turned to his assistant. "Start darkening her spine. I want the stripes to come from a single strip of black and wrap around her body. White between the nipples."

A tickle of spray passed over her butt crack, and her eyebrows shot into her hairline. Wesley laughed and lowered his voice. "I enjoy working with you newbies. I predict that three weeks from now, you'll be spreading your cheeks so that Andre can get a better angle."

"If you say so," she said through a smirk.

"High pony. No hairpiece. She has enough as it is. Black apron, black tail, black stilettos," Wesley practically barked the orders. The assistant took off toward a room in the back.

"We get to wear an apron?" Laina asked.

"Gotta have somewhere to put your tips," he said through an impish grin. "With a body like yours, I predict you'll make plenty."

Her cheeks went hot again, now under a coat of paint that clung and stretched like a leather glove.

The assistant returned and started fussing with her hair as Andre feathered another layer of paint under her arm. By the time they were done, her shoulders were cramping, but she didn't feel naked anymore. In fact, Nickie's prediction proved true; the latex coated her flesh like a wet suit, hairline to ankle. A lacy, scrolled black mask was placed over her eyes, and an apron the size of a micro miniskirt was tied around her hips. Andre affixed a black tail to the base of her spine with costume glue.

"Wait a few minutes more to put on the shoes," Wesley

said. Laina took the black stilettos in hand and headed for the full-length mirror on the wall. But when she looked at her reflection, a human-shaped zebra stared back at her. A contoured, curvy-as-hell zebra.

"Hot!" the cheetah said with a wink.

"Wow," Nickie added. "Wesley's a genius."

Wesley had made the blond bombshell into a doe, complete with dainty brown ears that poked from her chin-length hair.

"Thanks. It's not as bad as I was expecting. It's almost like…"

"Like you have a dirty secret." Her new friend arched an eyebrow. "Like for just one night you can be someone else. You can be anyone."

Exactly, Laina thought. Tonight, she *was* someone else. That was the plan. As Nickie and the rest of the models filtered through the door to the main part of the club, she dropped back and leaned against the lockers to put on her shoes. Once she'd double-checked that no one was watching, she unlocked her cubby and fished a tiny blue box from her purse. She dropped it into her apron. The box contained fairy magic, capable of attracting vermin from far and wide. An added enchantment made it invisible to humans when activated.

Laina closed the locker and squared her shoulders. It was time to do what she'd come to do.

With a tray of canapés balanced on one hand, Laina entered the crowded ballroom of Hunt Club. The members, although dressed in normal attire, also wore masks, all depicting animals. A curvy dark-haired woman in a black wrap dress scanned her from head to toe through a mask of dragon scales. She flashed Laina a lecherous smile.

A balding, portly man by the name of Nate, who she learned was in charge, gathered them in the kitchen and explained that the patrons paid a sizable fee for tickets to the grand opening. Tonight only, appetizers and house drinks were included with admission. Laina wouldn't be expected to take payment or make change for anything she served, but the guests were encouraged to tip her for her service. If the patrons asked for high-end wines or top-shelf liquors, they were available at the bar at an additional cost.

"Any other services you wish to provide are between you and your customer," Nate said through a lewd grin. "But those activities need to occur in the private lounge areas. Don't leave the floor without letting someone know."

"What services might those be?" she murmured under her breath.

Nate gave her a condescending look as if he'd heard her, but if he did, he didn't acknowledge her tongue-in-cheek question. He simply wished them a successful night before disappearing into the kitchen.

"Sometimes the members ask for a private audience," Nickie said from beside her. "You are allowed to say no, but you should totally say yes." She winked. "Lions, tigers, and bears, oh my! Just don't let them sink their teeth into you. Unless you're into that." She wagged her puffy white deer tail and strode deeper into the club, a tray of champagne flutes balanced on her hand.

The idea that one of these men or women might ask for a private audience made Laina's stomach clench. It wasn't vulnerability that set her on edge. On the contrary, as a werewolf on the night before a full moon, *she* was the danger, capable of ripping a man apart if she wasn't careful. No, what bothered her was the anonymity of it. Laina's past lovers had all developed from long-term relationships. Unlike her brother, she'd never appreciated the appeal of a one-night stand.

Wanting to avoid as much attention as possible, she worked her way around the outer edge of the crowd, along the line of potted trees and flowering bushes that gave the club the illusion of an outdoor garden. The green plants offered her a sense of peace and security in an otherwise dim room. All the tables were bar-height, and above them, white globe string lights drooped in zigzagging swags across the timbered ceiling. On a platform at the front of the room, an alternative rock band played a tune she'd heard before but couldn't remember the name of.

"Thank you," a young man in a panther mask said,

lifting a coconut shrimp from her tray and tucking a bill into her apron. His gaze darted to her breasts before turning back to a gray-haired woman in a leopard mask. They continued their conversation, something about pharmaceutical investments. The woman lifted a shrimp from her tray without looking at her. She didn't tip. Laina moved on.

At the next table, the men were too wrapped up in organizing a charity golf match to pay her any mind. They leaned across the table, trying their best to hear each other over the music. She extended the tray between them and smiled. They each took a shrimp, seeming to barely notice the as-good-as-naked woman offering it to them. Still, they stuffed her apron with bills before she moved on.

Near a set of stairs at the back of the room, a table of four women seemed more interested in one another than in her. They enjoyed what was left on her tray and handed her a tip directly, rather than tucking the money into her apron like everyone else.

By the time she'd finished her first round and returned to the kitchen, she'd decided this assignment was far easier than she'd expected. She picked up another tray and melded back into the crowd. In a few short hours, she'd discreetly drop the fairy box on her way out and put the entire experience behind her.

As the night wore on, she forayed deeper into the crowd, closer to the hall that led to the private VIP lounges in the back. Curiosity made her skin tingle. What went on back there? Should she go check it out? It wasn't like she planned to ever return to a club like this. Like Nickie said, tonight she could be anyone. Why not satisfy her itch to snoop? Smiling to herself, she looked over both shoulders and slipped behind the dark curtain that separated public area from private.

She strode down a long hall of poshly decorated rooms with velvet drapes in lieu of doors. Some were closed. Others were pulled back as if the guests inside enjoyed being observed. Laina snuck a peek inside the ones whose curtains were left open, noticing couples talking over drinks, some touching more than others. Near the end of the hall, she almost tripped over her stilettos at the sight of Nickie riding the lap of a man in a tiger mask. Flustered, Laina shuffled to the end of the hall and flattened herself against the wall, out of sight of their room. Jesus, she was lucky she hadn't dropped her tray. She knew things like that went on, but it was another thing entirely to see it in person.

She gripped the tray tighter and backed into a dark corner, trying to catch her breath.

Part of her wanted to wipe what she'd seen from her mind, but another part, the wolf that waited under her skin, was having a glorious time replaying the scene in her head. This close to the full moon, her animal instincts were near the surface, and this was too good not to indulge in. Her blood heated as she closed her eyes and pictured the act again.

A hand landed on her hip from behind, and she jumped. Only her werewolf reflexes kept the tray in her hands.

"You're not supposed to be here," a familiar voice said into her ear. *Kyle*, she thought, but no, it couldn't be. What would be the odds of him being a member here? The odds of him being here at all? Just someone who sounded like him, she thought. She glanced over her shoulder, but his face was covered in a lion mask. The door behind him was cracked open—a stairwell. So that's where he'd come from.

"I didn't know. It's my first day. Don't tell on me, okay?" She flashed a flirtatious smile and started to leave.

His hand landed on her waist. "Wait," he whispered in her ear. "Stay. It will be our secret."

The warm press of his thumb above her belly button made her body come alive. She inhaled deeply and parsed out the scent of human man, a spicy cologne, and the slightest hint of deep forest. Again, she thought of Kyle, and her wolf shivered beneath her skin, definitely interested. Her eyes widened. *It couldn't be.*

"Is this okay?" he asked, pulling her closer. "I just want to talk to you."

Her body thrummed, and she pressed her thighs together against a growing ache between her legs. "Yes," she answered, unable to deny herself. His voice...his scent... Whoever this was, she wanted him. Her wolf wanted him. The animal part of her rubbed up against the inside of her skin, chuffing for more of his touch.

As if he could hear her thoughts, he moved her tray to the corner of a decorative table with an ornamental vase. When he returned his hands to her, he stroked them over her back. His nostrils flared. "You even smell like her."

"Hmm?"

"You smell good," he said a little louder. He drifted his hand lower, hooking it under her bottom and pulling her flush against his chest. Goddess, she shouldn't be doing this, but her body loved the feel of him. It had been a long time since she'd been touched like this. She settled against him, giving herself over to the urge within her.

Tracing her nose along his neck, she inhaled deeply. "You smell good too."

His smile turned wolfish, and he gestured toward the room where Nickie was making guttural sounds. "Do you like to watch?"

"Not really," she whispered softly, her cheeks heating. "I... It was an accident."

"Hmm. I believe that. You don't strike me as someone who watches. You take what you want, don't you?" His breath brushed the shell of her ear, his voice and scent making her body go taut. Something heavy turned over deep within her. Pure instinct took hold, and she ground her belly against his erection, her palms smoothing under his jacket, along the fine fabric of his shirt.

His chest rumbled a low growl. He bent his head until his mouth was dangerously close to hers, and the heady, distinctly male scent of him filled her nostrils. Their lips brushed, featherlight. Damn, her heart was going to jump straight out of her chest, and the thump-thump under her hands told her he was reacting similarly. Her inner wolf edged close to the surface, making her skin tingle.

It had been so long since she'd had sex. She was always too busy or too distracted by pack politics to allow herself the pleasure. But tonight, she was no one. Anita Woody didn't exist. She'd never see this man again, and goddess, she ached for him.

Rising on her toes, she licked along the seam of his lips. Then fisted his hips and almost lifted him off his feet as she turned them both until her back was against the wall and his body nestled between her legs.

"Whoa," he said breathily. "You're strong."

She captured his mouth with hers. Hitching one leg over his hip, she arched, positioning herself until his hard length hit just the right spot. Hand in the center of his back, she pulled him closer, rubbing herself against him shame-lessly. He moaned, and she used the opening to stroke his tongue with hers.

"It's time," a familiar voice called. She looked over the

lion's shoulder to see Nate, the one she'd assumed was the manager, standing at the end of the hallway, pointing at his watch.

Swallowing hard, she tried to hide herself behind the man in the lion mask as he drew back, but thankfully, Nate hadn't stuck around. She picked up her tray, her eyes darting sheepishly toward the corners of the hall. Jesus, she'd just dry humped a perfect stranger.

"I have to go take care of something," the stranger said. "Will you wait for me? I want to see you again." He brushed the outside of her arm with his knuckles.

"Um… I…" What the fuck had just happened? As he moved into the light, she saw the build of him, his dark hair, the square jaw under the lion's mask. Her body clenched again. Shit, he was attractive, but this wasn't her. She didn't let random strangers kiss her in dark corners. Only, she had, and she didn't regret it. And if she were honest with herself, she would have let him do a hell of a lot more if they hadn't been interrupted.

"Please," the lion begged. He glanced at his watch. "Meet me back here in an hour. I want to talk to you." He left her side abruptly and strode through the curtain.

Laina let out a relieved breath when he was out of sight. What the hell was that? Never in her life had she felt this kind of attraction. It was…metaphysical…she was sure of it. The moon was to blame. Her wolf wanted him, and her animal was too close to the surface. *Fuck*. She needed to get out of here. If she saw him again tonight, she wouldn't be able to stop herself from doing more, maybe something she would regret.

She left the VIP area just as Nate was taking the stage where the band had been. He babbled something into the microphone about the success of Hunt Club and this being the sixth club opening this year. She wasn't listening. Her only focus was the restroom near the kitchen. She needed some alone time so she could decide what to do next. But she stopped when she saw the man in the lion mask step up behind Nate. Was he going to speak? Did he work here?

"And now, may I introduce to you the man who makes this all possible, the man we like to call 'The King,' Hunt Club's own, Kyle Kingsley!"

Laina's mouth dropped open as the lion in a suit, the one she'd kissed only moments ago, took the stage and removed his mask. Kyle, the man from her clinic, Milo's owner, her missed date, and her wolf's obsession, stood at the microphone behind a dazzling smile. The crowd applauded.

"Thank you for coming to the grand opening of Hunt Club, Sable Creek, where we cater to your inner beast," Kyle said.

He continued talking, but Laina's ears rang, drowning out his words. Kyle Kingsley...owner of Hunt Club. Shaking her head, she rushed from the room, remembering at the last moment why she'd come in the first place. Reaching into her apron, she retrieved the small box. As Monty had instructed, she turned the lid to activate the spell. With everyone distracted by Kyle's speech, it was surprisingly easy to navigate through the kitchen unnoticed. She slid the box into a dark corner under the sink.

Moments later, she'd gathered her things from the locker room and passed through the gate on the way back to Monty's, all the while ignoring her inner wolf, who whimpered bitterly over the lingering ache between her legs.

CHAPTER
ELEVEN

Laina slipped into a warm, soapy bath and started working the latex from her skin, peeling and scraping and thanking the good lord that Nickie had made her shave. How did the models do this regularly? Her feet and back were killing her, and her skin was tender where she'd extricated it from the clingy latex. Removing it from her nipples was almost as bad as detaching it from her inner thighs.

But when most of the paint was off and she could finally settle into the warm water, it was Kyle she thought about. Her near miss was now a hit-and-run. Remembering the feel of him grinding against her clit caused the rosy tips of her breasts to tingle and her legs to cross against the delectable pressure of desire growing between them. How long had it been since she'd had sex? Three years? Four?

A knock chased away her thoughts of Kyle and brought her to her senses. "Yes?"

"Can I talk to you?" Jason asked through the door.

"Hold on." She pulled a towel into the water to cover herself. "Come in."

When he entered the bathroom, her brother's eyebrows shot up, and he laughed. "What the hell were you?"

She grabbed a hand mirror she'd rested on the side of the tub and started scrubbing the remains of paint and makeup from her face. "Zebra."

"Damn. I'm sorry, Laina. You deserve better than that." At the sincerity in Jason's tone, she softened.

"It wasn't so bad," she murmured, trying to repress the memory of Kyle. "And now it's done."

"I'm relieved. After you left, all I could think about was that I should have gone instead. I sometimes forget how innocent you are. I'm sure you saw things you want to forget."

She laughed. "I'm not that innocent, and I didn't see anything I…" She was going to say she hadn't seen anything she hadn't seen before, but in fact, she had. She'd never watched a couple having sex, and the image of Nickie riding the man's lap filled her brain again. But the memory didn't bother her. It was shocking, yes, but she'd be lying to say it didn't intrigue her. "I didn't see anything I regret seeing."

Jason chuckled. "Well, all right. Maybe you are my sister after all."

"Can I ask you something?" She leaned her head against the back of the tub.

"Shoot."

"Have you ever heard of Kyle Kingsley?"

Jason snorted. "Uh, yeah. Anyone who hasn't spent the last five years under a pile of textbooks knows who he is. He's like a reclusive billionaire playboy. Every time the guy is seen in public, it's a social media event."

"Oh." She sighed heavily.

"What's wrong, La?" His use of his pet name for her coaxed the truth from her.

She took a deep breath and folded her arms over the towel on her chest. "My wolf seems to think he's breeding material."

Jason blinked at her for a moment, the corners of his mouth twitching. Eventually, he gave in to a deep, erratic laugh. "You. You, the feminist, princess werewolf...who refuses to marry and runs her own business like the queen of veterinary medicine...have a bitch boner for Kyle Kingsley?"

"You see the problem, then."

He leaned his elbows on his knees, his laughter dwindling to something more like concern. "Have you even ever met him?"

She rolled her eyes and sent a spray of water in his direction. "Yes! Actually, he brought his dog into Four Paws before we left Carlton City."

"Huh?"

"He was just passing through. The dog got sick. We were supposed to have a date, but I stood him up because of the ball. Then we ran into each other tonight."

Jason stilled. "Wait, is your cover blown? Did he recognize you?"

Laina shook her head. "No. I was wearing a mask. But I recognized him, and my wolf practically stuck her ass in his face."

The laugh that burst from Jason was so strong it almost knocked him off the toilet. "Damn! La has a crush. I did not expect that."

"*You* didn't expect it? How do you think I feel? The desire I felt for him, Jason, was so strong I almost... I might have done things if I'd had the chance." She narrowed her eyes, remembering how she'd pulled his hips to hers and ground against him. "It was like my wolf wanted to mark him like we do when we mate."

Drawing a deep breath, he leaned his elbows on his knees. "Shit, Laina. That's not good."

"What do you mean? Why?"

Jason's eyes narrowed. "You say your wolf wants him. Your wolf specifically wants *him*."

She nodded. "She's never wanted anyone like this before. Like it was almost outside my control."

"And you're sure she didn't just want sex with anyone?"

"I'm sure. Although, honestly, I would have had sex with *him* if given the chance. His voice…" She closed her eyes. "If he'd told me to do something, I'd have done it. My wolf pressed against my skin like Kyle was carrying the moon in his pants."

Jason groaned. "Laina, what you're describing isn't just attraction. Kyle's your *vice*."

"No!" She growled and bared her teeth in his direction.

"Yes. This is exactly what it's like." Jason's voice grew raspy with emotion. "Your wolf *wants* him. Maybe even as your mate." He lowered his voice. "I should know."

She leaned her head back and ground her teeth. The closest thing to a vice in the human world was an addiction; only, in werewolf world, the experience was metaphysical. The inner wolf attached to something unexpectedly, and denying it could become uncomfortable. A vice became stronger during the full moon. "What makes you think that my desire for Kyle is anything like your vice for sex?"

"I'm not talking about my vice for sex." Jason's voice held something so desperate, she turned her head to look at him. He was supporting himself on his knees with his elbows, his eyes closed as if in pain.

"Then what are you talking about?" she asked softly.

"Jessica Woods. Everything you're feeling for Kyle, I felt for her." He swallowed hard. "And she felt for me."

A chill traveled through her despite the warm bath, and she hugged the wet towel tighter to her chest. "What? Why have you never talked about this before?"

He turned watery eyes on her. "Because it was new, and before we could act on it—"

"She was killed by Alex." Jessica had gone to the theater with her parents the night Alex had struck. "Oh, Jason."

He rubbed a hand over his face. "I don't want your sympathy, and honestly, I never want to speak of this again. But yeah, the sex thing, that's just a balm, you know. A shallow vice to replace a soul-deep one. So I know what you're going through, okay, and it's serious. This could get hard for you."

Vices were serious business in wolf world. Different wolves had different vices. Some wolves were known to obsess over certain foods or have an irresistible craving to roll in dried leaves. A mild vice would pass if denied long enough. She'd known a wolf who'd given up their vice for coffee a few years back without many side effects. But other vices became all-consuming obsessions, denial causing painful detox symptoms. The best scenario was having a mate who was also your vice. The bond that formed was unbreakable and in their tradition was a sign the mating was fated by the goddess.

"I can't... I can't want him in that way. Kyle can't be my vice, and he certainly can't be my fated mate. He's not even a werewolf."

"Maybe your wolf can be distracted with sex, like mine is," Jason offered. "Try with someone else."

Laina stared at the ceiling. "Maybe, but my wolf has

wanted him since the minute we met. She's asked for him *twice.*"

"Shit." He ran his fingers through his hair. "You've got to stay away from him, then. If you don't, it's only going to get worse. With time and distance, you should be able to redirect her." In a quiet voice, he added, "It worked for me." Jason shifted uncomfortably, and she silently berated herself for not being more sensitive about his plight. Oh goddess, she hoped forgetting Kyle didn't require sleeping with practical strangers. It might work for Jason, but she just couldn't do it.

"Turn around. I'm getting out."

Jason slid to the other side of the toilet and stared at the door. She pulled the plug on the drain and stood up to grab a dry towel from the rack. Wringing out the wet one, she hung it up to dry before wrapping the other around her body. "Okay."

"What about the fairy box? Did you do Monty's dirty work?" Jason asked, turning back toward her.

"Yes. The box is activated and in the dustiest corner of the kitchen. The place will be crawling with rats by tomorrow. If the health inspector doesn't close Hunt Club down, at least temporarily, Monty hasn't bribed the right people."

"Good. Hopefully, that's the end of it. The packs should be here tomorrow. We need Monty to be cooperative."

"It's three o'clock in the morning. I think we can officially say the packs will be here later today, which is why I sorely need to get some sleep." She started for her room.

The toilet rattled as Jason removed himself from its porcelain lid. "Hey, Laina."

"Yeah."

"I know you think that if you work hard enough and study long enough, you can cure yourself of being a werewolf and escape what it means. You can't. This isn't a disease. There is no cure. You're a supernatural being. It's magic, not medicine. Do what you have to do to deal with these feelings you're having, and don't feel guilty about it for a second. No shame."

"Just like there's no shame in marrying someone I don't love to perpetuate the Fireborn bloodline? Like how there will be no shame in cheating on whoever the male might be because marriage is nothing more than a practical business arrangement and I am simply a wolf who needs to breed?"

"Come on, Laina..."

"No. Don't deny it. That's exactly how the pack thinks. That's how Silas thinks. Maybe that's how *you* think. Well, let me tell you how *I* think. I think I don't have to let the wolf rule my life. Love exists, real love, the kind of love that brings you to your knees and holds you tight during the storm. Sex means something, and so does marriage. And not because my inner wolf or the pack at large bullies me into wanting it."

He groaned, his gaze shifting toward the ceiling.

"Maybe it doesn't *have* to mean something, but I want it to. I don't want to grow old with someone who simply served a purpose in my life, like an ugly Christmas sweater I wear every year because it's become some kind of preposterous tradition. I don't want to dull my wolf's passions for someone by having sex with someone else. I need intimacy. I want tenderness and love. Yes, real love." Her voice took on a thready quality. "I want what Mom and Dad had!" Tears stormed her face with a vengeance.

"So that's it, then. This is about our parents."

She whirled on him. "Don't you want what they had? The pure, unadulterated affection we grew up with?"

Jason frowned. "Everyone aspires to that, Laina, but you

have to remember, they were both purebreds. And they were lucky. They were fated mates. It's not like one of them was human."

"Cameron asked me to marry him at the ball," she admitted.

"Cameron is gay."

"You caught on to that, huh?"

"Uh, yeah. I think most people know. They just don't talk about it."

"Well, is that good enough for me? Should I be happy that someone asked? Should I be satisfied with a platonic marriage?"

"Only you can answer that, but I would think choosing Cameron would be far preferable to having someone chosen for you. You're twenty-nine and female. You're running out of time. And on that note, I guarantee the last person anyone would choose for you is a human playboy who owns a lifestyle club."

"I know, I know. I'll stay away from him. I get it." Ugh. Her chest hurt. "As for Cameron's proposal, I don't think I want to be married at all."

Jason snorted. "You'd have to disobey Silas's direct order. You'd have to break your connection to your alpha."

"It's possible. It's been done before in extreme circumstances."

"You'd be shunned by the pack. It's suicide, not to mention it would break my heart. We could never shift together."

His forlorn expression caused her eyes to burn, and she wiped under each of them. Jason pulled her into his arms. "Don't cry. Whatever you decide to do, I'll always be here for you, pack or no pack."

She hugged him back. "I miss Mom and Dad. I hate Alex

Bloodright. I hate Jonah. I hate what they've done to us. What are we even doing in this godforsaken town?" She sobbed into her brother's arms. "Will we ever be free to move on from this…this nightmare?"

"I don't know, La. I just don't know."

TWELVE

The entire time he was giving his speech, all Kyle could think about was the woman from the VIP hallway. She'd reminded him so much of Laina. Certainly his body was just as interested. Her voice, her scent, it had set his blood on fire. It wasn't Laina, of course. Her hair was darker, and her eyes behind the mask were a different color. Not to mention that there was no way the talented veterinarian would be serving at his club. Still, she'd stirred the same kind of passion in him, and he couldn't wait to get back to her. He had to know her.

But when he finished speaking, Nate had a crowd ready to shake his hand. Business partners and VIPs asked for a moment of his time. Everyone wanted a picture with the King of Hunt Club. Over an hour had passed before he was able to excuse himself to look for her, and it didn't take long for him to figure out she wasn't waiting for him in the VIP lounge.

"What's wrong with you?" Nate asked. He'd followed Kyle from the area near the stage where the large and persistent group of admirers still gathered. "Did you lose your wallet or something?"

Kyle snorted. "No. The woman. Who was the zebra?"

Nate laughed. "She was a knockout. I'll give you that. Sorry to cockblock you earlier—"

"Is she still here?"

"Should be. The shift doesn't end for another hour."

Kyle scanned the floor, then started for the kitchen.

"Kyle, where are you going? There are more people who want to meet you. We have work to do. This is where you shine, remember?"

Waving a hand dismissively, he barked, "You do it."

Nate grabbed his arm, his head shaking and that shark's-tooth smile bending into a grin. "Not how this works, bro. You're the face. I'm the brains. Get over there and charm the dollars out of those fuckers."

Fuck. Nate was right. What the hell was he thinking, abandoning opening night for a woman? An employee, for Christ's sake. He cast one last lingering look toward the kitchen.

"Kyle, we have her name and number." Nate laughed. "She had to fill out forms to work here. I promise you, if you want to rail her later, it can be arranged."

Hearing Nate talk about her like that sent a brutal protective instinct through him. Made no sense. After all, he desperately did want to get inside her. But he couldn't suppress a snarl of distaste as they strode back toward the group. Nate shot him a curious glance, and Kyle coughed into his hand to disguise the sound.

What the hell was happening to him? Why were these women suddenly getting under his skin?

He pushed the thoughts aside. He was Kyle "The King" Kingsley. No attachments. All fun and games and animal instinct. For some reason, the thought left a gaping hole in his chest. Tonight, he felt as hollow as a carved pumpkin. He forced a smile onto his face anyway and returned to his admirers.

THE WOLVES ARRIVED IN SHIFTS, AND LAINA GUIDED THEM IN discreet units to the forest behind Monty's. Not the forest the humans could see, but one that could only be accessed through the door in the back of Monty's office, enchanted and otherwise inaccessible. Until Silas's witch friend could ward Cameron's property, the space was undeniably safer than Rivergate Manor, aside from the fact that an ogre with suspected tendencies toward organized crime guarded the door.

"How have you been?" Cameron asked as he helped her set up the tent that would serve as their mess hall for the next three days. It was possible for the pack to appear human and go about their business during the day, but they rarely did. Their preference was to stay together in a three-day wolfapalooza. Like a furry family reunion.

"As well as can be expected," Laina said. "Monty is about as agreeable as...well, an ogre."

He shook his head. "Thanks for doing this. I still can't believe your older brother offered you up like a sacrificial lamb."

"Speaking of Silas, have you heard from him?"

He shook his head. "Still undercover. Said he was going to track down Jonah and end this before anyone else got hurt. I haven't heard from him since." Cameron shrugged.

"Me either."

"It's my job to know where everyone is, yet Silas didn't tell me where he was going. I thought he'd tell you."

Laina shook her head. As much as her brother could be a pain in the ass, she loved the man. Where was he? He never missed a shift on purpose. She retrieved the burner phone from her back pocket, the one Silas had given her in case of an emergency, and texted him. A few seconds later, the device chimed as his response came through.

I'm fine. Won't be there. You can handle it without me.

She showed it to Cameron.

"Hmm. Spoken like a true leader." He stroked back his black hair, longer now that they neared the shift, as was his facial hair. "Shall we grab a burger before the main event?"

She started to say yes, but Monty interrupted her, bellowing her name from the pub door, the ogre's eyes sweeping the woods until he locked on to her. "Laina, you'd better get in here. We've got trouble."

She broke into a jog, Cameron right behind her, backing her up. "What is it? Has something happened to Jason?" As she broke through the protective enchantment, the trees and flowers faded away and were replaced by the illusion of a dark alley, complete with potholed lane and city dumpster. Monty motioned her inside, then slammed the door in Cameron's face.

"Hey—"

"Fucking Kyle Kingsley is standing in my bar holding a fairy box and asking for *Anna*." The malice in his voice was as real as his foul breath.

Feeling light-headed, she strode from the back room and into the bar proper. She came up short at the sight of the man her wolf had pined for since their last encounter. Kyle Kingsley.

His eyes widened in recognition. He knew who she was

—who she *really* was. Mouth pressed into a straight line, he shook his head. "I'm not sure what this is." He held the fairy box between his fingers. "But rats seem to love it." He tossed the box at her.

Catching it in one hand, she noticed the lid was closed. That explained why Kyle could see it but not who'd found and closed it. Those were not things a human could do. She forced her expression to convey total ignorance. "Why are you giving this to me?"

"Who the hell are you? The paperwork you gave Wesley said Anita Woody, but you told Nickie your name was Anna." He pointed a finger at her. "But I know you. You're—"

Monty coughed, cutting him off. "I think you've got the wrong girl. This one was here workin' last night. Wasn't she, boys?" Jeff and the other regulars chimed in affirmatively, no doubt hoping to be rewarded for the lie with a free beer.

"Really? My security cameras disagree." Kyle's hazel eyes narrowed. He pulled himself up to his full height, which almost rivaled Monty's. "I get it, Monty. You're worried I'm going to move in on your business. But this is a felony." He pointed at the box. "And if you think this shit is going to work, you don't know me."

"Lotsa girls got her colorin'. I think you're confused."

"Coloring, yes. Face and figure, no. This is the one."

"Aw, fuck you, Kyle. You're barking up the wrong tree. I had nothin' to do with this. If the girl's in your video, take it up with the girl."

Laina whirled on Monty, her eyes flaring with anger. Did he just throw her under the bus? *Bastard!*

"Don't look at me like that, Anna. It's you who's fucked up. Fucked up big-time by the looks of it." Monty placed both hands on the bar and glared at her with no remorse.

Laina turned back to Kyle, her wolf growling and snapping inside her head over Monty's betrayal. At least the anger was doing a good job of fighting back her lust and her fear. How could this happen? Especially now, with the shift happening in a matter of hours. What if he had her arrested? Becoming a wolf in a prison cell would be disastrous.

"Can I speak to you privately in the back room?" She pointed a trembling hand toward the storage area. It was all she could do to maintain her composure.

He nodded and followed her inside, allowing the door to squeal shut behind them in the same tone as a coffin lid. She faced him in the narrow aisle between the cases of alcohol. A bare bulb cast a harsh circle of light around them, but the ugly environment did nothing to curb her wolf's interest in him. Her heart galloped, and she shifted uneasily, trying to manage the growing ache between her legs.

"You came here instead of going to the police?" She breathed a sigh of relief. "Thank you."

"Don't overthink it. It isn't in Hunt Club's best interests to call attention to a rat problem in our kitchen, even if it was sabotage. If I file a police report, this will be all over the news. I'm sure Monty knew that when he hired you to do what you did. Although, I will do it if the two of you force my hand."

"You won't have to."

She waited patiently as he stared her down. Best to remain silent. Why offer information she didn't have to give? Information that might incriminate her?

"What happened at Four Paws the night of our date?"

Surprised, Laina spread her hands. "I thought Becca called you..."

He scoffed. "I think her exact words were, 'Due to a personal tragedy, the animal hospital is closing indefinitely, and details can only be released to immediate family members.' What the fuck happened? What I saw that night was..." He shook his head. "And why is a veterinarian from New Hampshire slinging beer in a hole-in-the-wall in rural Wisconsin? What are you doing here, Laina, besides trying to sabotage my club?"

"Shh." She brought her finger to her lips. "No one can know who I am."

His eyes narrowed to slits. "Explain."

Her thoughts darted, searching for some shred of truth she could share with him, although why it pained her to lie was beyond her comprehension. "I can't go into details," she said slowly, "but it was a domestic violence situation. I'm in hiding."

"Husband or boyfriend?" His voice broke as he asked the question.

"Neither. An enemy of my family. It's a long and twisted story. He's very powerful, and my survival depends on concealing my identity. I did what I did to your club because Monty would have thrown me out if I hadn't. I'm sorry. I'll do whatever you want to make it up to you."

She'd stepped in closer without even meaning to, her lids drooping low as she breathed in his scent. Her wolf had forgotten all anger and fear and was panting, tongue out in his direction. Oh, how she wanted his hands on her body, his mouth on hers. He was so close now, she could feel his heat, smell the cedar and pine scent that seemed to follow him everywhere. Had he moved that last inch, or had she?

"What do you have to offer me that would make up for

the deception you pulled last night? You could have ruined my business, Laina." His hands landed on his hips, and she looked up at him through her lashes.

Wolf whimpering, a vivid fantasy played out in Laina's head. She'd drop to her knees, unzip his pants, and take him between her lips, showing him exactly what she had to offer. With all the willpower left in her, she forced herself back a step. Her knees turned to liquid, and her ass landed on a crate of vodka.

"Hey, are you okay?" Kyle rested a hand on her shoulder, suddenly concerned.

She shook her head but didn't elaborate. "Kyle, I'm sorry. I think you know this wasn't my idea, despite what Monty says. He knows my secret and blackmailed me into it. What can I do but beg you not to get the Sable Creek PD involved? I'll do anything. Anything you want. But please keep my secret."

He tipped his head in agreement, and relief flooded her body. Tension she didn't even know she was holding eased. She blew out a deep breath.

"I won't tell anyone," he said softly. "On one condition."

"What?" she asked. "Money?"

He made a face as though she'd insulted him. "No, I don't want your money."

"Sex?" she whispered. *Please let it be sex.*

"No," he said curtly. "Jesus, Laina. I would never extort sex from you or anyone else."

She hung her head and forced her wolf, still trying desperately to show her enthusiasm for sex, down deeper into her psyche. "Then what can I give you?"

"I need you to train my dog."

Not what she was expecting. Her brows lifted. "Milo?"

"Yes, Milo. He's not adjusting well to the change in

ownership. He's made quite a mess of the place. I need you to come and stay with me for a while. Figure out what's wrong with him and teach me what to do."

"You want me... Wait, you want me to *live* with you while I train your dog...full time? Monty will never allow it. I have a job here."

"Oh, Monty will allow it, or Monty will need a lawyer. I'll talk to him." He pointed a thumb over his shoulder.

She swallowed. Even now, one look from Kyle made her squirm. How would she survive sleeping in the same house with him?

"Yes or no, Laina? Considering what you did, I don't think I'm asking too much here."

For a moment, she flipped the idea over in her brain. "I have an obligation to fulfill to my brother who is hiding here with me. Is three days from now soon enough for me to start?"

He nodded and offered her his hand. "It's a deal."

As they shook on it, he hoisted her from the crate and her momentum brought her flush against his wide, muscular chest. Her lips parted. Their eyes met and held.

"I was disappointed we never had that date," he murmured.

"Me too."

THIRTEEN

"I'm not comfortable with this, Laina." Monty clenched his fists, still reeling from his conversation with Kyle. "Who's going to take care of this place while you're playing with Pretty Boy's dog?"

"Do you want me to tell him no? I only offered because he threatened to get the police involved. If you'd rather handle this in the courts, I can stay." Laina knew the last thing Monty wanted was human law enforcement up in his business.

Monty's fish mouth bent in an exaggerated frown so pronounced it looked like an upside-down "U." "That fucking bastard. Fine. Go. Do what he tells you to do. But Jason better pick up the slack, or it'll cost you both."

Jason pulled her aside, his voice dipping. "Are you sure about this? After what we talked about last night, this is the worst thing that could happen."

He was right. If Kyle was her vice, her craving for him was only going to grow stronger the longer she was with him. "What other choice do I have?"

He rubbed a hand over his face. "I hope you know what

you're doing. Don't worry about Monty. I'll take care of things here. Although, I wish it were me staying at Hunt Club. I could keep those ladies busy." Jason smirked.

She rolled her eyes and returned to Cameron, who was more than a little peeved about having been locked in an ogre's enchanted forest. After accepting a supportive hug from her best friend, she told him everything, even about her strange attraction to Kyle and how Jason thought she might be flirting with a vice.

"Do you know what you're getting yourself into, Laina?"

She shrugged. "Yes... No... As of now, I'm just training his dog, despite what my wolf wants."

He extracted his phone from his pocket and typed "Kyle Kingsley" into the internet search bar, then handed her the results. She thought she might be sick. Kyle in a tux with a woman on each arm. A shirtless Kyle in the park with his head on the lap of one woman and another rubbing his feet, while yet another ate sushi off his abs. Kyle, naked in bed, the photograph taken through a woman's cheetah-painted legs as she straddled his hips. There were hundreds of photos, each more scandalous than the next.

"I've never had a vice," Cameron said. "I can't imagine what you're going through. But by the goddess, Laina, be careful. This guy makes your brother look like a prude."

THREE DAYS LATER, LAINA COULD ALMOST FORGET SHE'D PROMISED to live with Kyle Kingsley. Waking up after a night of being a wolf was a lot like waking up after a night of heavy drinking. Flashes of color, sounds, and scents came back to her as she blinked up at the clear blue sky. Leaves crinkled in her hair. Dirt coated her naked skin. But it was the stretched-out, used-up, mild ache of her muscles she liked best. The closest you could get as a human was the day after skiing or running a marathon. The compensating rush of endorphins created a sublime state of being. She was elated...and hungry.

A rustle and groan next to her signaled Cameron's waking. His manhood flopped against his hip as he rolled over and stretched. She giggled and averted her eyes. A few yards away, Jason was unfolding next to Lucile, the latter's curly gray hair matted with sweat. Even at sixty-five, she was as fast and strong as any of them. A living legend. Her sixteen-year-old granddaughter, Amanda, was already awake and desperately searching for her clothes in the tent near the door to Monty's. This was her first group shift. Time for Laina to be a proper princess and the alpha in Silas's stead.

She stood and joined Amanda at the pile. "It gets easier," she said to the girl. "You're new to this, and I'm sure the nudity is distracting, but you'll get used to it. Well, during the full moon. At other times, it will be just as awkward." Laina giggled.

Amanda pulled a Carlton City High School T-shirt over her head, her Fireborn tattoo disappearing beneath the sleeve. "Uh, I figured."

"Your tattoo seems to have healed properly," Laina said. The pack high priestess, or *Preotka*, administered the tattoos using a claw of the original Fireborn ancestor, called the primary. After a werewolf's first shift, which usually occurred in a private setting that included immediate family only, the tattooing ceremony was held to initiate the youngling into the pack. It was a ceremony most wolves considered as important as their mating or a birth.

"I can't believe how much I like shifting," Amanda said. "Last night… I can remember chasing an opossum through the woods. I was so fast. And the way the air huffed down my throat." Her fingers stroked her neck, her eyes misting over. "Will it always be like that?"

Laina, who had pulled on her own shirt in an effort to set the girl at ease, smiled warmly. "Yes. It will always be like this. It's important to be safe. Never shift alone. Stay away from humans. Plan ahead for a safe place to run. Try not to let it affect your employment. But once you've done those things, enjoy. For three nights, you're totally free."

Amanda gave her a quick, awkward hug. "Thank you, Laina. I'm so glad it was you here today. No offense, but Silas scares me."

Laina squeezed the girl's shoulders. "Silas scares us all. Now, come on. As the newbie, it's tradition that you help fire up the mess hall. I'm ready for breakfast."

THE PICKETERS FROM ETERNAL LIGHT MINISTRIES WERE OUT IN full force when Laina arrived at Hunt Club that afternoon. She honked her horn and revved her engine, and the protesters reluctantly parted to let her through to the gatehouse. This time, Taneesha recognized her and directed her to the main house rather than the service entrance.

From the front, Hunt Club Mansion was even more beautiful than what she'd seen from the service entrance, with gorgeous stone masonry and multiple towers that made her feel like she was driving up to Cinderella's castle.

An adult version, that is. The valet who offered to park her car was shirtless above a tight-fitting pair of cheetah pants and a tail. Was he wearing a collar?

"Welcome to fantasyland," Laina said to herself, cocking an eyebrow. "Wow, it's early for that much skin."

The door opened before she had a chance to knock. "Welcome to the King's Lair," an elderly woman in formal maid's attire said. Her half smile suggested the greeting was tongue in cheek, or else she personally couldn't take it seriously. The woman didn't fit the Hunt Club mold with her gray hair and bifocals. Laina liked her immediately.

She was about to introduce herself when Kyle jogged into the spacious foyer. If anything, he'd become better-looking since the day he'd walked into the animal hospital. The jeans he wore hugged his hips and skimmed softly over his lower body, bending and stretching in all the right places. His shirt was black, collared, with sleeves rolled past his elbows. Gorgeous and easy, as if he climbed out of bed looking like the goddess's gift to women.

Laina fumbled with her luggage, pretending to be immune. Her wolf chuffed inside her skin.

"Thanks for coming, La—"

"Anna," she corrected him.

He nodded and reached for her. For a moment, her stomach fluttered as she anticipated his touch. What was he doing? But he simply pulled the strap to her bag from her shoulder—his warm fingers brushing the skin near the scoop neck of her T-shirt—and transferred it to his own.

"Your room is this way." For some reason, she was surprised when he took it upon himself to carry her luggage, what with the housekeeper standing right beside them. When they'd reached the end of the hall, he placed her bags down on a four-poster bed in a room as big as the apartment she was staying in above Monty's.

"I'm right across the hall. I've been keeping Milo in my room, but now that you're here, maybe you can get him out more."

"Surely you don't keep him in there all day," she said incredulously, the animal lover in her perking to attention.

"I take him out in the morning and before I go to bed, but it's the best place for him while I'm working."

She cringed. "Dogs need exercise and socialization. He's not a toy you can put away. No wonder he's having behavioral problems."

Flinching as if she'd struck him, he collected himself. "Look, I don't think he's a toy." His tone was calm and gentle, completely unlike hers. "The dog doesn't listen to anyone. He drools all over the house, chews up anything he can get his mouth on, and scares the staff. I lead a very busy life, and Milo's coming here was unexpected. I'm trying my best to accommodate him." He spread his hands. "That's why you're here. You're going to teach me how to do this, right?"

She sighed. Maybe she'd spoken too harshly. Many new owners were completely unprepared to care for a dog like Milo. It wasn't fair for her to expect Kyle to have a lifetime of experience with canine behavior.

"Maybe you should introduce us again. The last time he saw me, he was sick. Better he associates me with a more positive experience."

He gestured toward the door. "Come on." Across the hall, Kyle showed her into a room even larger than the first, with a curved wall of windows overlooking miles of forest. The natural IMAX of the great outdoors created the perfect backdrop for the inner lair of the fairy-tale castle. A king-sized bed the width of a small island stood against one wall of the room, but as Laina entered, she couldn't miss Milo. The mastiff had destroyed what appeared to have been a couch at the far end of an attached sitting room, his guilt-ridden face turning up to hers from the center of a cloud of shredded stuffing.

"Milo!" Kyle dug his fingers into his hair. "Another one?"

"Another—" She darted a glance at Kyle and back at Milo. "Has he done this before?"

"Twice."

A giggle bubbled up Laina's throat, and she pressed two fingers over her lips to suppress it.

"I don't exactly see the humor in this sitch." He shot her a judgmental sideways glance belied by the ghost of a smile that drifted through his expression.

"How long has he been in here by himself?"

Kyle groaned. "An hour."

"Oh." The giggle returned, erupting from deep within her chest. She gave up and allowed the laugh to come full force.

Mouth in an exaggerated gape and hands on his hips, Kyle waited until she was finished before asking, "Can you help me or not?"

She straightened to her full height and strode directly toward Milo, who immediately assumed a submissive posture, head down, tail between his legs. "Oh, he knows what he did. Look how he's reacting. He's practically crawling into the floor. That's a good thing. That gives us something to work with."

"If he knows, why did he do it?"

She shrugged. "He's showing you he's stressed, Kyle. Dogs are pack animals. They don't celebrate when you leave the house with Netflix and ice cream. He doesn't know you. He doesn't trust you're coming back. He's bred to be a working dog, but he has nothing to do all day. He needs exercise and playtime. Social interaction. He needs to be with his pack."

Kyle scratched the stubble on his jaw and stared at Milo with a look of frustration. "I can't get another dog."

"Not another dog. *You*, Kyle. You need to be his pack." She stroked Milo's head while Kyle digested that nugget. "Dogs soothe anxiety by chewing. I sense he's coping with something more than loneliness and lack of exercise. Was Milo always nervous like this? What happened to his last owner?"

"As far as I know, Milo was a great dog. His owner died unexpectedly, and I offered to take him when no one else in the family could. I wasn't prepared to have a dog, but I thought he deserved better than the pound." Kyle sighed.

Something in his voice caused Laina's heart to sink. Milo wasn't the only one who'd lost someone recently. "How did you know his last owner?"

Kyle slipped his hands into his back pockets, trading his polished exterior for one bordering on exhaustion. "He was my father."

FOURTEEN

Kyle hadn't wanted to share that little tidbit of info with Laina within the first ten minutes of her being in his home, but once again, her presence loosened something deep within his chest, and he found he couldn't help himself.

"Your father passed recently?" Laina's eyes tightened at the corners. "Goddess, I'm an idiot. I'm sorry, Kyle. I didn't know."

He sighed heavily. "How could you have?" He shrugged. "It was a shock. My brother and I used to joke that the man was a cockroach—nothing could kill him. The guy smoked like a chimney, drank like he had a replaceable liver, and burned through women half his age while subsisting on a diet of bacon and butter sandwiches."

"Quite a man." Her lips twitched before she could force her face back into a solemn expression.

"It's okay. You can laugh. He would've liked a beautiful young woman laughing at his antics. Sort of his game, actually. You could say he was the quintessential American playboy. Hunt Club was his idea. It was the last business our company established with his direct involvement."

"When did he decide to get Milo?" she asked.

"About a year before his death. He died a few days before I came to see you. We didn't know he was sick until the end. Everyone assumed he was off sowing his wild oats. Turns out he was spending his days dying in a cabin in Red Grove, New Hampshire. The nurse said he'd wanted the dog for protection."

Laina raised an eyebrow as Milo shook his jowls, drool spraying the remains of the couch cushions around him. As he stared at the slobbery mutt, Milo's tongue lolled out the corner of his mouth, the billows of his leathery nose snorting. Kyle frowned. Gross. Laina may have plenty of experience with dogs, but this was a majorly unsexy way to welcome her to his home. And despite inviting her here under the pretense of watching Milo, Kyle wanted her here for other, more interesting reasons—namely, he wanted *her*.

"Protection huh? He may have chosen the wrong mastiff," Laina said lightly.

"He does seem more of a chewer than a fighter," Kyle murmured.

"Not just that, he's an English Mastiff, not a bullmastiff."

"There's a difference?"

"A big one. English Mastiffs are bigger but much less aggressive. Don't get me wrong, they can be protective of their owners and do make good watchdogs. His size and bark would be a major deterrent to most people. But it's usually the bullmastiffs that are used for security. They're more aggressive. You break in to a house with a bullmastiff, and his size would be the least of your worries. You'd likely get up close and personal with his teeth. English Mastiffs don't have a mean bone in their bodies naturally." As if to illustrate her point, Milo lay down near her feet and rolled onto his back. She knelt to scratch his belly. "The rash is completely gone."

"I changed his food like you said. He's been doing a lot better."

She gave him an appreciative nod. "Excellent."

"I don't think my father was worried about getting robbed," Kyle said, circling back to their earlier conversation. "His nurse said his first night there, something big scratched at the door and scared the hell out of him. He thought it might have been a bear and wanted a pet who'd scare away any wild animals who took an interest in the place."

Laina tapped her chin as she observed Milo and the couch he'd destroyed. When she was finished assessing the situation, she looked straight up into his eyes. And didn't that just make his blood pound in his ears and his dick twitch. All he could think about was what he'd like to do with her now that she was on her knees in front of him. He took a long blink, forcing his head back into the moment.

"I think we're dealing with more than an undisciplined dog here, Kyle. He's grieving—just like you. Your dad was his pack, his alpha. All the feelings of loss you're experiencing, he's experiencing too."

"He bonded with the old coot, huh?"

"Dogs weren't meant to be alone," she said, stroking Milo's ears. "Milo is lonely. He wants a leader. If you want Milo to respect you, you need to win him over, get him to see you as his alpha. Not only will he feel secure enough to stop eating your furniture, he'll be loyal and protective of you until the day he dies."

Kyle's polished smile faded into something more vulnerable. "How do I do that?"

"Two things." She stood, dusting Milo's hair from her hands. "The first is to earn his trust by caring for him on a predictable basis. That means he can't spend all day locked in this room. He must be fed a quality diet, be exercised regularly, and be socialized with both people and other animals. He needs a predictable schedule that includes work and reward."

Kyle snorted. "Don't we all. What's the second thing?"

She met Kyle's stare. "Love."

The intense and immediate reaction Kyle had to the word left him swallowing hard. He studied her expression. "Love?"

"Seriously. A dog can tell when you love him. They need love the same as food or water. The same as humans do." Her voice petered out at the end. Could she feel the charge in the air the way he did? He shifted his gaze toward the dog again to try to ease the tension.

"So, we start with trust," he murmured under his breath, then decided he had nothing to gain by hiding his attraction to her. Turning back to her, he stepped in closer. "There's something else I want to tell you."

"About Milo?"

He shook his head. "I wish we'd had that date. That first day I met you, you knocked me off my feet."

"Please," she said, rolling her eyes. "You are surrounded by supermodels. I highly doubt a woman with blood in her hair and smelling of fecal samples knocked you off your feet."

He allowed a languid smile to spread across his face. "There's something about you. You're different. Almost...wild."

"Why would you say I was wild?" Her scoff told him he'd touched a nerve. She tensed. Maybe she didn't like to think of herself that way.

He shrugged. "I mean it as a compliment. You just seem authentic, like the world hasn't shaped you. You have no idea how rare that is." She sighed, her body softening again, and he took it as an invitation to move even closer. "So, how about rescheduling our date?"

He was close enough now to kiss her, and the air crackled with their nearness. He desperately wanted to close the gap between them, take her face in his hands and direct all that heat and tension that was building in this room back into her. God, he wanted to press her against the wall.

LAINA COULD SMELL KYLE'S DESIRE FOR HER. IT HUNG IN THE AIR like rich spices, roasted nutmeg and cloves. Every part of her longed to kiss him. Every part. Especially her wolf. And by the way her beast awakened and begged for his mouth, she could tell Jason was right—Kyle was her vice. This was no simple attraction. She was on the other side of the full moon, but the draw to Kyle was so strong, she knew if she kissed him, she'd only want more. Already, his presence was magnetic, almost like he was emitting his own gravity.

The longer she stayed in his presence, the harder it was going to be not to throw herself at him. What then? They hadn't known each other long enough to form any kind of attachment or commitment. According to Cameron, Kyle was a known playboy. If he was only interested in casual sex, what would she do when he was sick of her? And she had other concerns. Although she'd been with humans before, her desire for those men didn't have the edge this did. As a wolf, she was strong, far stronger than a human man. Kyle had no idea what he was in for sexually. She fucked like an animal. Her inner beast would not be gentle with him. Maybe he was into that. Maybe he wasn't. But the truth remained, there was only one predator in this room, and it was Laina.

His lips parted. He was so close, so intent on her. She warred with herself. She should stop. She should back away. But in the end, it was impossible. Kyle was achingly attractive. Virile. Potent. Intense. Closing the last sliver of space, she planted her lips on his, teasing, tasting. His hands stroked her shoulders.

She drew a breath through her nose, detecting a subtle trace of woody cologne with a mandarin top note, the deep forest scent she'd come to associate with him, a light chemical residue she recognized as dry-cleaning solution, a hint of Milo, peppermint toothpaste, and underneath it all, the delicious spice of warm, passionate male she'd picked up earlier. His body warmed beneath her touch. His heart rate quickened. But the thing that made her wolf mad with passion was that despite living in this place and doing what he did, she could not detect even a hint of another female on his skin.

The slightest shift in his lips and the bend of his neck signaled his intent to end the kiss. She gripped his hips with both hands and pulled him against her, hard enough to make him grunt. She worked her hands under the tails of his shirt, enjoying the feel of smooth skin stretched over hard muscle. She clawed his sides, and when he gasped at the feel of her nails, she stroked his tongue with her own.

A wolfish growl rumbled from her chest, and she

doubled her efforts to gain control. What was she doing? If she didn't stop now, she never would. She called to mind the pictures Cameron had shown her of Kyle with other women, and the memory seemed to shake something loose, jarring her human mind back into control. Mustering her willpower, she removed her hands from his stomach and took a step back.

"Jesus." He ran a hand over his face.

"I'm sorry," she said. "That was... I don't know what came over me." She pressed her fist to her lips.

He released a shaky breath. "I cannot communicate strongly enough how much I feel you should go with what-ever it was if it happens again. It works for me. Oh holy hell, does it work for me." His gaze raked over her breasts, and he moved in, reaching for her waist.

She held up both hands. "Uh... I think it's a bad idea."

He stopped immediately. "Hmm?"

"I'll be honest. I find you attractive."

"Good. The feeling is mutual."

Her eyes shifted to the window, and she knotted her fingers in front of her hips. "I've spent too much time working lately, and the stress of what is happening in my personal life is overwhelming. It's only natural I'd be drawn to you." She placed one hand on her sternum. "But I don't think jumping into a casual sexual relationship is the right move for me right now, as much as I might want to. It won't happen again."

His lips pressed into a flat line, his arms folding over his chest. "I asked you on a date...for the second time," he said. "And *you* kissed *me*. What makes you think this was about casual sex?"

She was taken aback by his question and quirked an eyebrow. "You do have a reputation as a playboy."

His lip curled. "Ah, the tabloids. You read them, and you believe them?"

"Er, no, actually. I usually don't. I just... You own a club called Hunt Club," she said. "The thrill of the chase. Isn't casual sex what your business is all about?"

All emotion drained from his face, and a polished air of invincibility came over him. "I see." He adjusted his watch and pulled his phone from his back pocket. "As it so happens, I'm late for my afternoon orgy," he said through his teeth, his words dripping with sarcasm.

"I didn't mean—"

He closed his eyes and waved a hand through the air as if trying to clear it of what had just passed between them. "Never mind. Let's forget this ever happened. You get started with Milo. All his things are in the mudroom off the kitchen. I'll check in with you later." He gave her an entirely professional smile before leaving the room abruptly.

She stared at the door in shock, arms at her sides. A warm, wet nudge to her fingers reminded her that her charge was waiting. Milo's wrinkled face smiled up at her. "Don't look at me like that. How could I have known he'd take offense? The place *is* called Hunt Club, for crying out loud, and there are just short of a million incriminating pictures of the man on the internet."

The dog perked his floppy ears and tilted his head.

"Yeah, yeah. Come on. You need exercise, and I need air."

FIFTEEN

Clearly, Kyle had tried his best to provide for Milo. Laina found a basket of toys, treats, and a variety of leashes in the mudroom off the kitchen. Milo stuck to her side and examined each item as she pulled it from the basket, sniffing and licking each one. The mastiff was interested and friendly, snorting derisively and stomping his feet when she returned a rope toy to the pile.

She selected a training lead and positioned it on Milo's neck. Adding a handful of small treats to her pocket, she led the dog to the back door. "Okay, Milo. We can do this the hard way or the easy way."

The dog panted up at her, ears perked. A glob of slobber dropped from the corner of his sagging lips onto the toe of her shoe.

"I'm not going to hold that against you. I have a very good friend named Cameron who does the same thing sometimes." She rubbed the dog's tawny head. "Now, I'm going to open this door. You're going to wait and let me go through first. Understand?"

Pant, pant, pant.

"Sit." She pressed his butt to the floor and mumbled, "Here goes nothing."

Turning the knob slowly, she straightened, sending Milo every signal she could muster to indicate she was the alpha and he should stay behind her. But as soon as the door was cracked three inches, Milo bolted. Yanked by her leash-holding arm, Laina soared like a kite over the threshold, body flapping behind the massive canine. As he bounded across the pool deck, she leaped over chairs, limbs flailing until she could muster her inner wolf.

"Milo, stop!" she growled, giving the dog a sharp and firm correction.

Milo slowed to a stop at the edge of the yard. Panting, Laina took the mastiff's slobbery face in her hands. "Why did you have to do it the hard way?" The dog's tongue flicked out and up the side of her face.

"Ms. Whitehall, is everything all right?" the housekeeper called from the door Laina had left hanging open.

Laina waved. "Just fine." She nudged Milo and adjusted the training lead. "Let's try this again."

The backyard was ideal for a large dog like Milo. It was easily two acres, fenced, with plenty of shade trees. The swimming pool Milo had flown past might offer him an excellent form of exercise if the pool cleaner didn't protest the inevitable dirt and hair in the filter. Straightening, she began again, urging Milo to walk at her pace and correcting him when he tried to lunge ahead.

After a long afternoon of training, Laina concluded that Milo was further along than she'd expected. He could sit on command, as well as lie down, and, off leash, he came when called. He did not know the command to leave an object alone, and a ball she tossed for his amusement was promptly destroyed rather than returned.

But after several sessions around the yard, Milo followed her back to the house at an easy walk.

"I can't believe it." The housekeeper grinned from the door, her graceful gray chignon reminding Laina of a character from a children's book. "I never thought anyone but Herbert would bring that beast to heel."

"Herbert?"

"Kyle's father." She grinned, rubbing Milo's head. "Kyle was right about you. You are the best. I'm Gerty." The elderly woman held out her hand.

Kyle said I was the best? "Anna. It's nice to meet you."

"I'll call you Anna if you prefer. But ever since he brought Milo to see you at your clinic, he hasn't stopped talking about you, Dr. Flynn." She winked. "I can't recall a woman ever having the effect you did on him."

Laina narrowed her eyes on Gerty. So, the old woman knew her secret as well. "Did Kyle put you up to this? Half-naked supermodels twenty-four hours a day. Hundreds of pictures on the internet of his very *busy* lifestyle. I'm sure he has better things to talk about than a vet he met in New Hampshire."

Gerty pressed her lips together, her face growing serious. She seemed to want to say something but stopped herself. "Well, you would know better than I would."

Laina's eyebrows knit together, but the old woman turned back toward the kitchen before she could say another word. Clearly, Gerty had known Kyle longer than Laina, and the twist of the woman's thin lips would indicate her comment was sarcasm. But why? Why not address the realities of what Kyle did head on, one way or the other?

"Oh, Gerty?" Laina shifted her weight. "Is there a place nearby where I can order dinner?"

She clucked her tongue. "I should have told you that

Chef serves dinner in the dining room of the west wing at six o'clock. I'm afraid you've missed tonight's seating."

"Seating?" She laughed. "Does he cook for the staff every night?"

She stopped dusting and looked at Laina as if she were dense. "Yes. For the others. You're staying in Kyle's private wing, but there are always around twenty employees living in the west wing on any given day. Models, waitstaff, writers."

"Writers?"

"For the online magazine."

"Oh."

"I can make you a sandwich if you like," she offered.

"Don't bother, Gerty," Kyle said as he entered the kitchen. His outfit had gained a sport coat, and he looked as polished as when he'd left. "We'll fend for ourselves."

"Excellent." Gerty gave a small smile. "I'll be heading home, then, unless you have something else for me."

"Nope. Go put your feet up. How's Arthur?"

"Recovering. Knee's still sore, but the doc says that's to be expected. He's got his spunk back."

"Good. Send him my love."

"I will, Kyle. He can't wait to get back."

"We can't wait to have him." He kissed her on the cheek, and she left the room, along with Kyle's cordiality. When his eyes settled on Laina, his face turned impassive, a poker player with cards tight to his vest. Silence stretched between them.

When she was sure the housekeeper was out of earshot, she said, "Kyle, about what I said earlier—"

"Aren't you going to ask me how my afternoon orgy went?" He spread his hands. "You know, the thing about orgies, they're only fun if you're the last one to finish. Finish first, and you become an accessory. Easy enough for the females involved, but as a male..." He raised his eyebrows. "Plus, it's crowded, and remembering names is such a bother."

"I'm sorry," she blurted. "I obviously offended you. I made a rude and crass insinuation based on rumors and innuendo." She held up a finger, narrowing her eyes on him. "But in my defense, there are hundreds of incriminating photographs of you on the net. While you don't need a complete stranger accusing you of being a manwhore in your own home, I do think the evidence is on my side with this one."

"Thank you. I accept your apology." She balked at his graceful response to her self-righteous pseudo-apology. Deep down, she knew she should have done better, but now she didn't know what to say to make it right. His brows knit together, one corner of his mouth bending into a wry grin. "Do you still consider me a complete stranger? This is our sixth conversation. And let's not forget, I kept you out of prison, plus I know your deepest, darkest secret, *Dr. Laina Flynn*. I think we can officially bridge the gap to friendship, don't you?"

Not my deepest or darkest secret, she thought, but considering she'd explored the deepest and darkest regions of his mouth with her tongue, perhaps it was time to move beyond strangers. Through a crooked smile, she said, "Sounds reasonable. Friends, then."

He nodded, although the corners of his eyes tightened in a way that didn't match the rest of his expression. "Come on. I'm hungry. I'll make you my famous omelet. And when I say famous, I mean loved and adored by the only three people I've ever made it for." He leaned in close. "Just to warn you, they were all related to me and very hungry at the time."

"I'm up for an adventure," she said, shrugging. "But first, we need to feed Milo."

"Right." Kyle crossed to the corner of the kitchen and scooped three cups of high-end kibble into a stainless-steel dog bowl. Milo nudged his elbow, snorted, and stomped his feet. Kyle bent over to set the dish on the floor.

"Don't you dare just give that to him," Laina said, alarmed.

"Why not? You just told me to feed him."

"Look at his body language. In dog terms, he's calling you his bitch right now."

Kyle met Milo's unblinking stare. The mastiff woofed and nose-nudged the bowl. "What do I do?"

"Make him work for it. Tell him to sit."

"Sit, Milo."

Milo's mouth closed and he pounced. His front feet punched into Kyle's shoulders, knocking him to the kitchen's stone floor. Dog food sprayed across Kyle's face and scattered in every direction. Milo stepped over his owner and began slurping the kibble off the floor like a canine vacuum.

Laina leaned over Kyle. "Are you okay?" She hoped he hadn't hit his head.

He waved the empty bowl. Kibble skimmed from the shoulders of his suit jacket. "I'm my dog's bitch." He frowned. "He didn't even buy me dinner first. I bought *him* dinner."

"We can fix this." Laina held out a hand and helped Kyle from the floor, picking a piece of dog food out of his hand-kerchief pocket. She tossed it to Milo, who was almost finished cleaning up the rest.

Kyle rubbed the back of his head, his neck bending so that his defeated grin was wickedly close. "Are you still up for that omelet?"

In fact, with his mouth so near to hers, she was up for a hell of a lot more. Her wolf was quick to remind her that her vice was in the room, with a blast of heat that traveled straight to her core.

She nodded and backed away before she did something she'd regret.

He opened the refrigerator and retrieved a carton of eggs, before pausing to remove his jacket and roll up the sleeves of his dress shirt to wash his hands. Holy muscles of the gods. She slid onto one of the barstools next to the kitchen island and ogled the forearm porn with her chin resting in her palm.

"Since we're friends," Laina began slowly, "and we've established you are not a manwhore, do you mind explaining your public reputation?" She had to ask. The man was a walking enigma. It was driving her crazy.

"Only if you promise to stop using the term manwhore. What the hell does that even mean? A whore is someone paid for sex. Not even the tabloids say I'm *paid* for sex." The quirky grin was back, and she crossed her legs against the resulting ache it elicited in her.

"But you are in the tabloids, often, with several different women."

Kyle pulled out a cutting board and began chopping a tomato. "It's my brand."

"Your what?"

"My brand. Hunt Club deals in fantasy. We create an environment exclusive to people who want to feel in control of their pleasure. The thrill of the hunt. They are the predators, and their prey is more than willing. Men and women want to live vicariously through someone like me, someone with a new girlfriend, or two or three, every other week. Every aspect of the Hunt Club franchise is built around human desires. They can't get what we offer in the real world. It doesn't exist."

"Pleasure doesn't exist?"

"No. We don't sell pleasure per se. We sell pride. Powerful people want to feel powerful, like kings and queens of the jungle here. Hence the lion logo. They make the rules. They're in control. They lead the hunt. Even in matters of the heart."

She snorted. "So your brand is all about stroking the egos of the rich. Making them feel in control of everything." She sighed. "There are some things no one can control." *Like attraction,* she thought.

"Like I said, we deal in fantasy, not reality." He drifted to a cabinet at the far side of the kitchen and rummaged inside.

"Wine or scotch?" he asked. He glanced over his shoulder. "Or are you a teetotaler?"

"Scotch," she said, her wolf growling slightly from within.

He beamed at her over his shoulder. "I knew it. A woman who kisses like you had to drink scotch."

Cheeks warming, Laina rounded the island and selected a knife from the block. She began slicing the onion on the counter while he poured the scotch. "So, about those pictures. Your brand, as you call it... It's not real?"

He sipped the amber liquid, its color only a shade darker than his eyes, and gave her a condescending look. "I'm not a virgin if that's what you're asking." He raised an eyebrow. "I've had girlfriends. Some aspects of my public life are real. But most of the women you see in the magazines or online are actresses or models." He took a deep breath through his nose and stepped in close beside her, handing her the other scotch. With his shoulder brushing hers, he said through a smile, "I am a one-woman-at-a-time kind of guy, and I prefer to be all the man my woman needs."

She paused with the knife halfway through the onion and gulped.

"Careful," he said. "Your thumb."

Glancing down, she noticed she was dangerously close to cutting herself. "Thanks," she murmured, reaching for her scotch and thinking he was more than enough man for most women.

He grabbed the eggs and started cracking them into a glass bowl. "Recently, I haven't had time for anyone, to be honest."

"No? Been flying solo, have you?" She managed to make the words *flying solo* sound lascivious.

He rolled his eyes like she was a precocious eighth grader. "You know, you're sworn to secrecy about this. You could ruin me, spreading rumors I'm monogamous."

She grinned. "Your secret's safe with me. A secret for a secret."

He ignited a burner on the Viking range and positioned a frying pan over the flames. "That should be enough." He lifted the cutting board of chopped onions from the island and retrieved a bag of spinach and some feta from the fridge.

"Gerty says you have employees living on-site."

"At every location we own."

"How many locations are there?"

"Five others. Jackson Hole, Lake Christina, Pine Ridge, Dunes Island, Fern Gulch."

Kyle poured the egg into the pan and adjusted the heat.

"And you have private residences at each of them? I mean, for yourself and for the employees."

"It's easier that way. We choose remote areas to develop. Land is less expensive, but the talent we need usually comes from New York or LA. Offering them an apartment while they're here sweetens the deal."

"And you have a chef who cooks them dinner but not you?"

He smiled at her as he sprinkled the filling ingredients into the egg. "Oh, Chef offered. I sent him home. I wanted you to myself." The wink he tagged on sent her heart skittering.

When he turned back to the pan, she lifted her glass and tossed back the rest of her scotch, then poured herself another.

"I would like to take you out on that date you owe me, but this will have to do for now. Nate is expecting me back at the club later tonight." He plated one large omelet.

"There's only one."

"We'll have to share." He grinned. "Unless you insist on dirtying another plate."

"Share a plate. Save the planet." The smile he flashed in response made her pulse pound. Her wolf bowed her head and raised her haunches, ready to play.

Milo must have sensed the shift in her inner spirit; he leaped to his feet, barking and wagging his tail.

"What's gotten into him?" Kyle asked.

"I have no idea."

"Come on. It's a beautiful night." He gestured toward the patio.

She collected the glasses and scotch and followed him

outside to an umbrellaed table near the pool. She noticed he only brought one fork, but she didn't say anything.

Milo followed, off leash. She wasn't concerned, given the fenced yard, but he proved too tired to run anyway. The big dog curled up beside them.

"Did you always want to be a vet?" he asked.

She sipped her scotch and sat down beside him. "Always. I've had a special connection to animals since the day I was born, more so than I do to people sometimes. Caring for them just seemed like a natural extension of that."

"If your work with Milo is any indication, you made the right choice. You've been here half a day, and he's already glued to your side." Kyle offered her the first bite, and she accepted. The omelet was good, although the egg was slightly overdone. She presumed he didn't cook often.

"How about you? Did you always want to run a lifestyle club?"

He took a drink, looking a bit bored. "In short, no. This is one of over a dozen businesses I've run. Hunt Club was my father's idea. He grew up during the *Playboy* generation and wanted to create something modern but in the same vein. Something that would appeal to both men and women."

"For being the face of Hunt Club, you don't seem overly enthusiastic about the role?"

He shrugged. "My brother, Nate, is the actual CEO. He handles operations and is the true leader of the company. He has the passion for it. I'm part owner and on the board of directors, but I'm more of a figurehead when it comes to the details."

"Wait... Nate from the club is your brother?" There was absolutely no family resemblance.

"Half brother. We share a father."

It was easy to see why Kyle had been chosen as the figurehead for Hunt Club. As unfair as it was to judge a book by its cover, his carved-from-stone physique and Hollywood good looks would be far more effective in the media than Nate's overstuffed-Danny DeVito appearance, given the nature of their business.

"Is your mother also involved in the company?"

He shook his head and laughed. "I don't know who she is. Dad never married. Two boys from two different women. We've never met either of them."

She took another sip of scotch. "Must've been hard growing up without a mother."

"Gerty's been with me from the beginning." He shrugged and cut off the corner of the omelet. "Open."

She obeyed and was rewarded with another bite. As he pulled the fork from her mouth, he stared at her lips, his eyelids growing hooded. He fed himself while she chewed. The conversation diverted into the mundane: the unseasonably warm weather, where she'd gone to school, his time at Harvard, her first job at an animal shelter. By the time the eggs were gone, they'd talked and laughed for over an hour.

"Are you close to your family?" he asked, pushing the empty plate away and concentrating on his scotch.

She nodded. "Very close. To my brothers, at least. My parents were killed several years ago."

"Killed? How awful."

She nodded. "They'd gone to a play—a charity event— and were gunned down in their seats. You probably read about it. It was all over the news at the time."

"Does it bother you to talk about?"

"It used to. Not as much anymore." She frowned. "It still

bothers me that they're gone. Their loss left a hole in all of us. Enough time has passed that I can talk about it now. Was your father ill long?"

"We think about a year. No one knew until the very end. He had the cabin in Red Grove and would stay there with a nurse when he was too ill to function. We got the call when it was clear he was passing on."

"You couldn't tell before then?"

"My father and I...weren't close. Even when he was actively running the company, he did so remotely. Nate and I rarely saw him. I feel like I barely knew him."

How awful. Before her parents had been killed, her family had been undeniably close. And for all her complaints about Silas and Jason, the three of them would do anything for one another. She wasn't sure what she'd do without them. Laina tried to think of something comforting to say. "Maybe your father didn't want to burden you with his illness."

"If that's the case, it was the first selfless thing he ever did." He snorted. "But we loved the asshole. He provided for us. Funny as hell on the rare occasion he was around."

There was much more to Kyle Kingsley than met the eye, and didn't that just set her wolf to pacing? She'd counted on him fitting the mold—a spoiled, rich man whose playboy lifestyle flew in the face of her ideals—but he didn't. In fact, he didn't fit a mold at all. He wasn't a Boy Scout or a playboy. He was just a man. A man she found scaldingly attractive.

She threw back the rest of her scotch.

"You are a walking contradiction," he said, staring at her lips.

"What? Why?"

"You're obviously smart and independent, a young

veterinarian and successful entrepreneur. At times, you seem modest and conservative, but the way you kissed me in the club and then again earlier today, I don't believe that cover for a second."

Heat washed over her face. "I'm not a virgin either. I'm not saving myself for marriage or anything. But I am conservative in one regard."

"What's that?"

"I don't believe in casual sex."

He sipped his scotch. "Morals, convictions, strength, independence."

"And this makes me a contradiction?"

He shook his head as his gaze drifted over her. "It's a rare combination of traits to find in a woman," he murmured, his eyes drifting to her drink. "You drink straight scotch like it's Kool-Aid, and you were comfortable enough with your nudity to serve at Hunt Club in nothing but a coat of latex."

"Monty made me—"

"You can't force the kind of confidence I saw that night." He shook his head. "Or the heat in that kiss we shared. You kiss like something wild, like you know exactly what you want and how you want it. I've never been kissed like that. Not even close. Or by someone who could stop so easily."

"The stopping wasn't as easy as it seemed."

"And you're here, running from something, some family violence." He tapped a finger on the table and frowned. "Are you in the mob?"

"No!" She laughed like the idea was ridiculous but didn't elaborate. It would be too hard to explain her actual situation, even if she could tell him the truth.

"So, you see the contradiction." His gaze dug into hers,

and his fingers moved slowly to brush over the tops of her knuckles. She didn't pull her hand away. "You are a conservative academic with a streak of something positively animal. I can't put my finger on it." He shifted his jaw. "But there's no one like you."

"According to the sign out front, you want the thrill of the chase. Maybe what you're feeling is a desire to hunt me. What will you do if you catch me, Kyle? Will you try to tame me?" She asked it more to lighten the mood than as a serious observation.

"No." Darkness drifted in like a fog behind his eyes, and he held out a hand to her. "Actually, I was hoping you could teach me to be wild."

KYLE COULDN'T HOLD HIMSELF BACK ANY LONGER. THIS THING Laina had unleashed within him wanted her like he'd never wanted anyone. The heat of her skin, her hair, her face, her *scent.* Fuck, whatever perfume she was wearing was like a drug, earthy and warm with just a hint of spice. He reached for her, and thank God she came willingly, slipping her fingers into his and—Jesus Christ—straddling his lap. He cupped her ass. Fuck, she had a great ass. Churning his hips, he savored the delectable friction against his rock-hard cock, a frenzy building within him. He'd wanted Laina since the moment he'd first seen her at her clinic, but this was more than desire. It was obsession. All he could think about was being inside her.

He grabbed her lower jaw, tipped her head, and kissed her. Not gently. He couldn't be gentle with his blood heating the way it was. Thank God she seemed to like it rough, responding with a low moan. Their mouths warred, stroking each other. He sucked on her tongue. She nibbled on his bottom lip. And fuck if her hips didn't start moving with her mouth, riding him. He gripped her waist, wishing they were both naked.

Grinding against her, he slid his hand into the low scoop of her T-shirt, drawing it and her bra down under her breast. He brushed his thumb across her taut nipple, rolling and plucking it. The little gasp she gave was all the encouragement he needed. Hungry for her, he skimmed his hand up to her collarbone, noting the way her heart pounded against his touch, then lowered his mouth to her nipple, sucking, circling, flicking his tongue. She rewarded him with a growl of pure pleasure. When he drew back and blew across her wet flesh, she arched in his arms.

Feverishly, she buried her fingers in his hair and started moving against him in earnest, rubbing herself along his cock, her head tossed back and her lips parted. God, if she kept that up, he was going to come, and they were both fully dressed. He fumbled for her fly, practically tearing the button free and making short work of the zipper. Black lace thong. He wholeheartedly approved. Without hesitation, she undid the buttons of his shirt, spread the sides, and scraped her nails down his chest. Holy shit, she'd summoned lightning from his veins. God, he needed to touch her.

He slid his fingers between her legs, finding her soaked. "Jesus, Laina, you're so wet for me."

Her tongue met the curve of his earlobe. "Please," she gasped, as if she were in pain and the only thing that could relieve her was his touch. He was more than happy to oblige.

He moved her thong aside and dipped a finger into her,

shifting his body to cup her between her legs. Closing her eyes, she worked her hips overtime, riding his hand with abandon that made his cock throb. He took her breast into his mouth, licking in time with his stroking fingers.

His phone rang. He ignored it. It rang again.

"More," she cried. And he moved faster, harder, circling her clit with his thumb.

"Come for me, baby," he commanded. A shock rang though her body. She tipped her head back on a silent howl, her inner walls tightening rhythmically around his fingers. "Fuck, yeah." How good her orgasm would feel on his cock. He couldn't wait to get inside her.

"Kyle!" a man's voice barked from across the pool.

Laina whipped her head over her shoulder and growled. He'd never heard a noise like that come out of a woman before, but she was off him in the blink of an eye. Another blink and her jeans were zipped, her breast back in her T-shirt.

He swore as he spotted Nate watching them with that shark's grin of his. Fucking bastard. Kyle adjusted himself in his pants. "What the fuck are you doing here?"

"You weren't answering your phone."

"I'm busy." He reached for Laina, but she'd moved to the other side of the table.

"It's an emergency. I need to talk to you. *Now*." He pointed his thumb over his shoulder.

Kyle glared at his brother, but when it was clear the guy would not leave, he glanced in Laina's direction. "I'm sorry. Please excuse me."

"It's fine," she said, but her voice was clipped.

He crossed to the other side of the pool. "What the hell, Nate. What could you possibly need me for this time of night?"

He snorted. "She is a fine piece of ass, but this is business."

Kyle bristled. "Do me a favor and leave her out of this. Tell me why you're here."

"There's been a disturbance at the club. One of the picketers made it past security. The police have been called, but we have a few minutes to question the bastard. Maybe find out what they're planning next."

He nodded. Eternal Light Ministries had been increasingly aggressive as of late. It was worth a try. "I'll meet you at the security office in two minutes."

Thankfully, Nate took off, leaving Kyle alone with Laina. He returned to her at a fast clip, buttoning his shirt. "There's an emergency at the club. I have to leave. But...go out with me tomorrow, a real date to make up for the one we missed."

"Not in public. I'm undercover, remember?" she said.

"Leave it to me. I'll make sure it's private." Private, he could do.

"Okay," she said softly.

He gripped her shoulders and planted a hard kiss on her mouth. And then took off for Hunt Club at a jog.

CHAPTER

SIXTEEN

With Milo by her side, Laina retired to her room, fancying a cold shower and a good book. Goddess, her nipples were still hard, and the ache between her legs was almost painful. Her wolf wanted sex. She wanted sex. The orgasm he'd given her was barely an appetizer. She was wound up tighter than a spring.

With a sigh, she found an extra blanket in the closet and made Milo a bed in the corner of the room. She'd have to ask Gerty to obtain an extra-large dog crate in the morning. The big dog curled up obediently with his head between his paws. Then Laina headed for the bathroom, stripped down, and started the water.

Once under the spray, she started to feel more like herself again. It was probably for the best that Kyle had been called away when he had. Sex with Kyle now would only solidify him as her vice. Her attraction to him was already almost undeniable. If she fucked him, she'd be fully addicted in no time. And the way things were heating up, she would have been hard-pressed to stop that train from leaving the station. It didn't help that she genuinely liked

Kyle, even beyond the physical stuff. He was funny and kind, well educated, and forthright. She'd been relieved that most of what Cameron had shown her about Kyle had turned out to be pure fantasy.

Wrapped in a towel, she was digging a pair of pajamas out of her bag when her phone buzzed on the nightstand. She could count on one hand how many people had the number for the phone Silas had given her, and none of them would call her here unless it was an emergency. Bracing herself, she brought the phone to her ear, not even bothering to say hello.

"I don't like this," Silas growled.

"Nice to hear from you, big brother."

"Make an excuse and get back to Monty's."

"I'll do no such thing. I gave Kyle my word. I'm going to do what I said I would do. Anyway, the accommodations here are much more comfortable."

"It turns out the wolf that was murdered wasn't taken from the wild. She was stolen from the Carlton City Zoo."

"That bastard. Not even brave enough to give his victim a fighting chance."

"The good news is, his cowardice left us a clue. I found a fingerprint on the gate to her cage that didn't match any of the zookeepers' prints. Turns out Jonah has a record. I was able to track him to his last apartment."

"Did you apprehend him?"

"No, he was gone. But Laina, there were pictures of the three of us all over that place. He'd been taking pictures of you at Four Paws for months. There are pictures of me at Valentine's and Jason at the gym. Jonah's been following us since before Alex was killed."

"Where is he now?"

"I don't know, but his landlord hasn't seen him in three weeks. He's out there somewhere."

"We covered every footprint. This is the last place he'd expect us to go."

"True, but as an ogre, Monty can help protect you. He has enchantments to ward off dark magic. You're on your own at Hunt Club. Frankly, I'm concerned. Jason says the place is filled with strangers from all over the country every night. You're too vulnerable."

"No. Kyle has me staying in his private wing." She looked down at Milo. "The security here is top-notch."

"I'd feel better if you and Jason were together."

"Give me some time to do what I promised. I'll be back at Monty's before you know it. Before the next shift, for sure."

He groaned. "Be careful, Laina. Jonah is a master of disguise. He's an accomplished actor and fraud. Add that particular skill set to the fact that we are certain he's working with a member of the magical community, and it's entirely possible he looks drastically different. He could have a different skin color, be a different gender. Don't trust anyone. Stay out of sight. No one can know who you really are."

She thought of Kyle. Should she tell Silas he knew her true identity? Her first instinct was to keep it a secret, but then she remembered telling Jason. It would get back around to Silas sooner or later. She'd rather he heard it from her.

"Silas, there's something you should know."

"I don't like the sound of that."

"Remember how I told you I had a date the night of the ball, and you ordered me to go to Rivergate instead?"

"Yes."

"That date was with Kyle Kingsley."

There was a long silence on the other end of the line, lengthy enough for her to question whether the call disconnected.

"I don't like this, Laina. It's too much of a coincidence. This guy asks you out the night of the murder? Think about it. Becca didn't remember the exact time Jonah knocked her out and murdered the wolf in your operating room, but based on the time the plug was pulled on your security cameras, it was sometime after the ball started and before we found the body. The ball started the same hour as your date with Kyle. What if Jonah got wind of the ball at Rivergate and posed as Kyle?"

"Why would he do that? Why not just attack me at Four Paws Clinic?"

"Too public during the day. Too much visibility. If you went on the date, he'd kill you there, maybe poison your food. If you went to the ball, he'd lie in wait for you at your apartment. He murdered the wolf at your clinic. Jonah would know I'd send you home after the murder. Have you ever stopped to consider the heart on your surgical table was meant for me, for after I found your body at your apartment?"

"Jonah would suspect Stephanie was my Zafka."

"Exactly. Don't you think it's suspicious that then Kyle mysteriously ends up where you're hiding and wants you to play house with him?"

She could see where he was going with this, but it couldn't be true. "Kyle can't be Jonah. He's a public figure, Silas. Everyone knows who he is and what he looks like."

"And the person who murdered that wolf was able to place the body in the center of a crowded room without being seen or heard. Whoever Jonah has in his corner is a powerful magical being. Who's to say he didn't kill the real Kyle and take his place?"

"No. Trust me. He's not. I've spent time with him. I'd know, okay. Look, if he were Jonah, I'd already be dead."

"Unless he's using you to draw me out by gaining your trust. Has he tried to get Jason there? Has he asked about me?"

Laina's skin tightened, a chill wrapping her in its icy grip. She'd spent hours talking about her past tonight with Kyle, including stories of growing up with Silas and Jason. What Silas said was possible, but was it true?

"I'll be careful," she said. "But he smells human to me. I don't think you're right about this."

Silas growled. "He'll want to keep you alive to draw me in. That puts you at an advantage."

"Okay."

"There are three tests to tell if he's under a camouflage enchantment. The first is direct sunlight. It can cause color variations to his outer appearance, like an aura. If you're not looking for it, you might not notice."

Laina tried to remember if she'd ever seen Kyle in direct sunlight and realized she hadn't. That would have to change.

"If that doesn't work, try viewing his reflection in water or through water. If there is dark magic involved, water will reveal him for what he is, if only for a moment."

"And if that doesn't work?"

"If all else fails, you need to view his reflection in a mirror under moonlight. The right angle should give you a glimpse of who he really is."

"And if he passes all three tests, I can assume he's human?"

"You can assume he's not Jonah disguised as human. Kyle could still be working for Jonah."

Laina's eyes flicked to the ceiling. *Goddess give me strength.* "I don't think you're right about this, Silas, but I'll do it. I'll test him."

"The three tests aren't foolproof, but they'll catch most enchantments. Look for other clues. And if at any point you suspect him of being Jonah or working for Jonah, don't hesitate to kill him." It was a direct command from her alpha. She prayed she'd never have to act on it; doing so would mean killing her vice. Just the thought cut her to the quick.

"I love you, sis. Stay safe."

"Love you too." The call disconnected. Laina stared at Milo for a moment, trying to process what she'd just heard. If Silas was right about Kyle, she was sleeping across the hall from the enemy. Worse, her wolf desperately wanted to fuck the enemy. Even now.

"Time for bed, Milo." The dog looked up at her from his nest of blankets but didn't move. Double-checking that the door to her room was locked, she wedged a chair under the knob for an extra measure of protection. Inspections of the bathroom and closet turned up negative for anything suspect as well. Satisfied she was safe, at least for the moment, she crawled under the blankets of the large bed. But although Milo's snores echoed through the room soon after, sleep eluded her.

SEVENTEEN

Something warm and wet slid across Laina's temple, and she came awake with a jerk, springing from the mattress and landing in a defensive position on the other side of the bed. It took her a few moments to comprehend that it was Milo who had woken her with a lick to the face, both massive paws planted on her side of the bed. He smacked his lips at her expectantly.

A glance at the clock revealed it was almost nine. No wonder Milo woke her up. He probably had all four legs crossed. She washed her face, brushed her teeth, and gathered her hair into a messy bun. Donning jeans and a T-shirt, she declared herself ready to go in less than ten minutes.

After unbarring the door, Laina clucked her tongue to call Milo to her side. The house was quiet as she crept into the hall, the jingle of his collar the only sound. She stopped short at Kyle's open door, the ache between her legs returning with a vengeance. *For the love of the goddess.*

Asleep on his stomach, arms tucked under his pillow, he faced away from her, affording her a view of his broad back. The deep dimples formed by his shoulder muscles mirrored the two narrower grooves above his buttocks, the latter peeking from under a swath of his white comforter. From the mess of his sleepy dark hair to the swell of his rounded ass, he was a perfect specimen of a man, and that was a problem. Were his extraordinary good looks authentic or the result of dark magic? Her wolf salivated, begging her to cross the threshold and place a kiss between those shoulder blades. But if it was Jonah lying in that bed, she'd been a fool. He would relish using her body before taking her life.

A daydream of running her tongue along his spine had hit her full force when Kyle cleared his throat and adjusted his head on the pillow to face her. His eyes opened, their pale sherry color staring blankly in her direction. He rolled his hips against his mattress.

"Laina?" he whispered, his voice all grit.

"Time to get up! Milo needs a walk," she said brightly, internally wrestling back her wolf. After her conversation with Silas, it was more important than ever that she maintain control.

He groaned and rolled onto his back, the covers falling low across the front of his hips. A trail of dark hair descended from his navel and disappeared beneath the white duvet.

"Something you'd like to see?"

Her eyes snapped to his. "No!" she squawked. "I mean, yes! Yes, I would like to see you out of bed and downstairs, ready to walk your dog, in five minutes."

"You do realize I worked until three in the morning."

"But Milo didn't, and unless you want a mess on your hands, we need to go."

With a look of defiance, he grabbed the corner of the blanket and tossed it back, revealing everything she'd imagined just moments ago. She inhaled sharply, infuriated by the smug grin he gave her when he caught her staring. She ducked out of the frame of the door and jogged silently down the stairs to the main floor, Milo at her side.

Kyle may have been well-endowed—ridiculously, unbelievably well-endowed—and beautifully built, but she would not allow herself to react like a horny schoolgirl. She was a grown, accomplished woman. Romantically experienced. A professional. Crossing her arms over her chest, she decided it would take more than a pretty face and an enormous, mind-blowingly large dick to win her over. At the prospect of her will trumping her desire, her wolf howled in pain and curled up at the back of her brain with a pronounced pout.

Thankfully, when Kyle joined her in the kitchen, he was fully dressed in jeans and a Hunt Club T-shirt, the latter sporting a tribal-style lion on the breast. It reminded her a little of her pack tattoo.

She thrust Milo's leash into Kyle's hands. It was a sunny morning. Time for test number one. "I'm going to open this. Try to be the first over the threshold. It's a display of dominance."

He shrugged. "Okay. Sounds easy enough."

With a glance at Milo, she threw open the back door.

Kyle's feet left the tile floor and his head snapped back as Milo took off like a bullet. Laina snickered as Kyle leaped over a padded chaise in a desperate effort to keep his feet under him. "Miloooooo!"

"Milo, stop!" Laina snapped when he'd reached a sunny patch of grass. The mastiff obeyed immediately, stopping abruptly and almost tripping Kyle. With both dog and owner in direct sunlight, she raked her eyes over him from head to toe. Aside from a beautiful constriction of his pupils that brought out the multilayered hues of his hazel eyes, she detected nothing unusual. Certainly no aura. Just a man holding his chest and resting his hands on his knees. Test one passed.

"Oww," he said.

"Big dog," she said.

Kyle was athletic, as tall and muscular as any werewolf, but she'd personally seen a mastiff slightly larger than Milo pull over 5,000 pounds on wheels. They were working dogs—all muscle and grit.

"Did you know he was going to do that?"

She repositioned the leash in his hands for optimal control. "In the future, Mr. Kingsley, I would hope you could keep your private parts private."

"You were the one who came into *my* room. It's not my fault you told me to get out of bed and I happened to be naked."

She ignored him. "Stand tall and keep Milo at your side. If he starts to get ahead of you, correct him with a sharp snap of the leash. We'll take him around the yard and work on control. Try to keep him behind your heel."

"Can we talk about this?"

Laina redirected the conversation back to Milo. "He'll have to relieve himself, so you can give him a little leash when he's ready."

With a cluck of her tongue, she urged the dog forward. Laina wasn't angry about seeing Kyle naked. On the contrary, she'd enjoyed it. But anger became a shield she could hide behind until she knew for sure Kyle was human. Drop that shield and she'd be in his bed before the day was through.

"And what is with this Mr. Kingsley shit?" Kyle asked. "You didn't mind calling me Kyle when you were straddling my lap last night. What happened between then and now?"

He turned his attention to her. Immediately, the dog lunged ahead.

"Milo, heel," she commanded. "Concentrate, Mr. Kingsley. He knows when you're not paying attention."

The muscles of his lips tightened faintly. "I'd prefer you call me Kyle. Actually, I insist you call me Kyle. And unless you want to answer for the stunt you pulled in my club, you'll call me Kyle."

"Fine. Kyle, your dog needs to poop."

Kyle stopped abruptly, finally noticing that Milo had fallen behind slightly and was attempting to squat. He winced when nature took its course. "Ugh. Wow."

Laina shrugged. "Big dog. This is what you signed up for. You can use one of the bags at the end of the leash for now, but you might want to invest in an in-ground disposal system."

"In-ground…"

"A system to compost it underground. You could also flush it if you're willing to carry it inside every day."

"I'll tell Gerty."

Laina placed her hands on her hips. "No, Kyle. Gerty can't always do this for you. This is your dog, and you are building trust. You need to take care of his needs." She folded her arms and waited. Milo, now relieved, looked between the two of them. One thing was for sure: if Kyle was Jonah in disguise, his ego would be too big for him to pick up after Milo.

"Oh, for God's sake, you are a pain in the ass." Kyle tore a bag from the roll, turning it inside out around his hand.

Laina held back a smile. It wasn't proof, but she was more confident than ever Kyle was human. When he was done, he tied off the bag, looking positively disgusted.

"Happy?" he asked.

She nodded. "Just leave it here. We'll pick it up on the way back to the house after one more time around the yard. You're doing really well."

He dropped it and wiped his perfectly clean hands on his pants. "What happened between last night and today, Laina?"

"Anna."

"There's no one out here but us."

She sighed, walking quickly to keep up with Kyle and Milo's pace. "I think the scotch went to my head."

"Are you saying you didn't want to kiss me?"

Even then, with Milo between them and in the bright light of day, her desire for him felt like a neon badge she wore on her chest. How could he not see it on her? Lying would be futile.

"I did. I do," she murmured.

"So why the icy attitude this morning? I thought we had something. Are you angry that I had to leave to handle that situation at the club?"

"No. I just think, with everything going on in your life and mine, the only responsible thing to do is keep a professional distance."

"What about our date?"

"I think it's a bad idea."

They arrived back where they'd started, and Kyle picked up the baggy without saying a word. He led the way back toward the house, tossing it in the garbage can near the pool. The tight set of his jaw told her he was more than a little confused and frustrated.

"We should feed Milo," Laina said, then thought to offer an olive branch. "Would you like to have breakfast together?"

He shook his head. "I have a board meeting at ten. Another time."

Her heart constricted at his emotionless tone and flat smile. He nodded, handing her the leash once they were inside the door. "Thanks for the lesson." He scooped three cups of kibble into Milo's bowl. "Milo, sit," he said firmly. This time, the dog obeyed. Laina could feel why the mastiff had a change of heart; the energy coming off Kyle sizzled against her skin. He dropped the bowl and turned to leave.

"He'll need another walk and to be fed tonight," she said. The note of hope beneath the words was less about Milo and more about wanting to see him again. She hated herself for it, but she was already looking forward to their next training session.

He nodded once and headed for his room.

"You have to let me help," Laina told Gerty, picking up a rag and loading it with wood polish.

"You're Kyle's guest— hired to train the dog, not to clean. It's not your job."

"Milo is sleeping, and I'm bored. I need something to do."

"Why not explore the library?"

Laina shook her head. Not only did she feel useless sitting around, she wanted the company.

"If you help me, what will I do when I finish early?" Gerty quirked a brow.

Laina smiled at the old woman. "You'll sit down in a chair and drink a glass of lemonade with me."

Gerty made a noise deep in her throat and waved her hand in the air. Without hesitation, Laina started in on the wood-work in the dining room. "How long have you worked for Kyle?" she asked, desperate for the distraction of conversation.

"Since he was a baby. Herbert hired Arthur and me to look after Kyle and his brother, Nate. I was the nanny and Arthur was the butler until the boys grew up and I became the housekeeper."

"You never felt the urge to move on and do something else?"

"And trust my boys to a total stranger? Never!"

"Hmm. You think of them as your own."

"Of course I do. Other than Arthur, I'm the only one Kyle allows in his private residence. There are eight other housekeepers in the west wing, but Kyle's very private. He rarely allows anyone in here, aside from my husband and me."

"He's allowed me to stay here."

Gerty gave her the side-eye. "And isn't that saying something?"

Laina polished in silence. Why would Kyle invite her here if he wasn't Jonah? She wanted to believe he was human and that it was because he was drawn to her in the same way she was drawn to him. But what were the odds? Laina's attraction to Kyle, though initially driven by her wolf, grew deeper the longer she was in his company. There was no such reason why Kyle would be attracted to her. The whole thing was a headfuck. Was it love or magic?

When they'd finished in the dining room, she followed Gerty upstairs to Kyle's room. She was surprised to find the couch Milo had destroyed had already been removed and replaced as if Kyle had a room full of identical couches at the ready.

"When Kyle was six, Arthur and I took him and his brother to the beach," Gerty said as she ran her duster over the antique dresser that perfectly fit the fairy-tale charm of Hunt Club Mansion. "Kyle's brother, Nate, had no trouble making friends. He spent the rest of the day with a crowd of boys, bodysurfing and playing games along the shore. Kyle was always different. He was obsessed with the tide pools, the starfish, the tiny crabs. All he wanted to do was build sandcastles with Arthur, houses for those tiny ocean dwellers to enjoy. Such a quiet, introspective boy. Never wanted the limelight. Never cared to be part of a crowd. Completely different from his brother."

"Far off from the media sweetheart he is today." Laina laughed.

Gerty paused, becoming serious. "You know, an expensive education and high expectations go a long way toward conditioning behavior." She nodded at Milo, who had followed them into the room and was curled on the floor. "You'll train this one to sit when you say sit and heel when you say heel, but he'll always be a dog. He'll always want to run."

"Are you saying Kyle is somehow a prisoner to expectations? He hardly seems like he's suffering here."

"No. Not suffering. But I sometimes wonder if he's left behind a piece of himself to live this life." Her eyes twinkled wistfully. She shook her head and chuckled. "I'm an old woman. Don't listen to my babbling."

If there was anything that Gerty could have said to make her desire Kyle more, Laina couldn't think of it. As the princess of her people, she understood the demands of external expectations and how they could easily extinguish the flicker of light someone carried in their soul.

Laina allowed her eyes to drift around the enormous

room, noticing for the first time that there were no pictures or mementos. No family portraits. No snow globes from trips to Lake Tahoe. Kyle's bedroom might have been staged for a photograph. "This home wasn't built until recently when they built the club, right? Where was home before this?"

"We've followed Kyle and Nate from New York to LA, Wyoming, Minnesota, South Carolina. We move when they move. I think Kyle wants to stay here this time, though."

"Why do you say that?"

There was a long pause, and Gerty seemed to choose her words carefully. "Just a hunch. I sense he's tired of being a rolling stone." Laina helped her make the bed, closing her eyes when Kyle's deep woods scent wafted up from the billowing sheets. "Plus, this is the first time he's demanded separate living quarters from his brother."

"Gerty," Laina said, desperate to put aside the fear Silas had instilled in her, "have you noticed a change in Kyle the last couple of weeks?"

"What kind of change?"

"You know, not acting himself, wanting to eat things he previously disliked, doing things he normally wouldn't do."

"Only when it comes to you."

Laina dropped her arms to her sides and stared at the old woman.

"I've never seen him so smitten."

As she opened her mouth to protest, her mind went blank, her wolf reveling in the idea that Kyle might be as interested in her as she was in him. She stood, speechless, as Gerty plugged in the vacuum cleaner but hesitated to turn it on.

"You should enjoy the magic of this moment, dear," Gerty said softly. "Arthur and I had a similar courtship. Not everyone experiences love at first sight. Life is short, passion is fleeting, and love is a risk worth taking."

Laina snorted. "I think it's much too early to use the word love in the same sentence with Kyle and me."

Gerty smiled until her rheumy eyes were lost in the folds of her face. "You're probably right. Guarding your heart is the sensible thing to do. Like I said, I'm an old woman. Don't listen to me." She turned on the vacuum and got to work.

EIGHTEEN

For the next week, Laina fell into a routine with Kyle. She'd wake him to work with Milo in the morning, then meet him again at the end of the day. To her wolf's dismay, Kyle took her request to maintain a professional distance to heart. She found his door closed in the morning and his conversation, although open and friendly, completely appropriate for mixed company.

Milo thrived on the routine. Since she'd come to Hunt Club, the mastiff hadn't destroyed anything but the daily chew toy Kyle gave him for that purpose. Laina would care for the dog during the day, in between helping Gerty with her chores. The housekeeper had become her good friend.

And reluctantly, she had to admit, so had Kyle. After they walked Milo in the evening, it had become a habit for them to stay up until the wee hours of the morning talking about anything and everything. His favorite food was Korean barbecue. He'd played baseball until the tenth grade when he'd sprained his wrist. He spoke French and just enough Spanish to survive in an emergency. And he was completely addicted to HGTV.

She'd shared things with him too, those things she could share. He knew she liked to drive fast and loved the beach but hated the sand. She'd rather eat a steak than a slice of chocolate cake and had spent a summer in Europe with her parents before they were killed. He knew she was a sucker for animals and gave an unholy amount of money to the ASPCA each month. Only on this night, a storm had moved in, and the thunder and lightning had cut their usual walk and post-session talk short.

"Are you tired?" he asked. Of course she wasn't. It was nine o'clock, and she wasn't eighty years old. Sherlock Holmes, she was not, but it was obvious he was giving her an out if she wasn't interested in his company without the excuse of Milo.

"Not yet," she said. With the full moon in her rearview mirror, her wolf's voice had quieted, and she could be in Kyle's presence without the aching need she'd felt before.

"Come on. I want to show you something."

He led her to the back of the house, to a room with floor-to-ceiling books, saddle-brown leather furniture, gold fixtures, red tapestries, and a shiny black baby grand piano. "It's a beautiful library."

"What do you like to read? Let me guess..." He tapped his chin and studied her. "*Jane Eyre*."

She snorted. "Why would you say that?"

"Jane breaks out on her own, would do anything for a friend, makes a life for herself. Seems like a character you could relate to."

"I like your thinking, but I'm more of a Mary Shelley fan."

"Oh, *Frankenstein*?" He knit his brows.

"She published it anonymously, you know, because no one in 1818 would read a book written by a woman. But the entire tale is a work of feminism. It's a warning about what would happen if a man tried to create life without a woman."

"Hmm. I never thought of it that way. I always read it as a warning that just because we can do something scientifically doesn't mean we should." He sat down on the piano bench and started playing a simple, plodding version of Bach's Prelude in C.

"How about you? What do you read?" she asked.

"Financial reports, the *Wall Street Journal*, legal documents."

She giggled. "What do you read for fun?"

"It's been a long time. Maybe I'll pick up *Frankenstein*." He stopped playing, and a heaviness settled over him that made her heart ache.

"I know what it's like." She slid in next to him. "I buried myself in school and work for years. It starts as an escape. It's safe. There's routine. But eventually, it takes over, and that's all there is." He frowned at her. "I say we make a pact, right now, to do something fun every day for as long as I'm here."

The corner of his mouth curved toward his ear, and he arched a brow. "Deal."

She threaded her fingers and stretched them over the keyboard. "Fun thing number one, I am going to show you what this bad boy can do."

"The piano? You play?"

"My parents insisted all three of their children suffer refinements that included music. I chose piano."

He scooted to the end of the bench to give her room.

With a deep breath, she positioned her hands and allowed her fingers to dance across the keys, playing Mozart's Piano Sonata No. 16. She was cheating, she knew.

As a werewolf, she was endowed with unnaturally fast speed and agility, which made the finger positioning far easier for her than it would have been for him. But she held nothing back, showing off to her full potential, at one point leaning her head back to smile cheerfully at his awestruck face. By the time she finished what she could remember of the piece, he'd stood up and was staring openmouthed.

He slow-clapped through her final note. "Take a bow, Laina. That was truly extraordinary."

She shrugged. "I try."

His laughter faded to an expression far more serious. "What the hell are you doing here?"

"I'm training your dog."

He shook his head. "It's a travesty."

Before she could respond that she rather liked him and his dog, his phone buzzed.

"Nate. He needs me in the club. I'm sorry, but I have to go."

"The fate of an overachiever."

"Thank you for the entertainment."

With a few cordial words, he left the house again, looking tired and empty. Milo jogged to the closing door and whined. "Come on, boy. Let's go to bed." The dog turned and followed her.

As she topped the stairs, her cell vibrated in her back pocket. Silas. "You need to finish testing Kyle. You've been there too long. If he's Jonah, he's pulling you in deeper, clouding your judgment."

"I will. I haven't had a chance. The man works constantly." She chewed her lip. "He passed test number one. I don't think you have anything to worry about."

"Get it done, Laina, or I'm pulling alpha on you."

She ended the call, knowing what she had to do.

KYLE STRODE THROUGH THE DOOR JUST AFTER NINE. WHAT A DAY. What a fucking day. Hunt Club was under attack from so many directions, but those fucking protesters were going to send him over the edge. They really were.

"I walked and fed Milo for you." Laina appeared before him, and all the stuff going on in his brain quieted. God, she was beautiful, all that dark hair and golden skin. "He couldn't wait. He's already curled up in his new crate."

"Thank you. I'm sorry I'm late. Important meeting. I couldn't leave." He swallowed. It was the first time he'd been late since she moved in, but still, he regretted it. Lord knew he would've rather been with her than in that meeting. Although she had every right to chew him out, she simply watched him as he poured two glasses of scotch and handed her one, then led the way outside to the pool deck. Slumping into a chaise lounge, he stared up at the moon. It was a beautiful fall night, every star visible in the clear sky. God, the moon always eased him.

"Rough day?" Laina took the chair beside him.

"Our online magazine subscriptions are flagging. The analysts say we need to do something to break through the noise, gain some publicity." He sipped his scotch. He should've brought out the bottle.

Those beautiful green eyes scrutinized him. "And you don't want to do that?"

He shook his head slowly. "I don't want to talk about this. I know it's late, but will you just sit here with me for a while? Your presence is...grounding. I'm beginning to think it's some kind of drug."

"I'm a drug?"

He closed his eyes. It was too much and he was probably making her uncomfortable, but he couldn't hold his feelings back. "Lately, the only time my life seems real is when I'm with you."

She took a fast sip of air.

"Sorry if that crosses the line."

As she leaned into the cushion of the deck chair, a breeze coursed over the pool, the heated water fogging where it touched the cool night air. "No. It's fine."

The corner of his mouth twitched, but he forced himself not to flash her a stupid grin by refocusing the conversation. "What were your parents like, Laina?" She raised her eyebrows. When she didn't answer right away, he added, "I'm just curious what a nuclear family is like when they all live together." Kyle hadn't meant for the question to sound quite so sad. He finished his scotch and hoped she wouldn't notice.

Laina hugged her knees to her chest. "My mom was a botanist. I can't remember a time when there wasn't something growing in our house—trees of all types, green plants, flowers. But it wasn't just plants... She grew people too. She had this softness about her that brought everyone around her to light, especially my father. Dad was a lawyer. Not the grandiloquent type you see leading class action suits on TV, but a taciturn professional with a narrow focus on a specific niche of corporate tax law. Most of the time, we thought he was lost inside his head. Until my mother was in the room, and his face would grow younger, his smile would come alive, and I'd see it."

"See what?"

"Love. The connection that cuts through all the bullshit in life, exposes you for who you really are, without your job or your money, right into your soul. Love looks right through you and loves you anyway."

He inhaled sharply. "I'm not sure I've ever witnessed that."

"Now that they're gone, I get a glimpse of it now and then with my brothers. It's a different kind of love, but there's a permanence that comes with family." Her expression turned wistful.

"Yeah." Kyle's brows contracted until his head hurt. He'd never had that with Nate.

"We made a pact, Kyle. We said we'd do something fun, every day." Laina smiled impishly at him.

He groaned. "I'm not sure I have the energy for much fun tonight."

"I have an idea." Her gaze fixated on the water and then up at the crescent moon. "How about a swim?"

He arched an eyebrow at her. "Isn't it a little cold?"

Laina stood and pulled her sweatshirt over her head, her white lace bra barely visible in the sliver of moonlight. "Pool's heated." She unbuttoned her jeans and slid them down her legs, toeing off her shoes and socks.

Kyle's pulse picked up the pace, the thump, thump of his heart loud in his ears. All his blood was in a terrible rush south. Fuck, he was already hard. He set down his glass. "What happened to keeping things professional?"

The look she shot over her shoulder was heavy with invitation. "As far as I can tell, we are both off the clock." In nothing but a bra and a stretch of lace, she rounded the pool and dove in, the warm, clear liquid undulating over her muscles. Breaking the surface, she smoothed back her hair with both hands, a siren calling to him in the glow of the underwater lights.

For a moment, he didn't move, just stared at her from

his pool chair, his gaze drifting to the place where the surface of the water lapped over her nipples, clearly visible beneath the wet white lace. His eyelids lowered to half-mast, and his fingers moved to the cuff links of his shirt. He stood and removed his jacket.

"Laina, we're too old for games." He had to have her. That wild thing inside him was back, and every instinct in his body was begging him to mount her, to claim her, to *mark* her. "I've respected your request to maintain a professional distance, despite wanting you every minute you've been here. If I dive into that water, it won't be just to swim. Tell me now if you want me to walk away. I can't pretend I don't want you. Not tonight." Damn, what had happened to his voice? It gritted out of him like the rusty growl of an old engine.

She snaked her arms through the water, blinking up at him. "Come closer. I want to see you."

Stripping down, he stepped to the edge of the pool, making no attempt to hide the erection that tented his boxer briefs. Her eyes darted to his reflection in the water, then up to the moon behind his head, and back again. Everywhere, it seemed, but at him. "Laina, look at me." Her eyes finally snapped to his. "Yes or no?"

For some reason, when she smiled, she seemed... relieved, although he couldn't puzzle out why *she'd* be feeling that emotion. "Come in," she said, her voice husky. Now, the relief was all his.

He dug his thumbs into his briefs, pulled them off, and cast them aside. The way she stared at his erection as it jutted toward her left him breathless and buzzing from the electric charge growing between them. He jumped into the shoulder-deep water and waded across the pool toward her. As his fingers found her waist and his thumbs stroked between her navel and bottom rib, his gaze raked over her face and settled on her lips. He pressed her against the side of the pool, the only sound the movement of the water around their bodies and the soft current of his breath. He lowered his face toward hers.

"There's something you should know about me," she whispered into his mouth.

"Hmm?"

"I'm strong, really strong. And I like it rough. If something I do hurts you, you have to tell me."

The corner of his mouth lifted. "Give it all you've got. You won't hurt me, and I won't hold back."

Greedily, his lips crashed down on hers, tongue diving into her mouth. Stroking. Exploring. Staking a claim. She let him in, her hands finding the back of his head, gasping for air as they repositioned to go even deeper.

She hitched a leg over his hip, and he pressed his erection into the thin, wet lace between her thighs. He used the weightlessness of the water to hold her up with one arm and wrap her other leg around him without effort. He thrust into her mouth, showing her with his tongue what he planned to do between her legs next.

Cupping her under her ass, he ground his massive erection against her belly, eliciting a carnal moan. He coasted a hand up her side to squeeze her breast through the wet lace, thumb flicking the nub to a hard peak. His touch traced the material under her arm to the center of her back, where he unclasped her bra and paused from kissing her, panting heavily, to toss it aside.

When she reached for his face again, he caught her wrists in his hands and spread her arms, the angle forcing a subtle arch to her upper back. "You are beautiful." He lowered his head to suck her nipple into his mouth, rolled it over his tongue, and bit it gently. A guttural sound came from deep within her throat.

"You like that? God, Laina, I've wanted to bury myself in you since the first day I saw you. I want to make you scream." He released her wrists and cupped her breasts with both hands, the water lapping against their skin.

She kissed him wickedly, biting his bottom lip until he groaned. "Then do it."

It was as if the words popped the cork on the thing inside him. He surged into her, his hands gripping her waist and lifting her until her bottom was perched on the edge of the pool. With one hand, he tore the lace panties right off her, while he lifted her leg over his shoulder with the other. He dove between her legs, licking up her center and sucking her clit.

"Oh...oh..." She leaned on her elbows, tilting her head back.

He didn't let up. Spearing into her, he lapped and sucked, worshiping her clit with tiny flicks and circles of his tongue. She was a banquet, and he intended to feast. The little sounds she made as he worked her were driving his cock wild. He couldn't get enough of her slick heat.

In a rush, she clamped her thighs around his ears, and her panting breaths morphed into a howl. Fuck, he'd never heard a woman make a sound like that, like a goddamned wolf. She was still spasming when he leaped from the pool, grabbed her around the waist and carried her to the nearest padded lounge. Tossing her facedown, he hooked his hands into her hips and yanked her ass into the air. She barely had time to grip the edges before he was slamming into her. She said she liked it rough. All he had was rough. Tonight, his edges had edges, and all his instincts told him to grind them down on her.

Her howls turned into a low, lusty growl. He wasn't going to last long. Already, a tingle was gathering at the base of his spine, and his hips were pounding faster, chasing the orgasm that remained just out of reach. His instincts drove him to bend over her and bite the space between her neck and shoulder.

That did it. She howled as she came again, her inner muscles milking him as his orgasm pumped into her, filling her. He held her with his teeth until there was nothing left in him to give her. Only when he came back down to earth did he realize he'd broken the skin. She panted as if she couldn't catch her breath.

"You are mine, Laina Flynn," he said into her ear. "Tell me I don't have to share you with anyone."

She met his eyes over her shoulder. "You don't."

"Good. I couldn't bear it." He pulled out of her, then helped her up, brushing her hair from her neck and rubbing a thumb over the spot where he'd bitten her. "Did I hurt you?"

She shook her head. "No, it just surprised me."

"Me too," he admitted. "I've never done that before." Noticing how cold it had become, he quickly gathered their clothes and led her up to his room. Without a word, they both crawled under the covers, her heat finding his. With her tucked into the curl of his body, his mind blanked under the gentle caress of her fingers on his chest. "Laina, I want you to stay with me tonight. All night. In here."

She sighed. "Good, because I want to stay."

He pressed a kiss to the top of her head. With her positioned in the nook of his shoulder, he listened as her breath evened out, and then he fell with her into a fast, deep sleep.

<h1 style="text-align:center">CHAPTER
NINETEEN</h1>

When Laina woke, she was being bopped in the nose by a wet snout that protruded from beneath a set of giant brown eyes. Milo blinked at her unapologetically. She must've forgotten to lock his crate last night. He stomped and wagged his tail before licking her face.

"Milo…" She wiped the kiss away.

"You can hardly blame him. You are positively delectable." Kyle rolled her beneath him, propping himself on his elbows and settling between her thighs. He kissed her gently. Damn, feeling him like this, hard, warm, distinctively male, she felt her desire rise again. But in the light of morning, there were things she had to know. She had questions. The way he'd bitten her last night, it was almost as if he were marking her. He wasn't a shifter, but she wondered if she'd awakened some dormant instinct in the man.

She ran her nose along the side of his, inhaling his scent. "Kyle…"

"Morning."

"I need to ask you something."

He pulled back and looked at her. "Ask."

"Did you mean what you said last night?"

He gave her a wry grin. "Remind me what I said."

"You said I was yours and you couldn't bear for me to be with anyone else," she whispered. "Was that just talk in the moment, or did you mean it?"

He snorted, his eyes growing hooded. "Oh yes, I meant every word." Any hint of humor left his features, and he held her eye contact as if he were searching her soul. "How about you? Any hesitation to agreeing to those terms?"

She closed her eyes and smiled. "None at all."

"Good." He slid his arm under the arch of her back, and he shifted between her thighs until his cock nudged her entrance.

"What about Milo?"

"Milo can wait." Kyle entered her in one quick thrust, and she arched into him as pleasure gripped her. Her body was already humming. She bucked against him, urging him faster, harder, deeper.

She fisted his shoulders, flipping him over and rising above him so that she was in control. His hands found her hips, guiding as she ground against him, frantic with need. He sat up and captured one of her nipples in his mouth, fluttering his tongue across the sensitive tip. It sent her over the edge.

Her orgasm plowed into her and took him with her, both of them clinging to each other as they rode out the aftershocks.

In the aftermath, Milo whimpered softly. "He really does need to go out," she said. "I can take him."

"No. Get dressed. I'll come with you. There's something I want to show you."

The world's fastest shower later, Laina met Kyle in the

backyard, where he was already waiting with Milo. "So, what did you want to show me?"

"It's back there, in the woods, behind the fence." He pointed to a gate on the other side of the expansive yard.

"Let's run. Milo needs the exercise."

"What? Why?"

She grinned before breaking into a jog as much for her own sake as for Milo's. Her wolf was unusually close to the surface, and she was desperate to burn off the raw energy. Milo loped easily beside her, but Kyle struggled to keep up. She tempered her pace.

How could she possibly have entertained the idea he was Jonah? Sure, he was athletic, but his gait was slightly uneven and his pace was entirely human. Then again, he'd marked her last night as wolves did. That was strange but didn't necessarily mean anything, she told herself. When she reached the back of the massive yard, she slowed to a stop and waited for him.

Huffing, Kyle rested his hands on his knees. "Running. Isn't. My. Thing," he said between breaths.

"What is your thing?"

He grinned and scratched the back of his head. "Bossing people around. Isn't it obvious?" He nodded toward Hunt Club.

"I don't believe it. It doesn't suit you. You can barely boss Milo around." At the sound of his name, Milo perked his ears up.

The morning sun made Kyle's eyes blaze butterscotch with just enough flecks of green and brown to remind her they were hazel. The smile faded from his face. For a moment, she felt like the polished veneer he commonly wore moved aside and she was staring straight into his soul. He cocked an eyebrow. "Bossed you around well enough last night."

"I stand corrected. I rather like your bossiness under the right circumstances."

He straightened. "Come on. There's a trail back here."

He led her to a gate in the fence at the back of the property, where they melded into the woods on a narrow and twisting dirt path. An intense peace came over Laina as the forest swallowed them, the songs of birds overhead joining the whirr of cicadas and Milo's panting. Behind her, Hunt Club became a distant memory, completely concealed by the changing trees, their auburn, evergreen, and saffron leaves celebrating the early fall. There was nothing else. No traffic. No voices.

"How much land is yours?" she finally asked, curious as to how far they could go.

"Just over five hundred acres."

Her eyebrows shot heavenward. "Why on earth do you need that much property?"

"I'd like to turn this Hunt Club into a resort. Horses, tennis, skeet shooting, snowshoeing in the winter."

"I thought Hunt Club was a lifestyle club—essentially liquor and sex."

"It is, for now."

"You want to make it something more?"

"Maybe. Nate's not a fan of the idea."

Laina analyzed his guarded expression. "Gerty thinks you want to make this your permanent home."

"Gerty knows me better than anyone."

"Why here? Why now?"

Kyle waited a long time before responding. "The other ones weren't for me. This is the only club designed with my permanent residence in mind. There's something about the woods, the wild. Plus, it's the place I can practice my hobby." He turned down an even smaller branch of the trail, then came to a stop at the base of a clearing. Milo sat and waited as they'd trained him to do.

"Good boy," Laina said, ruffling the dog's ears. When she looked up from the mastiff, she followed the exposed roots of an enormous oak tree to a rustic tree house intimately designed within its branches. Intimate because the craftsmanship gave the illusion the house was a natural extension of the tree. Her lips parted in amazement at the design.

"Who made this? It's beautiful. The artistry is incredible."

When he didn't answer, she looked at him. "Me," he said simply. "You asked what my thing was. It's this." He pointed a hand at the tree house. "When I'm not being the boss of people, I build tree houses."

Eyes wide, she shook her head. "It's impossible. It's like something out of a fairy tale."

"Come on. I'll show you inside."

"What about Milo?"

"He can come too. There's a ramp." He walked around to the back of the tree, where a selection of cleverly placed shrubs concealed a plank bridge that sloped to the bottom of the structure. As the three approached the door, she inhaled deeply. Cedar and pine—the source of Kyle's unique scent.

Kyle pushed open the rounded door, which reminded her more than a little of a Hobbit hole, and ushered her and Milo inside. The interior was equally charming. Maple floors flowed into roughhewn log walls, the bark preserved in places to continue the illusion that the tree had bloomed a house rather than simply supported one. The only furniture was a small daybed and a driftwood end table with a battery-powered lantern.

"It's possible to build these with modern amenities, but I'd need help for that. It would be too hard to hide the crew."

"Why do you need to hide the crew?"

"Like I said, this is my dirty little secret. When my father was alive, he'd call it wasting time. My brother would say it was a distraction."

"You built this yourself?" She exhaled in amazement. Dropping Milo's leash, she ran her hands along the sanded wood of the windowsill. The big dog trotted to the daybed and curled up on the multicolored afghan spread.

"Not entirely. Gerty's husband, Arthur, helped me. He has a passion for it as well. But aside from him and Gerty, you are the only one who has ever seen it."

She bit her lip. "But why would you keep this a secret? I get that your family might not like you wasting your time, but you're exceptionally talented. I've never seen anything like this."

The grin that spread across his face told her he appreciated the compliment. "My time is not my own. My father was a businessman, his father was a businessman, and so on, as far back as anyone can remember. If my cave-dwelling ancestors could be tracked down with a time machine, I'm sure we would find Ogg Kingsley peddling flint and slingshots from a rock near the communal watering hole. Nate would flip if he knew the hours I'd put into this, hours that could have been earning the family more money."

Laina smiled faintly. "So, Nate isn't supportive of your hobby?"

"Nate, the board, our partners. My father might have punched me in the face."

"I hope you're joking."

"He was the type of guy who felt actions spoke louder than words."

"Actions? More like child abuse."

He chuckled. "Rich people don't abuse their children, Laina. Don't be silly."

She crossed her arms over her chest, her wolf baring her teeth at the thought of anyone punching Kyle for any reason. "Is part of you glad he's dead?"

With a visible jerk of his head, Kyle's eyebrows pinched over his nose.

"I'm sorry. That was completely uncalled for. I don't know what came over me." A complete brain hijack by her wild side would be the only explanation. She was mortified.

His face softened. "Laina, this is why I'm drawn to you. You're honest and genuine, probably the only person in my life who cares to see things for what they are. The truth is that my father was not a nice man. Herbert Kingsley provided for us. He was a talented business partner. But he wasn't a father to me, not emotionally."

"I'm sorry." Running her fingers through the back of his hair, she glanced toward the window as the ping of rain against glass signaled a coming storm. A heavy feeling settled in the space between her heart and her stomach. As genuine as Kyle thought she was, he still didn't know she was a werewolf. He could never know. In just ten days, she'd have to shift again. What excuse would she give him to leave? How long could this go on?

"Last night, I noticed the tattoo on your shoulder. It's a phoenix, right?"

She nodded.

"Did you design it?"

She tapped her fingers on the windowsill. "I know what it's like to have a controlling family. It's like you have no will of your own, like your choices don't matter." Her gaze drifted through the window to the rain-soaked shades of green beyond.

"What happened to you, Laina? How did you end up here, really?"

A long, heavy silence settled in the tree house. "You asked once if I was part of the mob."

"You told me you weren't."

"I'm not. No organized crime involved." She looked down at her trembling hands. This was a delicate truth, fragile as butterfly wings. "My family belongs to a rare subculture...a society different from your own."

"Different, how?"

She rubbed the back of her neck, trying to find the words. "Our culture is ancient. We have strong bonds and maintain a careful balance with others of our kind, families of the same culture. Our rules and traditions hold us together and maintain our bonds." She tapped her right shoulder. "For example, this tattoo represents my family group."

He narrowed his eyes. "So, why are you in hiding?"

"One of our own decided he didn't want to live by our rules anymore. He wanted more power. He wanted power over all the families, to make his own rules, and use our society's resources for his own gain. He wanted it so badly he was willing to kill for it."

"Kill?"

"The first day I was here, I mentioned my parents were murdered several years ago in a theater."

"I remember."

"My parents received an invitation to a production of Shakespeare's *Macbeth* from a local animal rights charity. All proceeds were promised to advance the organization's goals. My mother loved animals almost as much as I do, but I couldn't go. I was finishing veterinary school, and my brothers were busy with their own lives at the time. None of us could attend with our parents."

She swallowed the lump forming in her throat and tangled her fingers on the windowsill. "When they arrived, other families were there too, families from my...culture, along with others they'd never met before. During the final act, a masked gunman shot and killed everyone in the first four rows, including my parents and my best friend's parents."

Kyle winced.

"The police assumed it was an act of terrorism. They never caught the gunman. Over a year later, there was another murder, two more elders from my society found dead. This time, they did catch the perpetrator, the son of one of our leaders. He confessed to killing my parents. That's when we learned the tragedy wasn't a random shooting. My parents were murdered by a man named Alex Ravien Bloodright. He wanted to rule my society. The man killed his own parents out of a bottomless thirst for power. Thankfully, the authorities captured him, and he was imprisoned."

"But..."

"Recently, he escaped. My brother Silas is a detective. He hunted Alex down, and there was a confrontation. Alex was killed. But his supporters have vowed revenge and threatened me directly. Specifically, we think Alex's right-hand man, Jonah, is targeting my family. I'm in hiding because what you saw in Four Paws the night we were supposed to have our date was Jonah targeting me. He's trying to kill me. And if I didn't come here and change my identity, I'd probably be dead." Her voice petered out at the end as though she'd run out of air, and she rested her forehead against the window. She'd told him too much, too close to the truth without revealing the furry details.

Strong hands gripped her upper arms, and Kyle's face reflected in the window over her shoulder. "I'm sorry, Laina," he said genuinely. "You're safe here. Hunt Club has the finest security in the world. I won't let anything happen to you."

She turned within his arms to face him. "I wouldn't blame you if you wanted me to leave."

"Why would I want you to leave?"

"Aren't you afraid I'll bring a killer into your life? Why would you want this...drama?"

"Isn't it obvious?"

She shook her head weakly.

"From the moment I saw you in Four Paws, I've been enamored. You're enchanting. You had me when I saw you care for Milo like he was your own. I fell deeper when I saw how, instead of collapsing as most people would, you cared for your assistant when your clinic was in ruins. Then you stood up to me after the incident at the club. Fuck, you're made of steel. You're fearless. You own me, Laina. It's like this magnetic connection, a pull at the center of me that leads only to you. I couldn't stand to see you working at Monty's. I had to know you. I *had* to make you mine."

Laina's nostrils flared on an inhale, the warm, heady scent of Kyle flooding her senses; the sharp tang of hunger; grit and sweat; the cotton of his shirt; a hint of Milo; finished wood; and under it all, the faint whiff of his arousal. The urge to bury her face in his chest was almost overwhelming. What Kyle had said to her was romantic, but the pull he described could be nothing like the deep, gnawing desire that ached in her core. He was her wolf's vice. If she'd had any doubts before, that was over now.

He moved closer, a simple shift of his body, and she lost all control. Rising onto her toes, she slammed her mouth into his, fisting his shirt. Kyle grabbed her ponytail, wrapping it around his hand until it tugged her head back. He trailed tiny, nipping teeth down her neck.

"Bite harder," she said. He obliged. She moaned appreciatively.

"Last night, you said you like it rough," he whispered.

"Yes," she rasped. "I won't break."

He bent her backward over his arm and trailed his teeth and lips along her collarbone. Releasing her hair, he pulled aside her T-shirt, tugging her breasts from her bra. He took her nipple into his mouth, nibbling softly on the tip. The sucking grew more intense until her nipple stood at attention; he switched to the other, his thumb thrumming her rosy flesh.

"I like them like this," he said in a husky voice. "I bet this makes you wet. Let's see if I'm right." He skimmed his hand down her torso and plunged it under her waistband.

Laina inhaled sharply as he brushed his fingers over her sex, his middle finger massaging her opening. "Mmm."

"You're wet and ready. Fuck, I love that." She squirmed on her feet and was forced to steady herself on his shoulders. With one hand bracing her back, he flicked his tongue across her nipple while he massaged inside her in long, languid strokes. Abruptly, he pulled his fingers out and plunged them into his mouth. "Oh, Laina, you taste good."

She trembled as he dropped to his knees, hitched his fingers in the waistband of her sweats and tugged them south. He buried his nose in her mound, and his tongue continued the work of his fingers, eliciting a moan that filled the tree house. With a slight bend of her knees, she spread her legs as far as she could with the sweats around her ankles. His tongue darted inside, then flicked and sucked her clit.

Laina didn't stand a chance. The wolf inside was hyper-sensitive to his every touch. The orgasm plowed into her, her nerve endings lighting up like a thousand blinking fire-flies. Her knees gave out, and he popped off the floor to catch her in his arms, his eyes hooded, his breathing heavy.

"I love to feel you come," he whispered in her ear.

She collected herself, kneading his sides with her fingers. Once she regained control of her limbs, she smiled slowly. "My turn." She shoved her hand into his pants, threading her fingers into the soft curls below his belly button. When she wrapped her hand around him, he inhaled sharply through his teeth.

A shrill ring sent Milo into a fit of barking. Kyle grabbed her wrist and cursed, pulling his phone from his back pocket. "If I don't answer this, he'll just call back," he mumbled. "Not a good time!" he shouted into the phone.

There was a long pause, during which Laina played mercilessly with Kyle's cock, circling her thumb over the bead of moisture at the tip. His face reddened.

"Yeah. Running late. I'll be there." He tapped the screen and tossed the phone on the daybed. "Sorry about that."

In answer, she dropped to her knees and slid her lips around his cock, drawing him deep into the back of her throat. He moaned and fisted the back of her hair.

"Laina. Oh my god."

With long strokes, she worked her tongue over his shaft, sucking hard to the tip, swirling her tongue over the head, then swallowing him down again. She reveled in the growing urgency of his thrusts and gently fondled the heavy weights between his thighs.

"I'm going to come," he rasped, pushing gently against her shoulders.

She grabbed his hips and pulled him in deeper, hollowing her cheeks. When his body jerked with his orgasm, she swallowed, his scent burning in her nose, her wolf howling in her head, and her own body revving up again at the erotic feel of him at the back of her throat.

"Jesus Christ, Laina." He pulled back, stroking the hair from her face. "You are... I can't find the words..."

"I want to roll in you," she said. "I want to cover myself in your scent and spend three days with you inside me."

A low growl came from deep within him, one she could have easily mistaken for a wolf's. "Oh yeah, baby." He shook his head slowly. "We'll do that, but..."

"But..."

"I hate to leave you, but I'm late for a meeting with some investors from Japan. Nate threatened to have my head."

She stood and called Milo, who'd fallen asleep, apparently uninterested in what had occurred moments before. He trotted to her side while Kyle collected himself. At least the rain had stopped.

As the three of them walked back to the mansion, Laina couldn't help but feel like Kyle and Milo had become her second pack, her home away from home. And although she wasn't ready to broach the subject with Silas, she could no longer picture a future without them.

The next morning, after feeding Milo and having breakfast, Laina found herself wandering the east wing, daydreaming about Kyle. It wasn't long before sheer boredom drove her to seek out Gerty.

"Someone's bed didn't need making this morning." Gerty grinned like she held a juicy secret.

Laina's face blazed, blood rushing to the surface of her skin.

"Oh dear, don't be embarrassed. It's a suitable match," she said with a throaty chuckle. "Any fool can see you're good for him, and I'm willing to bet he's good for you."

Laina was formulating a response to Gerty in her head when the door opened without a knock and Jason entered, sliding his sunglasses back on his head. "The driver told me not to bother knocking."

"Jason! What are you doing here?" Laina rushed to him and tossed her arms around his neck.

"Kyle sent a car for me. The driver insisted I come immediately. Even convinced Monty. He told me to pack a bag." Jason tapped his shoe against his suitcase.

Gerty smiled and took the bag from him. "You'll need a room. I'll go get it ready for you." She hobbled upstairs, refusing Laina's and Jason's help.

"I thought you were hurt or something," Jason said.

She shook her head. "No, I'm fine."

"Then why the dramatics?"

"I have no idea why Kyle would send for you. I can't even ask him. He's in a meeting."

The delicate tinkle of a woman's laugh reached their ears, and Jason raised an eyebrow in Laina's direction. When another laugh filled the space between them, they navigated the house to the pool area and discovered the source. Nickie, the platinum blonde who'd helped Laina the day she'd served at Hunt Club, crossed the pool deck in a plush white robe gaping enough to reveal a sparkling blue bikini underneath. She headed for the hot tub, her laughter in response to a phone pressed to her ear.

"Put your tongue back in your mouth, Jason," Laina said.

"I think we should go hot-tubbing." He was out the door before she could protest.

"Anna!" Nickie called when she saw her, jogging across the pool deck in a way that caused her massive breasts to bob like buoys beneath the robe. They turned out to be quite firm when they pressed into Laina's chest as the woman embraced her. "I ran into Kyle, and he said I could come over for a soak. The west wing pool is being cleaned." She eyed Jason. "And you! I thought you were going to call me?"

"I thought you were going back to Chicago."

"They made me an offer I couldn't refuse." Nickie bit her lip as she pulled him into a hug that lasted ten seconds longer than a hug between strangers should last. Laina drilled Jason with a stare, then realized that Nickie must be the model he'd spent the night with when they'd first arrived in Sable Creek.

"Come, soak with me," Nickie said. She threaded her fingers into Jason's and led him to the hot tub. Jason raised an eyebrow at Laina before shedding his jacket and lifting his shirt to expose a torso that was ripped by human standards. Despite all the corded muscle, Laina winced at how much weight he'd lost the last three years and wondered if losing Jessica at the same time as their parents had affected him in more ways than he let on.

Jason reached for his fly, making it obvious he intended to go in sans swimsuit. Laina glanced away until dual splashes signaled he and Nickie were under the bubbling water.

Kicking off her shoes and rolling up her pant legs, Laina settled on the edge opposite Nickie and dipped her feet in.

"Oh, how cute. You two have matching tattoos." Nickie eyed the phoenix on Jason's shoulder.

He darted a glance to Laina, who unconsciously rubbed the sleeve of her sweater.

"Oh, I can't see it now, but I remember the design from when you were being painted. I've never seen a brother and sister with the same tattoo before." Her platinum bob swayed as her glance darted from one to the other.

Jason's gaze drifted across the pool. He ran a hand through his hair and tugged at his earlobe. Clearly, he didn't know how to answer the question. Laina rolled her eyes. She supposed she was technically alpha in Silas's absence.

"Did I say something wrong?" Nickie asked.

The muscles around Laina's lips tightened. "We got them when our parents died. It's a painful subject." It was also a lie. Their pack tattoos had been inscribed into their skin as part of a sacred ceremony following their first shift, well before their parents' deaths.

"Oh," she squeaked in an almost cartoonish voice, placing her perfectly manicured fingers over her lips. "I'm such an idiot."

"You couldn't have known," Jason said with a smile. "Don't worry about it."

"Let's talk about something else," Laina suggested.

"Yeah. Like, why are you living in the east wing?" Nickie glared at Laina. "Are you sleeping with Kyle Kingsley?"

Laina almost choked on her tongue and started coughing furiously. "Why would you think that?"

"Because the rest of the girls stay in the west wing. You do know you are the first girl ever to stay in Kyle's private residence. Not just here, but anywhere."

"I'm training his dog. I have my own room." Laina scratched her nose, her gaze darting toward the pool.

Nickie leaned back and brushed a hair from her face. "Hmm. I guess I read that one wrong. The day he found that box you left, I thought he was going to blow a gasket. I didn't see what the big deal was. I had a theory that it was just an excuse to find you."

Laina stiffened. "Did you say Kyle found the box?" She'd assumed it was someone else, perhaps an ogre or fae who'd been working in the kitchen. Jason made eye contact. She knew what he was thinking. If Kyle could find the box, it meant he wasn't human.

"No. I think it was Kyle. I didn't actually see the box—I was in the locker room—but he came into the staging area, yelling about finding it and grilling everyone. He'd printed your picture from the security cameras and demanded any information anyone had about you. I told him you went by Anna. What was in the box anyway?"

"I'm not supposed to talk about it," Laina said.

"Oh." Nickie shrugged. She snuggled in next to Jason in the water. Laina quickly felt like a third wheel.

"I better check on Milo."

"Later." Jason gave her a little wave, before focusing all his attention on Nickie.

Laina scooped up her shoes and headed inside, leaving them to each other's company.

"The housekeeper said I'd find you in here." Jason entered the library two hours later, looking slightly disheveled but, thankfully, fully dressed.

"Enjoy yourself, brother?"

He chuckled. "More than you know. Nickie and I are seriously compatible when it comes to sex. If I hadn't been so concerned about you, I might have followed her home for round three."

"Concerned about me?"

"What do you think it means that Kyle found the box?"

"I don't know, but I tested him, and he isn't under a camouflage spell or enchantment."

"That doesn't rule out trouble. He could be a supernatural creature or be working for the enemy. We should call Silas."

"Don't you dare. I'll kick your ass, Jason. I mean it." She locked eyes with her brother, conveying in no uncertain terms that she meant what she said.

All humor bled from his expression. "Shit, Laina. You're in deep. He really is your vice."

"He's a kind, generous, and successful man, and yes..." She looked down at her hands in her lap, almost ashamed to say the words. "He's my vice. And I'm falling for him."

Jason shook his head. "Don't confuse it for love."

"I'm not confused. Kyle and I, we are similar creatures, Jason. I really think he might be the one."

"The one?" Jason stared at her in disbelief. "That's crazy talk. You do realize that even if you two were somehow fated to be together, he'd forever be relegated to the sidelines. You're royalty. You'd never be allowed to mate with a human."

The words hit her in the heart like a wrecking ball. Her throat constricted into a tight knot. "Excuse me," she rasped. She rose from the leather sofa and headed for the staircase. To his credit, Jason didn't come after her.

TWENTY-ONE

Laina lay awake well past midnight, staring at the ceiling and waiting for Kyle to come home. He'd sent a message with his driver to say he'd be very late and that she was welcome to sleep in his bed, but she decided to stay in her own. What Jason had said was true. Her relationship with Kyle was doomed. How would she break it to him? She couldn't tell him the truth. Would she just disappear? Say nothing? Create an elaborate lie to let him down easy? How would she survive after tearing out a corner of her heart and casting it aside?

Or worse, would she continue the relationship as a lie? Marry Cameron and keep Kyle on the side, a long-distance crutch to appease her wolf with no chance of ever becoming more than a fling? It depressed her even to think about it. He deserved better.

She was so disturbed by her predicament that when the sunrise finally broke her sleepless night, she decided to take Milo for his morning walk alone, desperately needing the solitude to process her feelings.

Love was a dangerous sport, played without the benefit

of safety equipment. She would have gladly paid anything for a helmet that fit her heart these days. For someone who hadn't had much use for the opposite sex up until then, she'd certainly learned why the term used for fast affection was a crush. Everything about her relationship with Kyle was crushing.

"Good morning," she said to Gerty as she breezed through the kitchen.

"Would you like some coffee?" the old woman offered, holding up the empty pot. "The matching baggage under your eyes suggests you do."

"I'd love some, but it will have to wait. I'm afraid we'll have a Milo-sized accident on our hands if I don't walk him soon." She smiled warmly as she snagged Milo's leash from the coat hook and clipped it to him. On a whim, she decided to take the mastiff out front, unable to face the memories the pool and yard afforded. She needed clarity. Before this thing with Kyle went any further, she had to decide what to do about it.

She hadn't even made it past the fountain when Milo lifted his leg on a bush lining the circular drive.

"Feel better?" she asked him. He looked up at her, tongue lolling out the corner of his mouth.

A car pulled up beside her, a shiny black cube she recognized upon second glance was a Mercedes G-Class. The passenger's side window rolled down, and Nate's frog-like face smiled at her from behind the wheel. "I see Milo is in good hands."

"I hope so."

"Dad loved that dog almost as much as he loved beautiful women. He'd be pleased. Two of his favorite things."

Not knowing what to say to that, she gathered the leash in her hands. "Milo needs a walk. Nice to see you again."

"Is Kyle up yet?" he asked quickly before she could move.

"When I left the house, he was still in bed."

"I'd want to stay in bed all day too, with a woman like you between the sheets. Only, you're out here, which begs the question why he'd be in there."

"I'm here to train the dog. I wasn't in bed with him," she said matter-of-factly. "I just noticed he wasn't out of his room yet." What was his angle? She and Kyle were mature adults. It was none of Nate's business if they were sleeping together.

He nodded. "Well, that's a relief. When I walked in on you sitting on Kyle's lap next to the pool a couple weeks ago, you looked at me like you might bite my head off. I assumed there was something going on. That must have been part of your training program."

Her stomach sank, and the hot flare of a blush burned her cheeks. She shouldn't be embarrassed, but she was. Tongue-tied, she searched her usually quick mind for a clever retort but came up blank.

"Kyle isn't for you, sweetheart," the frog mouth said. "In fact, becoming involved with someone like him could be dangerous." Nate gave her a threatening smile.

"What is that supposed to mean?"

One side of Nate's mouth curled. "Plenty of girls would kill to get closer to Kyle."

"Kyle is perfectly capable of deciding who to get close to. Let's get something straight—I'm training his dog, not marrying him."

He tugged at the sleeve of his dress shirt. "He hasn't been himself since you came here."

"How so?" she challenged.

"Short-fused, reluctant to be photographed with the

models, distracted, late to meetings, early to leave, unwilling to party with business partners. You'd think he had a ring around his finger. I don't know who you are or who you work for, *Anna*, but I'm watching you."

As she opened her mouth to tell Nate to go fuck himself, the threat she saw in his expression stopped her short.

"Hey, wait up!" Kyle called. They both turned their heads toward the mansion as Kyle jogged out, dressed in jeans and a Hunt Club T-shirt, with two travel mugs in hand. "Gerty said you needed coffee." He handed her one of the mugs and gave her a quick kiss on the mouth. "Cream and sugar, right? If it's too sweet, you can have mine."

"It's perfect, thank you," she said without even trying it.

"Nate, what are you doing here? It's Sunday, my day off, brother."

"I invited Tanaka to a formal dinner this Friday night at my place. It's imperative that you be there. Which of the models would you like to accompany you?"

Kyle glanced at Laina. Her eyes drifted to the leash in her hands. Would he ask her to go? Silas would never allow her to be that exposed. Not to mention, the full moon was Saturday. She'd be cutting it close. An emotional tinderbox.

"I'll go alone this time," Kyle said.

"No." Nate shook his head. "Absolutely not. Out of the question, Kyle. It is not within the Hunt Club brand for you to be seen alone."

Kyle braced himself against the hood of the car, eyes darting toward Laina. "I'll give you an answer by the end of the day."

Nate nodded. "How's Milo working out? I wasn't sure what you'd be dealing with, considering."

"He's settling in just fine, thanks."

Nate nodded. "Care to join me for lunch? Personal, not work."

Kyle glanced at Laina and back at Nate. "Uh, not today. Sorry, I have plans."

With a curt nod, Nate shifted the Mercedes into drive and waved at Laina, his eyes drilling into her. "A pleasure, as always." His gaze darted to his brother. "I'll catch you later, Kyle." The Mercedes circled, then drove off in the direction of the gatehouse.

"I'd better give Milo some exercise. He's getting restless," Laina said. In fact, the mastiff was pulling against her wrist and weaving from one side of the walkway to the other.

"Let me," Kyle said, shifting his coffee into his opposite hand to take the leash from her.

"You don't have to."

"Didn't you say that walking him was a key part of earning his trust?" His hazel eyes twinkled in the late-morning light.

She nodded and fell into place beside Kyle. He positioned Milo at his side expertly. Laina watched the dog heel, proud of what they'd accomplished. Milo trusted Kyle implicitly as his alpha. They'd be okay if she had to leave. Her heart turned to lead at the thought.

"I hope you didn't turn down lunch because of me," she said.

Confusion morphed into disappointment before Kyle's polished grin snapped into place again. "I thought we could spend the day together."

"I would love to. I just know you both recently lost your father. Family is very important. When my parents were killed, my relationship with my brothers was instrumental in helping me heal emotionally."

"Thanks, but it's not the same for us." He glanced in the direction Nate had gone.

"Speaking of brothers, what made you invite Jason?" she asked.

He looked down at his coffee. "When we were in the tree house yesterday, your story about your family and that Jonah guy made it occur to me that Jason might not be safe at Monty's. We have much better security here." He took a sip of his coffee, sizing up her reaction before adding, "I want you to stay with me, Laina. I thought it would be easier for you if Jason was here too. He can stay as long as he wants. Silas is welcome as well. I would have sent for him too, if you'd said where to find him. Where is he staying?"

Laina frowned. She was sure Kyle was trying to be helpful, but sending for Jason without talking to her first crossed the line. She ignored his question about Silas and jumped to the point of the matter. "But you know Jason will have to go back. We both will. I can't stay here permanently."

"Why not? If I haven't made it obvious, as far as I'm concerned, you never have to leave." His face lit up with hope.

"There's something we have to do next weekend, family business. But even if we come back after that, once this is all sorted out, I'll go home to New Hampshire. I have a business, a life. I can't stay forever." She hadn't wanted to do it this way, not now, but Nate had made her realize the effect she was having on Kyle. She had to be honest with him. Leading him on would only make the inevitable worse.

He scratched the back of his head and stared at her. "I'm sure we can figure something out. You're important to me. I don't want this to end."

Laina walked faster.

"Will you go with me Friday night? To the Tanaka dinner at Nate's?"

She looked at him, jaw going slack. "I can't. Who would watch Milo?"

"No one needs to watch Milo. He hasn't chewed anything in over a week. One of the models can give him his evening walk. I'll ask Nate who he was expecting to use as my date. If she was free to spend the evening with me, she should be free to walk Milo."

Laina laughed. "I'm sure that won't burn."

"Please. I can't go with someone else. Not now. It wouldn't feel right."

She sighed. "This thing between us, Kyle, I want it to work, but..."

He shook his head. "You can't deny we have a connection. I've never felt anything like this. No way am I quitting because of geography."

"I don't want to quit. We do have a connection," she said.

"Then what is it?"

"He said it was dangerous," she murmured, thinking of Nate.

"Who said it was dangerous?"

"Your brother," she said, choosing to share what truth she could. "He implied I was distracting you and said it would be dangerous for me to become involved with you."

"That asshole!"

"He would have probably preferred I keep that to myself."

"Forget about Nate. He's a dick."

"But maybe he's right, Kyle. Maybe I'm not what you need. I don't fit here."

Silence wedged between them, their feet crunching rhythmically on the stones. They turned the corner of the drive that led to the gatehouse. Kyle slowed his steps. The picketers from Eternal Light Ministries were back, lined up on the other side of the gate. At least fifteen signs waved in the air. *God hates fornicators. Porn dooms America. Repent and be saved!*

"Don't they ever leave?" Laina shook her head.

"Never." He grabbed her elbow and tugged her back up the drive. "I should have known better than to come this way. Come on."

Laina wasn't sure she'd have noticed the man if she weren't a wolf; they were still far enough away that he'd be a blur to human eyes. Dark blond hair, a baseball cap, and a hand that reached behind his back and pulled a pistol from his waistband.

"Get down!" she yelled, releasing Milo. She shoved Kyle off the path and into the grass. The pop of the gun discharging reached her ears moments before the bullet drove into her shoulder, knocking her off her feet.

TWENTY-TWO

"Stop! Get on the ground!" Taneesha yelled. From the place where Laina landed, with her cheek pressed to the grass, she watched the security guard draw her gun on the shooter. Taneesha's partner rushed the man and bound his hands behind his back.

With the wind knocked out of her, Laina struggled to draw tiny sips of air into her lungs. Meanwhile, Milo barked furiously toward the gate. Intense pain radiated from her shoulder, causing waves of nausea to pitch her onto her side.

"Fuck, Laina, you're hit!" Kyle pulled her into his arms. "We need to get you help."

She didn't have the breath to argue. With a hand pressed to her shoulder, she thanked the goddess that the bullet hadn't pierced any internal organs but cursed when she realized it hadn't passed all the way through. As a shifter, she'd heal quickly once the bullet was out. Every moment it stayed inside her flesh, though, would cause torment as her body attempted to heal around it.

Her gaze darted toward the gatehouse. Some of the

picketers had cell phones pointed in her direction. She gripped Kyle's shirt and positioned her face against his chest. He narrowed his eyes, seeming to understand her need to protect her identity.

In one motion, Kyle swept her into his arms and stood up, keeping his back to the gate. He walked her to the house at a steady clip, Milo trotting behind. The mastiff whined occasionally and poked her hand with his giant wet nose.

"When we get back to the house, I'll call my personal physician. He's signed a nondisclosure."

"No," she rasped, shaking her head. "Get Jason. He'll know what to do."

Gerty opened the door for them. "Should I call 9-1-1, Kyle?"

"No. Find my brother. I need Jason," Laina insisted. "Take me to my room."

The grimace on Kyle's face told her he wasn't happy about it, but he dutifully obeyed. When he tried to set her on the bed, she squeezed his arm. "No. The tub. Too much blood."

"Exactly. Too much blood. Now, will you let me call someone?" He lowered her into the tub and carefully helped her out of her jacket. She stopped him when he reached for her T-shirt.

Jason appeared over Kyle's shoulder with the trauma kit from her bag. She always carried one. When you became a wolf once a month, accidents happened. Bites and abrasions were par for the course, and as a vet, she had the know-how to treat pack injuries. "You'll need this, sister." He handed her a pair of scissors.

Laina cut away the section of T-shirt over the wound. "Forceps," she said to Jason.

"Which forceps?" Jason asked.

"The ones that look like extra-long tweezers. The longest ones." He held up a pair, still in their sanitary packaging. "Yep, those. Try to hand them to me using the wrapper."

Like a pro, he pulled the packaging back, touching only the paper and plastic. She tugged the instrument out and tucked in her chin to try to better see the wound. Gritting her teeth, she dug the tips of the forceps into the entry point. Kyle grunted. When she glanced up, he was three shades whiter and unsteady on his feet.

"What the fuck are you doing?" he asked.

Jason rested a hand on his shoulder. "Relax, Kyle. She's done this before. If you need to leave the room, it's okay."

"Jason, hold up the hand mirror for me," Laina said.

Kyle knocked Jason's hand out of the way and grabbed the mirror, taking a seat on the side of the tub. Laina guided his hand until the mirror was in the right position. As she suspected, her body had already started to heal around the bullet. Fuck, this was going to hurt. She'd have to break through the flesh to get to it. "Now or never," she murmured, then used her opposite hand to pound the forceps deeper into her wound.

She grunted, but it was Kyle who yelled as if she'd stabbed him.

Jason snorted. "I don't suppose that felt like the nudge of a soft kitten."

Kyle gave him an openmouthed scowl.

"Just about..." she said as she maneuvered inside the wound, listening for the metal on metal scrape. "Got it!" Clenching the bullet between the tips of her forceps, she yanked. The small piece of metal slipped from her grip as it exited her flesh and chinked against the side of the tub. Its exit was followed by a spurt of blood that splattered the knee of Kyle's pants.

"Sorry," she mumbled.

His jaw dropped, and he ran a hand over his face.

"Jason, the suture kit." She pointed toward the trauma bag.

He pulled it from the kit, donning a pair of gloves to thread the needle for her without being asked. "Maybe I should do the stitches," Jason said.

"No. Yours are too sloppy. You'll leave a scar," Laina said.

"Please tell me you are not going to give yourself stitches!" Kyle tipped his head back in exasperation.

"Unless you'd like to do it," Laina said.

He blanched.

"I've done this before," she said to him reassuringly. "Luckily, I'm a righty and the bastard hit my left shoulder."

Jason helped glove her hand and clean the wound, then handed her the sterile needle. With a deep breath, she steadied herself and began. Although the process was painful, she sutured using tight, even, continuous stitches. This would be folly on a human shoulder, but she'd be healed in twenty-four hours. Fast healing and resistance to infection were hallmarks of her kind. She tied off the end.

"Cut," she said to Jason. He obliged.

"Who are you people?" Kyle asked, eyes narrowing as she dabbed her stitches with antiseptic.

"You know who I am. I'm Laina Flynn, DVM."

"I just watched you take a bullet, remove it from your own shoulder, and stitch your own wound as if you did it every other day."

"I do! I'm a vet. I'm trained for this."

Kyle squinted at her. "You're trained to give animals stitches, not yourself."

Jason met Laina's eyes and raised his fist behind Kyle's head. He paused, offering to knock him out.

Laina shook her head. Jason lowered his arm.

"How?" Kyle asked. "How is it you've done this before?"

"I told you, my family—"

"This is insane."

She frowned. "I need to rest." Closing her eyes, she tipped her head back against the tub.

"Not in the tub." Kyle retrieved a washcloth from under the counter, wet it in the sink, and carefully washed the blood from her face and arm with long, even strokes. "Get her a new T-shirt," he ordered Jason. To Laina's surprise, her brother complied, although it must have been painful for him to do the bidding of a human.

Jason handed the shirt to Kyle. He gently removed the remains of Laina's bloody one before stretching the fabric of the clean top over her head and injured shoulder. Then he scooped her into his arms and carried her to the bed, tucking her in. She grunted in pain as he repositioned her.

"I'm going to call my personal physician. You need painkillers. Maybe antibiotics."

"Don't make me have to hurt you, Kyle," Jason said. "She can't be seen by a doctor, and that's that."

Kyle frowned and shook his head. "Laina?"

"Food. Something to drink." Her lids were too heavy to keep open. "It will help. I haven't even had breakfast."

"I'll get you something," he said.

Jason hovered over his shoulder, giving her a nod that he'd make sure Kyle did nothing more.

She mouthed *thank you* before sinking into a deep and much-needed sleep.

CHAPTER

TWENTY-THREE

Kyle set the tray of food on the dresser and moved to stand beside the bed. He desperately wanted to call his private physician but didn't want to betray her trust. After all, she'd told him no—twice. But the longer she stayed asleep, the more he considered doing it anyway. He placed a hand on her forehead. No fever.

Her eyes fluttered open in the dim light. "What time is it?"

Thank God. "It's after midnight. You've slept more than twelve hours."

She ran a hand over her throat and pointed toward the water. "Please."

Quickly, he poured her a glass. The ice cubes clinked against the side as he returned to the bed, scooping an arm behind her shoulders to help position her to drink.

She tipped the glass back, chugging down every cool drop. "More. Please."

He stood and refilled the glass.

Again, she drained it dry. When she'd finished, Kyle crossed to the other side of the room to make her a plate.

She needed to eat so that her body had enough calories to heal. She was too thin already. He picked up a strawberry, noticed a small bruise, and tossed it back on the tray. Another strawberry passed inspection and made it to the plate along with several slices of cheese, deli meats, and Gerty's fresh-baked bread. He returned to her side and held a perfect strawberry to her lips, relieved when she took a bite.

"You made a plate just for me." The tone of the statement sounded a lot like "aww," and he couldn't help but preen under her appreciative gaze.

She bit into another strawberry, savoring the fruit's perfection before licking the tips of his fingers. Fuck. His dick jumped in his pants, and he swore silently at himself. Until she healed, he wasn't going to do anything to put her at risk. He used his thumb to wipe a bit of juice from her lip.

"Can I ask you something, Laina?" He built a simple sandwich from the bread, meat, and cheese, and held it out for her.

She took a bite and nodded, although he saw hesitancy behind her eyes. Undoubtedly, she had secrets. Big family secrets. He knew there were questions she might not be able to answer. So, he tried to keep things simple.

"Why did you throw yourself in front of me?"

Her eyes widened. She wasn't expecting that one. "I didn't. I was walking slightly in front of you and was in the wrong place at the wrong time."

He shook his head. "You were right beside me. I know because Milo was heeling between us as he always does. Somehow, you saw the gun and pushed me out of the way. You took a bullet for me." He frowned. "I think I deserve to know why."

She chewed another bite and swallowed. "I couldn't bear to see you shot."

"Why?"

"Because I care for you." Her voice cracked.

"Care for me enough to risk death and potentially revealing your identity."

"Yes," she said honestly.

He fed her another bite, stroking her hair back from her face while she ate it. "That kind of caring... A person could mistake a thing like that for love."

She swallowed and looked down at her hands, and he felt his stomach turn over with yearning. "Do you love me, Laina?"

Her throat bobbed again. Maybe he was wrong about this. Shit. But there was no turning back. Not for him. "Because *I* love *you*," he added. Her eyes snapped to his. "I think I loved you from the moment you walked into Milo's exam room. There was something about you, something otherworldly. You were nothing like any woman I'd ever met, but all I could think about, all I've thought about since that day, was what I could do to get closer to you."

"You can't love me." She pressed a hand to the center of her chest. "Trust me on this. It will never work."

He set down the plate and leaned over her, one hand on each side of her body. "I love you, Laina. Whatever this secret is, this thing with your family, it's okay. Absolutely nothing you can tell me will undo what has already been done. Something deep within me, something I never knew existed, woke up when I met you. It's yours. Completely yours. I love you. I will always love you."

He took her face in his hands and kissed her, long and hard. By the time they came up for air, he'd decided that if she didn't feel what he did by now, she never would.

Her voice trembled as she said, "I love you too, Kyle. I took the bullet because I couldn't bear to see you hurt... because I love you."

Overwhelmed with emotion, he embraced her, kissing her harder and squeezing her against his chest. Until, horrified, he remembered her shoulder and released her. "Did I hurt you?"

"It's fine," she said.

He pulled aside the neck of her T-shirt to expose the blood-soaked gauze. "We should change the bandage. Let me have a look. I'm still not convinced I shouldn't call the doc over here." He dug his fingers under the tape.

"Really, Kyle. It's fine." She brushed his hands away, but he already had hold of the corner, and he took the gauze with him. What he saw underneath was nothing short of a miracle.

He studied the bandage in his hand and then her shoulder again. Although the gauze was bloodstained, the wound underneath was almost completely healed. The stitches came away in pieces with a brush of her hand, as if her flesh had already dissolved the parts inside her.

Kyle backed away from the bed. This was *not* normal. "What the fuck is going on, Laina?"

TWENTY-FOUR

As Kyle backed away from the bed, Laina thought of one thing and one thing only: she loved him, and if their relationship had any hope of working out, she had to find a way to tell him the truth. It was forbidden for a werewolf to reveal his or her true nature to a human. She couldn't tell him the entire truth, and she doubted he was ready for it anyway. But she could give him enough information to allow him to make a choice.

"Remember what I told you in the tree house? My family is not like other families. My community is not like other communities."

He nodded.

"My body is not like other bodies either. It's why I couldn't let you take me to the hospital. The doctors would see I was different, and everyone would know, and then Jonah would find me."

He scrutinized her face. "We did a story in *Hunt Club* magazine about a guy whose bones can't break. A freak genetic mutation makes them the density of marble. Is that what we're talking about here?"

She nodded. It was true; she was a medical miracle. Of course, she was also magic, but that was something he wasn't ready for. That was something she'd have to reveal slowly, over time, and with special permission from the pack if she could get it. "You can't catch it or anything. I'm just different."

He gave a quick, curt nod. "And your brother?"

"Also like me."

"This murderer who's after you, he knows your secret?"

"Yes. Silas will find Jonah and he will bring him to justice, but until then, I have to be careful. No one can know who I am or where I am. He's deadly and dangerous. That's why I was so worried about the cell phones today."

"The shooting is all over the news, but your face isn't in any of the footage. My security team interrogated most of the picketers and threatened legal action. Some shared the videos despite our efforts, but as far as we can tell, the only part of you visible in any of them is your feet. You're completely concealed behind my chest." He took a step closer to the bed but didn't sit down beside her.

The generic buzz of Laina's cell phone broke through the tension in the room. She bounded from under the covers and snatched it from the bedside table. "Hold on," she said to Silas before he had a chance to speak. She held the phone to her chest before turning back to Kyle. "It's my brother. Would you...?" She glanced toward the door.

Eyebrows pinched over his nose, he nodded once and left, closing the door behind him.

"Okay. I'm alone."

"We need to get you out of there." Silas's tone was urgent.

"Why? What happened?"

"I got a call from a friend working at the Sable Creek PD. The man who shot you disappeared, Laina."

"What do you mean, disappeared? Did he get away?"

"No, sister. He vanished from the back of a police cruiser. Left behind a set of still-locked handcuffs on the seat."

"You don't think…"

"Jonah has found you. You've got to get out of there."

"No, Silas. The shooter was trying to hit Kyle, not me. The protesters were here well before I was. And if this guy is powerful enough to beam himself somewhere from the back of a moving car, he is certainly powerful enough to blip in here and carve me to bits. I've been passed out for the last twelve hours. Jason is asleep right next door. Believe me, if Jonah was targeting me, I'd already be dead."

"Something's wrong here. I've got red flags flying in my head like you wouldn't believe. Did you test Kyle?"

"Yes. He passed all three. I saw him in direct sunlight and through water. I saw his reflection in the water by moonlight. No aura. Nothing strange."

"What about the mirror? Did you view his reflection in a mirror by moonlight?"

"Well…no. It was in the water. But there's no way it's him. He's not Jonah. I don't want to move, Silas. I feel safe here."

A growl of frustration rumbled in her ear. "The shift is this weekend. I'll join you and Jason at Monty's Saturday morning to discuss this. That will give me time to investigate further."

"I understand."

There was a pause on Silas's end and murmuring in the background. When he came back on, he sounded resolved to something. "Grateful has agreed to come to you."

"Grateful Knight? The witch? Why?"

"She'll walk through the property, looking for residual magic. If Jonah has been anywhere near you, she might be able to trace him to where he's hiding."

"How am I supposed to explain her being here?"

"Make something up," Silas said, obviously annoyed. "Tomorrow morning, go outside at sunrise and face east. She'll be there."

"I don't trust this witch, Silas. All I hear about Grateful Knight is how trouble follows her wherever she goes."

"Fine. Don't trust her. Trust me."

She sighed heavily.

"Stay safe, Laina."

"Wait, what about Jason?"

"I'm calling him next. He'll be right beside you."

TWENTY-FIVE

"Which way is east?" Jason asked.

Laina held up the compass on her phone and turned toward the path where Kyle had taken her to see his tree house. "That way."

"So we just wait here? In the dark?" Jason frowned.

The slightest bit of silver lined the horizon, but Laina empathized with her brother's foul mood. They were both exhausted, having stayed up late talking about the shooting and then rising before dawn. Neither of them had personalities that thrived on less than four hours sleep. Plus, Laina's shoulder was barely healed; she needed her rest.

"Let's move away from the house. I don't want to have to explain this to Kyle. As it is, we're lucky Milo didn't give us away."

"Seems like you have no problem explaining things to Kyle."

Laina looked over her shoulder toward the mansion as they walked toward the back of the property. "What's that supposed to mean?"

"I have wolf hearing, and I'm staying in the room next

to yours. Do you think I missed the profession of love between you two last night?"

"Jason, I—"

"You came wickedly close to breaking pack law and telling him what we are. You know you're just making things harder on yourself. He's your vice. It's going to be exponentially harder to break the habit now that you've fed it."

"I love him, Jason."

He gave a short laugh, then sobered when he saw she was serious. "But... It's not like you can marry him. You know that, right? You've got to frame this up in your mind as an affair, nothing more. Love can't change the world."

Tears spilled over her bottom lids. "I don't want to talk about this right now." Even if he couldn't see her tears, it was impossible not to hear them in her voice.

Jason did a double take and pulled her into his arms, kissing the side of her head. "I'm sorry, La. Truly."

"I know."

Light broke the horizon and spread through the trees beyond the gate, fanning out and casting shadows in their direction. One shadow morphed into a woman's silhouette, another into an enormous man's.

"What the actual hell?" Laina whispered.

The silhouettes stepped forward, transforming into solid shapes. The woman, a curvy blond in black leather pants and a racer-back tank, stopped at the gate. The man waited behind her, completely naked, a tower of muscle who gave off seriously deadly vibes. Laina raised an eyebrow and forced herself to close her mouth and look away. Jason murmured, "Holy shit, that guy is big."

"Laina Flynn?" The woman waved.

"Yeah, that's me."

"Silas sent me. I'm Grateful Knight, the witch who's helping your pack."

Laina stepped forward and opened the gate. "Come inside. If we hurry, we can walk through the house before Kyle wakes up."

The witch took a step forward, then balked as if she'd bounced off a sheet of glass. "Interesting." She narrowed her eyes at the empty space between them.

"What just happened?"

"I can't come inside. This entire place is surrounded by a protective ward." Grateful looked up as if following the line of a glass dome that rose above Laina's head. She raised her hand, passing it over an invisible barrier. "Rick, come look at this."

Rick approached, his eyes a creepy shade of black. After a cursory inspection, he said, "Impeccable magic, *mi cielo*. I cannot discern the source, although the signature is not elemental."

"Right. Not another witch. Something else." Grateful frowned. "Whoever put this here knew what they were doing. It's as strong a spell as I've ever encountered."

Laina led Jason through the gate and stared in the direction Grateful did. "I don't see anything."

Grateful smiled and tilted her head, her honey-colored waves falling over one shoulder. "Let me help you with that." She removed a sword from a holster on her back and tapped the invisible boundary with the tip. Purple light rippled from the point of contact. The magic was beautiful and alive, like the aurora borealis shaped into a dome over Kyle's yard and home.

"What is that?"

"It's a selective protection spell," Rick said. "No supernatural or enchanted creature can pass through it without an invitation."

"I made something similar for a friend once. It's the same sort of thing I'm setting up around Rivergate Manor," Grateful said. "Although, I admit, this one is far more sophisticated than any spell I've cast. It looks like it's been here for some time."

"Excuse me," Laina said, "but *what* type of spell this is isn't nearly as important as *who* put it here."

"Or why," Jason added. "Are you sure it's for protection?"

Grateful nodded. "As Rick mentioned, this type of spell keeps out supernatural beings, yet you and your sister can pass through. That means you were invited intentionally. Whoever built this enchantment knows what you are and allowed you in."

"So what do we do?"

"Stay where you are. I think the spell is keeping you safe. If it was Jonah who shot at you, Laina, he did it because he can't get to you physically. Someone is protecting you here, although my gut tells me this spell was here before you. Is there anyone you've met who could be responsible for this enchantment? Maybe the ogre?"

"Monty? No way," Jason said. "Magically capable but fundamentally unwilling."

Grateful stroked her chin. "Hmm. I'm sorry I can't be more help."

"What will you tell Silas?"

"Your brother is a dear friend of ours. I'll tell him you should stay right where you are until the shift," the witch said. "He loves you. I'm sure he'll agree once he knows the facts."

"Thank you."

"I'll have the protective enchantment in place around Rivergate in a few days. One more week and you two can come home." She gave them a cheerful smile.

While she nodded politely, Laina couldn't bring herself to thank Grateful as Jason did. At that moment, she realized she did not think of Rivergate or Carlton City as her home. When she thought of the word home, she thought of Kyle, and although she wasn't ready to admit it to either of her brothers, she was already devoting a large percentage of her brain to the problem of remaining in his presence.

"It was a pleasure to meet both of you," Grateful said, "but we have to go. Our son—let's just say, odd things seem to happen when we're away." She waved a hand. "It's a long story."

Tall, dark, and brooding behind her folded in half, and in the most painfully twisted shift Laina had ever witnessed, transformed into some kind of dragon beast. Grateful ran and vaulted onto its back.

"Good luck," she called. Witch and dragon vanished into the light.

"Well, that was a bust," Jason said.

"No joke." Laina cast her eyes toward the now-invisible spell above them as they returned the way they'd come, wondering who her secret benefactor might be.

TWENTY-SIX

When Laina reached the mansion, she expected to find Milo in need of a walk and Kyle still asleep. After all, when he'd left her side after midnight, he'd put in several more hours at the club. But while Milo was still in his crate, what she found outside Kyle's room chilled her to the bone. A camera crew had gathered in the foyer, a girl with a shield-sized reflective disk jogging up the grand staircase as if she were late for a meeting.

"What's going on?" Jason asked from behind her.

"There's a camera crew. They must be interviewing Kyle about the shooting yesterday," she said.

A man with a fistful of cables paused, having overheard her comment, and shook his head. "Nothing that exciting. Just a routine photo shoot for the magazine. Do you want to come up and watch?"

She shrugged. "After you." She followed the man up the stairs, navigating cords and a crowd of assistants and technicians who had assembled in the hall outside Kyle's room.

"Maybe we shouldn't." Jason grabbed her arm from behind, turning her away from Kyle's room. His expression confused her. Embarrassment? Yes. That was it. But not for himself. Jason was embarrassed for her. But why?

The two workers in front of her parted, and she turned her head to look straight into Kyle's room. Her breath caught in her throat, and ice water poured into her veins. Kyle lay in the middle of the bed, his head resting in a nest of his fingers. A rail-thin redhead with creamy skin curled against his right side, her perky rose-colored nipples peeking over his chest. A platinum blonde, tucked into his opposite side, had her nude back to Laina, her lean muscles feathering out from her spine, while a brunette with a complexion like roasted cinnamon kneeled in front of him, straddling his legs.

"Lower your face to his lap, Bailey. I need to be able to see Kyle over the top of your head," the photographer said. Wesley. He squinted into the camera viewer as the brunette spread her knees and lowered her chin toward Kyle's crotch. The sound of the shutter clicking preceded Wesley saying, "That's it. That's it. You look beautiful."

Laina took a step back and crashed into a girl with a nightmarish tray full of sexual props—dildos, floggers, a leather dog collar.

"Hey!" the girl yelled.

Kyle's eyes caught hers in the doorway.

"Excuse me." Cheeks hot, Laina navigated around the girl. Jason was right behind her, trying to calm her with a flurry of words she couldn't hear through the pounding in her head.

"Wait!" Kyle called.

"Kyle, we don't have the shot!" Wesley said.

"Just a minute."

Laina broke into a jog, slipping into her room. "Lock the door," she said to Jason. He did.

"Laina, let me in, please," Kyle begged. "We need to talk."

A deep growl rumbled up her throat.

"Give her some time, Kyle," Jason replied. "I think everyone needs to take a beat and process this situation."

"No. This isn't what it looks like!" A thump that sounded a lot like Kyle's forehead hitting the door sounded through the room.

"It looks like you're being photographed naked with three equally naked women!" Laina's wolf raged inside her, turning her voice gritty.

"It's just for the magazine," he called back. "It isn't real. Nothing is going on."

An uncomfortable facial tic twitched over her right eyebrow, and her wolf surged inside her. Fantasies of ripping the three women she'd seen in Kyle's bedroom apart with her teeth filled her brain.

"Laina," Jason whispered, reaching for her. "Your eyes. What's happening?"

She backed deeper into the room.

"You need to get a grip. Your wolf's really upset. I can see her under your skin." He stared at her arm as a ripple moved from wrist to shoulder.

Laina closed her eyes and swallowed. A few deep breaths, and the wolf inside her calmed. She didn't want to put this off. "Let him in, Jason. Then leave us."

Eyes wide, Jason shook his head. "You could hurt him."

She poked her tongue into her cheek and nodded. "It's a chance I'm willing to take."

Jason frowned. "I don't like this."

"I'm fine. Open the door."

With a heavy sigh, Jason unlocked the door. Kyle charged into the room, still naked.

"I'll be next door if you need me," her brother said.

"I won't. Take the dog. He needs a walk." Laina gave Milo a silent command to go with Jason.

With one last warning glance in her direction, her brother disappeared into the hall with the mastiff by his side.

Kyle closed and locked the bedroom door behind him. Hands up and open, he approached her as if she had a gun pointed at his heart. "I know this is difficult. I wanted to warn you, but I didn't have a chance."

"I don't think we should see each other anymore, Kyle," she said through her teeth. He balked as though she'd yanked the trigger on that metaphorical gun. His body jolted from the impact of her words. "This is never going to work."

"Don't do this. You knew this was part of my job."

"I'm not the kind of person who can share, even for pretend."

"You don't have to share. This isn't real."

"It looks real."

"If it upsets you this much, I'll tell them to go."

"For now," she growled. "But there will be other photo shoots. Other women. It's your *brand*." She spat the word like a curse.

"Laina..."

"It's better if *I* go." She eyed the door. "I have a life and a career in Carlton City. This was never supposed to be long-term. I'll go, and you can move on with your life."

"I don't want that."

"What do you want, Kyle? You hate what Nate makes you do. You feel trapped in your own life. You keep a secret hobby out of fear of upsetting the applecart. How can I have a relationship with someone who lets his work rule his life?"

With his next inhale, something changed. Tiny muscles in his torso flexed, his jaw set, and his eyes narrowed on her. As if someone had flipped a switch, Kyle appeared bigger, taller, and more powerful than she'd ever seen him. He swaggered toward her, an imposing figure that made her wolf whimper in her head. "How can I be with someone who allows her family to rule hers?"

The verbal blow knocked her off-balance, and she steadied herself on the nightstand.

"You want me to end this? I'll end this." He turned on his heel and strode from the room, slamming the door behind him.

LAINA WANTED TO BE STRONG. HER HEAD TOLD HER THAT THIS WAS inevitable and things with Kyle weren't meant to be permanent. But her heart wouldn't listen. She cried longer and harder than should have been necessary. She cried until the tears gouged out her innards and left her a hollow, empty shell. She cried like she had the day she'd learned her parents had been killed.

And then she stopped crying, and a drill sergeant voice inside her head bellowed, "Get up. Keep going." She'd heard that voice before. It was her soul, that fire within that refused to be snuffed out. Dr. Laina Flynn did not allow a man, any man, to ruin her. She would sweep up the pieces of her broken heart and build a beautiful mosaic in her chest. And she would guard that work of art from this day forward.

Like a machine, she searched out her duffel from the closet and started packing her things. It didn't take long. She hadn't brought much to begin with. But after all the drawers and hangers were empty, she noticed one outfit was missing. After a moment, she remembered that Gerty had collected laundry the day before. No matter how many times she protested and said she'd do her own, the good woman had insisted on washing her clothing.

Splashing cold water on her face, Laina tried her best to calm the puffy red blotches that marred the skin under her eyes. Once she was reasonably presentable, she headed for the laundry room, noticing there was not a trace of the camera crew that had been in the hall hours ago. No trace of Kyle either. She hurried, hoping she could retrieve her items without running into him. But when she reached her destination, she found her things were in the washer, midcycle. She plopped down on one of the chairs next to the folding table and waited.

"There's a black cloud above your head," Gerty said. *When had she entered the room?*

"Oh Gerty, I'm just sad. It's time for me to go back home. Milo is trained." She nodded. "We all knew this day would come. I just wasn't ready for it."

"What about you and Kyle?"

"What about us?"

"The fact that you love each other."

She met the old woman's eyes. "I can't be in a relationship with a partner who regularly takes nude pictures with his employees." As much as she tried to temper her emotions, the words hissed from between her teeth.

"But he sent them all away. Didn't he tell you?" She adjusted her bifocals, frowning. "Kyle met with the board this afternoon to announce he would no longer be available to photograph for promotional purposes."

"What?"

Gerty spread her wrinkled hands. "Personally, I can't believe he finally did it. Kyle has been his father's and his brother's pawn for so long, I began to believe he enjoyed the life they built for him. But Arthur and I always hoped he'd see things for what they were someday. It seems today is the day."

"He's not going to be the face of Hunt Club anymore?"

She shook her head. "He's part owner. He can choose. Nate won't be happy. The company will likely try to force the issue. There will be a considerable expense involved. But I've never seen Kyle so resolved."

Laina stared at the front loader, watched the clothes tumble against the glass, the whoosh-whoosh-whoosh of the spin cycle echoing through her brain. *I'll end this.* Had Kyle meant his relationship with her or Hunt Club?

Gerty cleared her throat. "The one thing we can count on in life is change. You came here seeking it. You found what you were looking for. Change won't leave you if you return to your past life. What you've experienced here will go with you. The two of you can survive apart—I have no doubt about that. You're young and strong. The question is, why would you want to?"

Laina stared at her hands a good long time. Why would she want to? Why *would* she want to? She looked at Gerty. "Thank you."

The old woman inclined her head and took off toward the kitchen.

TWENTY-SEVEN

"I don't think I've ever seen a room clear out so quickly." Jason tossed the ball for Milo in the backyard, and the mastiff loped off to retrieve it. "I'll have you know, I had to console the three girls who lost their jobs today."

Laina folded her arms. "Poor you. They call them working girls for a reason. I'm sure they'll find another job to do."

"Don't be a snob, Laina. They're not whores. They're models, and this is their work. It's not as easy as it looks, and everyone is entitled to find his or her own path in life. They're not bad people."

She sighed. "I know."

"You do?"

"Yes. Logically, I understand these are women trying to make their way just like everyone else. But considering I witnessed their naked bodies wrapped around the man I love, you'll need to give me a few days to get over it."

"Love. Doubling down on that one. You're sure?" Jason grimaced.

"Love." She pried the ball from Milo's slobbery face and threw it again. "And he loves me too."

Jason scrubbed his short brown hair. "So that's why he couldn't complete the shoot? He's going to go domestic for you."

"I can't be with someone who poses in bed with naked women. My wolf wanted to rip their heads off."

"But Laina, you can't be with him anyway. You're not the same *species*." He held out his hands to her. "Seriously, Laina, if you loved him, truly loved him, you wouldn't screw up his business by pretending he had a real chance with you."

She set her jaw. The argument with Kyle came back to her. *How can I be with someone who allows her family to rule her life?* "But he does have a chance with me, brother," she said softly. "A very good chance."

Jason froze. "You're thinking about leaving the pack."

"I've been thinking about it for a long time. You know that."

"Where will you shift? You can't tell him the truth. If you share our secret, the supernatural community will have your head. I'm not even talking about Silas. I don't think he'd have it in him to hurt you. But a witch like Grateful Knight? She exists to judge the supernatural, and the first law of being supernatural is—"

"You shall not reveal your true nature to humans, nor interfere directly with their history, nor threaten their lives or livelihood," she recited.

"Exactly. Hate to break it to you, sis, but the jealousy shit is, by definition, interfering with Kyle's livelihood. You publicly domesticated Kyle 'The King' Kingsley today. You tamed the world's playboy."

She frowned. "I didn't force him to do anything."

"You're too close. We should leave now. Go back to Monty's."

She faced him head on, hands on her hips. "I've watched you fuck anything that could walk since Mom, Dad, and—"

"Don't say her name." She swallowed against a swell of guilt for dredging up painful memories for her brother.

"Since the shooting. You've been trying to fill some hole in your heart that nothing can fill. You know what I figured out? Our vices aren't rooted in the things we desire. They're rooted in our overlooked and unfulfilled needs. You need love so badly, you think you can get it with sex. I need it too. That true intimacy we lost, along with so much of our innocence the day they were killed—I found it. I found what they had. And it makes me feel whole and wanted and like nothing else matters. So you can take your nos and your can'ts and go shove them up your ass. Because nothing is going to make me leave Kyle. Nothing."

She stormed off toward the house, heart heavy with the burgeoning distance between her brother and herself. It was like being ripped apart. Like her body was split in two. But she knew without a doubt which side would win. Something had changed today, and it would take a hell of a lot more than a werewolf or her pack to keep her from Kyle.

Jason left for Monty's that hour without saying good-bye. No doubt he'd tell Silas what she'd said. There would be consequences. She waited with Milo in the library, taking books down, flipping through them, putting them back.

"I have to get home to Arthur. Are you sure you'll be all

right? Do you want me to fix you something to eat before I go?"

"I'll be fine, Gerty. Go home. Get some rest."

She nodded and took her leave.

Laina walked and fed Milo before giving in to her wolf and eating some leftover chicken she found in the fridge. She'd just put the big dog to bed when she heard the front door open and saw Kyle at the base of the stairs.

"It's done," he said to her. "I am no longer the face of Hunt Club. What you saw today will never happen again." He looked tired, exhausted, like he'd spent the day jackhammering concrete rather than in a board meeting.

She descended the stairs. "I almost left today. I thought we were over."

"Are we?"

"I hope not."

"You were right. I let Nate and the company run my life for too many years. I ended that today. But there are two sides to this coin, Laina. I did my part. Are you willing to do yours?"

Twisting one finger in her hair, she approached him cautiously, afraid to make any sudden moves and risk jinxing a reconciliation. "Jason left today. I told him I'm staying. I'm not sure what will happen next. Jonah is still out there. I won't have the protection of my family."

"I'll protect you."

"I'm willing to try to make this work." She didn't know how or when she'd tell him she was a werewolf. She had no idea what she'd do about her business. But she couldn't think about those things now.

"I need you to come to the Tanaka dinner with me on Friday. It was a condition of my change in position. I can't go without a date."

"Someone might recognize me."

"This is a private dinner between us and our Japanese business partners. We'll have full security. I promise it couldn't be safer."

"It's here, at Hunt Club?"

He nodded. "At Nate's place."

She wanted to say yes, but she knew Silas wouldn't approve. Then again, this was where the rubber met the road. Was she willing to choose Kyle over her family? The witch, Grateful, had said Laina would be protected by the mysterious spell that covered the property. If the man who had shot at her was Jonah, he already knew she was alive, and he'd proven he couldn't reach her here. What could be safer?

"Either you serve as my date, or I have to choose a model. Nate will never settle for my going alone," Kyle said softly.

Rubbing the space over her heart, she said, "I'll go."

"You'll need something to wear. I'll have Gerty bring you a few choices tomorrow." He pressed a firm kiss against her mouth. "I love you, Laina Flynn."

She met his eyes. "I love you too."

"Don't talk about leaving me again."

"There are still things I'll need to take care of."

He stepped into her and cradled her head in his hands. "I don't want to hear reasons you have to leave—I want to hear ways that you can stay."

She searched his face...and it hit her. Life didn't mean much without him in it. "Okay," she whispered. "We'll find a way."

TWENTY-EIGHT

Laina sat facing Kyle in a plush leather seat that belonged in a living room rather than the back of a limousine. He handed her a glass of champagne as the driver closed the back door and took his seat behind the wheel.

"I thought Nate's place was on Hunt Club property. Why the need for the car?"

"It is...on the other end of the forest. Five hundred acres might be a long way to walk in high heels, especially considering the only direct way between there and here is a dirt path through the woods. Driver will take us out and around on Route 36."

"Gerty says this is the first time you and Nate have lived apart."

"It was time. Nate's lifestyle was becoming incompatible with my own. As much as Hunt Club made me out to be the playboy, Nate was always the real thing and more."

"Hmm." Laina laughed. She could only imagine what a man like Nate was into.

"Just to warn you, Nate isn't happy about my change of

227

heart. I doubt he'll cause a scene, but you might want to keep your distance."

"Understood. So who are the Tanaka people anyway?"

"Japanese company interested in licensing the Hunt Club name for a new chain there."

"Interesting. I'd think the concept was a uniquely American one."

"It's universal. No matter how modern a world we live in, no matter how much we say we've evolved, no matter how they live their daily lives, deep inside, people are either predator or prey. Our members want to be alphas."

Laina froze. "That's a strange choice of words."

"What? Alphas?"

She nodded. "What made you put it that way?"

He shrugged. "I don't know. Just seemed like an apt comparison. Hunt Club members want the fantasy of being the top of the food chain sexually. That's what we sell."

Laina stared out the window at the blur of trees that seemed to cut through her reflection in the glass.

Kyle sighed. "Laina."

She blinked, trying to make sense of the firestorm of emotions raging in her chest. The last thing she wanted was to leave her pack, only to be dominated by someone else. She loved Kyle, but if she gave up her life in Carlton City to be with him, was she the prey? Was she putting him in the position of being her alpha, no pack required? She'd spent too long building a life for herself and fighting the expectations of Fireborn pack to willingly make that sacrifice.

"Laina, it's fantasy. I'm talking about the brand, not about us. If you want to be the alpha in this relationship, so be it." He scoffed.

She turned from the window to see him staring at her,

gravely serious. "You'd be okay if I took charge?" She gave him a devilish smile.

He raised an eyebrow. "Hell yeah. Bring it on."

Nate's house was a modern architectural marvel constructed of glass and steel, with slabs of black granite that added to a reflective, transparent quality. Kyle helped Laina from the limousine and threaded his arm through hers as they followed a Japanese couple toward the house. "This is so different from Hunt Club Mansion."

"Castles aren't Nate's thing."

"What is Nate's thing?"

Kyle groaned. "Power. Control. He's my brother, but he can be a scary man when he wants to be. It's why Gerty chose to work exclusively for me when we parted households."

They were welcomed by one of the models she'd worked with at the club. The peacock. Laina couldn't remember her name and only had a moment to greet the woman before she was ushered toward a magnificent room of white-clothed tables. Each was dressed with silver charger plates that reflected the purple orchid sprays adorning the candelabras at the table centers. The bright moonlight shone through the windows and melded with the candlelight to give the table setting an almost magical quality.

Kyle placed a hand in the slope of her back. "Mr. Tanaka is a man who enjoys the finer things in life. I suspect the meal will be memorable. Nate wants to make an impression."

She followed him into the throng of people, shaking hands and making small talk like a pro. At the center of the throng was Tanaka himself, a height-challenged waif of a man in a suit that cost more than Four Paws.

"May I be photographed with your guest?" Tanaka asked Kyle, holding Laina's hand far longer than necessary for a simple greeting.

Kyle opened his mouth to respond, but Laina interrupted. "Of course." She shifted into Tanaka's side and smiled at the camera.

"*Arigatou gozaimasu,*" Tanaka said, bowing to her.

"You're not afraid of being recognized?" Kyle asked, pulling her into his side.

"I am, but Tanaka is important to you. I don't suppose you can make sure that picture never gets published though?"

He ran a hand down her arm. "I'll do my best."

A sound above her drew her attention up. Nickie watched her from the balcony above the main staircase. She was dressed for the event in a shimmering red-and-black-sequined dress.

"Oh, Nickie's here," Laina said.

"Who's Nickie?"

Laina snorted and pointed toward her friend. "The doe from your club. Looks like she came as someone's date. She's not painted like the others."

Kyle glanced up. "Oh, the one who found the box you left in the kitchen."

"What?"

"That's how I found you. We couldn't figure out where the rats were coming from, but she brought it to me and told me where to find you."

Laina froze, her thoughts spinning. "Kyle, did you give

Nickie permission to use your hot tub the day your driver picked up Jason?”

“Huh? No. The employees have their own attached to the west wing. It’s against policy.”

She threaded her fingers into his. “We need to go.”

“What? Why?”

She turned for the door so quickly she knocked into one of the beautifully set white tables.

Nate grabbed her arm to steady her. “Clumsy.”

A flash of crimson caught her eye. The silver charger on the table next to Nate flashed as if it cradled a lit match in its belly. Nate’s reflection in the silver burned with magic, fiery ripples distorting his features. His normally brown eyes were the color of a snake’s, bright yellow and pulsing.

“Can I talk to you alone for a moment?” Nate asked.

Kyle frowned and took her other arm. “Why would she need to talk to you alone?”

“You can come too, brother. I have something to discuss, with both of you.”

Tanaka and his executives turned to stare in their direction. Kyle placed a hand on Nate’s arm. “This isn’t the time or the place.”

“I agree.” He smiled that gaping, amphibious smile. “Just one moment, Kyle. That’s all I’m asking for.” He pointed at a door near the back of the room.

Laina held her ground. “Don’t go with him. He’s not who you think he is.”

“What are you talking about?” Kyle chuckled nervously, looking confused.

With a tilt of his head, Nate locked eyes with Laina and lowered his lips to her ear. “You don’t want to do this out here, Princess. If you think I’m above taking out this entire place to get to you, you don’t know me.”

"What did he just say to you?" Kyle asked. "I couldn't hear."

"Just explaining that there's a problem at Hunt Club I need to discuss with you right away," Nate said.

"I'll go. Anna can wait here and enjoy herself."

Nate shook his head in warning. "This has to do with her as well, and if she doesn't come, I'll have to take action."

"All right. I'll come." Her voice cracked as the truth settled like a red-hot ember in her belly. Either Nate was Jonah or he was someone working for him, and she and everyone in this room were in terrible danger, especially the man she loved. "I'll come if you let Kyle stay here."

Kyle looked at her like she was out of her mind. He laughed and threaded his fingers into hers. "While I have every confidence in your abilities, I think I should be in the room if there's a problem at Hunt Club." Laina tugged at his arm and shook her head, but the look in Nate's eyes held menace. A tremor flowed through the ground under her feet, strong enough to rattle the plates.

"Did you feel that?" Nate asked.

Kyle snorted. "Weird. Felt like a mild earthquake. Are we sure we're not in California anymore?"

Nate laughed, his eyes boring into Laina's. "Who knows, a fault could crack open and swallow us all."

Anxiety raged like a swarm of bees inside her. That was terrifyingly strong magic, and by the wicked gleam in Nate's eye, she knew it was no idle threat.

"Come on. Let's get this over with. It shouldn't take long." Kyle placed a hand in the center of her back.

With an evil grin, Nate grabbed her elbow and ushered both of them through the door he'd pointed out. "Let Kyle go," she whispered in a voice she knew only Nate could hear.

"Laina, you're, uh, sweating. Are you all right?" Kyle did a double take, his worried expression making her heart squeeze. He held the back of his hand to her forehead.

She didn't have a chance to answer. As soon as the door was closed behind her, a sharp pain exploded at the back of her skull, and then everything went black.

TWENTY-NINE

Laina came awake on a hard marble floor with her wrists bound and secured to the wall by a length of chain behind her. The back of her head ached, and it took her sitting up and shaking it for her vision to clear. She was in some kind of dungeon. Across the room from her, a familiar mass of human muscle lay in an unconscious heap.

"Kyle! Kyle!" she called, trying her best to rouse him.

"He'll be out for a while," a voice said from her left.

Scrambling to her feet, she turned her head to face the dark figure in the shadowy corner of the room. He was tall, lanky, with dark blond hair and eyes that twinkled purple when the light hit them a certain way. The dragon fae amulet hung around the man's neck. Without a doubt, under his tuxedo, his right upper shoulder sported the tattoo of a harvest moon with three claw marks ripping through it.

"Jonah," she said.

"Think again." He stepped into the light. "You don't remember me, Laina? I kissed you in the game room at Rivergate when we were children."

"No…"

"And then there was that time I murdered your parents."

"Impossible. We found your body."

"You found my *old* body. I rather like this new one. My Zafka, Jonah, worked out regularly—more than I ever did. It was brilliant, if I do say so myself, to use the amulet to switch bodies with Jonah when it was clear your brother Silas had the advantage. It was the last magic I performed with this"—he fingered the amulet—"before they took it from me. Before your brother took *everything* from me."

"Alex," she spat. She shook her head, pulling against the chains binding her.

"I love to hear you say my name." He smirked. "Now, here's how this is going to go. In approximately twelve hours, you're going to shift."

"Shift? What are you talking about?" Nate said from across the room. The big, balding man hovered over his brother, patting Kyle's face and feeling his neck for a pulse. He hadn't been there before and wasn't chained to the wall. Laina looked between Alex and Nate, confused. Nate was still alive, which meant he'd cooperated with Alex to some extent, but clearly, he wasn't happy about the state of things.

Alex ignored him and focused on Laina. "As I'm sure you know, those chains are not meant to hold you in your wolf form. By that time, you should be fairly hungry, practically starving with your accelerated metabolism. How much control do you have over your wolf, Princess? Enough not to make a meal of your boyfriend?"

"What do you want, Alex?" Laina desperately tried to work the manacles over her cupped hands, but they were hopelessly tight.

Alex laughed through his nose. "Only my true place. For me to obtain what's rightfully mine, your two brothers must die. Then, Fireborn pack will bow down to me. Oh, I'm not so crass as to believe the Lycanthropic Society will accept me as their leader, not at first anyway. But blood rules. I will take you as my mate, and we will sire a legion of purebred children. Eventually, the other packs will have no choice but to recognize our superior race."

"You're insane."

"Probably. Love will do that to you."

"Love? You don't love me."

Alex stepped closer to her, squatting down to her level. A wicked smile spread across his face. Close up, his skin took on the appearance of plastic, not quite human or werewolf. A sourceless breeze cycled through the room. "Silas returned the amulet to the dragon fae himself. How do you suppose I got it back, Princess? No, I don't love *you*, but thankfully, that emotion is not necessary to sire werewolf children. The one I do love understands the importance of my work and my rule and supports my use of you."

Laina's thoughts swirled. Rumor had it that a dragon fae princess had fallen deeply in love with Alex and had given him the dragon fae amulet as a gift, but he'd left her and chosen to murder his own parents rather than return it. What if the dragon fae princess still had feelings for him? What if she was helping him now? Laina tried to remember the name of the princess but couldn't. Why hadn't she paid closer attention to Silas?

"Now, you will help me call your brothers out to play."

"Go fuck yourself." She sucked her teeth and hurled a wad of spit that landed wetly on the side of his face.

Alex paused for only a moment to wipe away her saliva with a handkerchief before pulling a phone from his pocket.

Her heart sank when she realized it was hers, the untraceable phone Silas had given her for emergencies. He tapped the screen a few times.

"Laina?" Silas's voice came from the speaker.

"Tell him to come for you." He held the phone toward her face.

She sliced her head tot he left in refusal.

"Laina!" Silas yelled.

"Do you know why Kyle was attracted to you? Do you want to know the magic behind love at first sight?"

She glared at him, a dark ribbon of preemptive grief unraveling like a worm in her torso.

"It seems his father had a penchant for supernaturals. Kyle is a dormant. His mother was a shifter. That hole, the missing thing, the something wild he's felt deep within his soul, recognized you. He would have never shifted on his own—his mother's blood was too diluted, but I have the power to make him."

With a wave of Alex's hand, Kyle bucked off the marble floor, waking with a scream and contorting with the grotesque snap and slurp of breaking bones. Kyle's screams grew more tormented until Laina could stand no more.

"No! Stop!" Forcing the shift on a dormant was said to be pure torture. Depending on their physiology, it could even be deadly.

"Tell Silas to come, or we'll find out if Kyle has what it takes to survive a forced shift, or five, or seven. I can shift him back and forth all day if you prefer." Alex raised a hand, and Kyle screamed again, arching off the floor.

"Stop!" she screamed, tears streaming.

He held the phone toward her. Kyle's body slapped the floor, rattling his chains. He groaned and curled into the fetal position, facing her.

"Silas, Alex is alive. He has me," she whimpered. The connection ended. "He hung up."

"Don't worry, Princess. Your brother heard enough. He's on his way."

Nate glared at Alex from Kyle's side. "This was not our deal, Alex!"

"What did you do?" Laina barked at Nate.

Ignoring her, Nate pointed a chubby finger toward her nemesis, as if his human self had any hope of controlling the evil beside her. "You said you wanted the girl. Let us out of here. My brother needs help."

"Hmm. You are correct. I did promise I'd only take the girl in exchange for you planning this event and providing me with your blood. That was our bargain." Alex nodded slowly.

"So, unlock Kyle. Let us go," Nate gritted out.

Alex stepped closer to Nate, his wicked grin growing. "Can you guess what Nate's mother was, Laina?"

"What the fuck are you talking about?" Nate said.

Laina kept her eyes on Kyle, willing him to be okay..

"Half ogre. I almost think the senior Kingsley had a goal of sleeping with every type of supernatural there is. What other explanation is there for bedding an ogre?"

"Hey! Fuck you." Nate crossed the room in a huff, his fist connecting with Alex's chin. He might as well have punched stone. Nate cried out, shaking his hand in pain, but Alex only smiled wider. Surging forward, he clutched Nate by the lapels and dragged him across the room, tossing him into a cage between a row of floggers and a rack of canes. Ignoring Nate's struggle and protests, Alex locked him inside and stored the key in his pocket.

"You should know," Alex said, eyeing Nate, "that I rarely keep my promises. I'm kind of a bad guy that way."

"Let me outta here, Alex. We had a deal."

Alex shrugged. "No. Now, silence yourself, or I'll remove your voice box."

Nate distractedly rubbed the base of his throat.

"I need your brother for what I'm planning to do to this one." He pointed his thumb in Laina's direction. "Considering we are in your playroom, Nate, I'll assume you understand that sometimes playthings need to be broken. Laina here has always had an indomitable spirit, even as a little girl. But when I'm done with her, she'll obey my every command."

"Not fucking likely," Laina hissed.

Alex fixed her with a wicked grin. "You'll come around, after I make you kill the man you love."

All color drained from Nate's face. "What do you want? Money? I can make you very rich."

Alex laughed. "Your money is worthless to me, as are you. And you've broken the rules." The amulet around Alex's neck glowed to life. He snapped his fingers. Nate's protest turned into a cough. His lips moved as if he were trying to speak, but nothing came out. A growing panic seized the heavier brother, and he banged against the bars, eyes red and chest heaving.

"Don't make me remove your arms as well as your voice," Alex said softly. "Here's how this is going to go down. I'm going to kill Laina's brothers, Silas and Jason. Meanwhile, Laina is going to shift right out of those chains. She'll be hungry, and Kyle will be easy prey. You get to watch, Nate—that is, if she doesn't make short work of those bars and kill you too. Goddess knows she's strong enough."

Kyle scrambled to his knees. "Laina, what is he talking about? Who is this?"

Alex chuckled wickedly and tipped an invisible hat in her direction. "That's my cue. The sun is rising. This is going to be a good day. A very good day."

He climbed the stairs and exited the dungeon without ever opening the door, leaving Laina staring helplessly at the look of confusion and betrayal on the face of the man she loved.

THIRTY

"What's going on?" Kyle glanced between Laina and Nate, his head reeling. He'd never felt such pain as he had moments ago. It was like every bone in his body had splintered at the same time, and although he felt better now, there was still a lingering ache in his muscles, a pain that didn't hold a candle to what was going on in his heart. "One of you start talking."

Laina's voice trembled with her answer. "H-he could come back at any time. We have to get out of here. See if you can reach one of those silver...things behind you to pry your chains off the wall."

As much as Kyle needed to know what was going on, he couldn't argue with the pragmatism of Laina's suggestion. The man who'd just left the room had carried a certain Hannibal Lecter quality that Kyle had no intention of getting to know better. Besides, it was possible that what he'd said to Laina was nothing more than the ramblings of a madman.

Kyle tugged at the chains binding him to the wall while he scanned the room. A Wartenberg wheel hung from the rack closest to him on his right. Damn, his brother was into some sick shit. But maybe, just maybe, his perversion would be their salvation. The steel handle ended in a flat edge.

He reached with his toe and knocked the tool toward him onto the floor. Once it rattled to a stop, he slid it closer, until he could pick it up with his bound hands. He dug the point of the handle behind the metal plate of the iron ring bolted to the wall and attempted to pry it away from the marble.

"Nate, why the hell did you help that guy?"

Nate gasped like a fish out of water.

"He can't answer you," Laina said. "Alex took his voice box."

"You can't take someone's voice box by snapping your fingers."

"You can if you have a magic amulet. And Alex does."

Kyle sighed. "You need to start talking, Laina. What do you know about this? You said his name was Alex. Was that the Alex you told me about? I thought you said he was dead."

"We thought he was. We were wrong."

"So, he wants to kill your brothers and impregnate you?"

"Yes."

"Why?"

Laina grew quiet behind him.

He stopped working his makeshift lever and turned to face her. "Since the day I met you, I've known you were keeping something from me. I have no doubt there is more to this dark family secret than what you've told me. It's time to come clean. Tell me the truth. All of it."

Her body shook like he'd demanded something impossible of her, something that made her physically ill to accommodate. She closed her eyes tightly, parted her lips.

"I love you, Laina. Nothing you could say to me is going to change that. But the truth could save our lives."

"I told you my family is not like other families," she blurted out. "But I didn't tell you how we're different."

"You said you were medical miracles. You're strong and you heal fast."

"But that's not all. There's more to it. We are also...magical."

"Magical."

"Alex left you here because he wants me to kill you."

"I heard. But you won't. Why would you kill me?" He succeeded in wedging the handle deeper between the metal and marble. "And what did he mean about you *shifting?*"

"Because when the sun sets and the moon rises, I will change." Her voice cracked, and tears spilled from her eyes. "I will change into something that could kill you."

He snorted. "I've seen you after sunset. I've spent the night with you. I think I would have noticed if you were a killer after dark."

"It only happens during the full moon," she said in a voice so soft he could hardly hear it.

"The full moon? What, are you, like, a werewolf or something?" He chuckled and rolled his eyes.

She wasn't laughing. In fact, she was crying harder. Her head bobbed once. "Not just me, my entire family. Alex, too, although fairy magic has warped him into something else altogether."

Kyle closed his eyes for a beat. "Don't fuck with me on this, Laina. It's not funny."

"No, it's not." She bowed her head. "When the sun sets, I will shift into a wolf. My fur is dark brown, like a mink.

And I won't necessarily know you, not like I do now. When I'm the wolf, I'm completely in the moment, in the animal brain. When I'm myself again, I remember flashes of what I did as a wolf. But shifted, I can't control her. She'll be hungry. She could kill you, Kyle. If it comes down to that, promise me you'll use something in this room to kill her first."

Kyle turned his back to her and used his foot as leverage against the handle. It worked. The bolt slipped a quarter of an inch.

"Kyle, are you listening to me?" She sobbed.

He braced a foot on the wall and pulled with all his weight against the chains. One of the bolts gave slightly. He dug the handle in again.

"Say something. What are you thinking?"

He paused, staring at the veining in the marble. "When I was getting my business degree, I took some classes in psychology. I've read about this. You probably have some kind of schizophrenia. I mean, you talk about this wolf like you have another person in your head."

"No... No... Kyle, this isn't that."

"I'm guessing that if your family believes it, it's a sort of mass hysteria. I'm going to get us out of here, and then I'm going to find you help." He leaned his entire weight against the handle and tried a different angle, carefully avoiding the sharp pins at the end of the wheel.

"You sensed something wild in me. You weren't wrong. You sensed my wolf."

"Yep," he said, hoping that by agreeing she'd give up on trying to convince him.

"You know in your heart that this isn't in my head. You've known for a while there is something different about me. How fast I can run. How easily I trained Milo, almost as if I could communicate with him in his language. How I can take a bullet and be healed the next day. How I make love."

He stopped, took a deep breath, and let it out. He couldn't deny that she was freakishly strong and unlike any woman he'd ever known. Whatever this was, it was weird and it was wrong, and at the moment, he couldn't process anything but the problem in front of him. He braced and pulled until the chains cut into his palms. This was taking too long.

He looked at Laina over his shoulder. "Hey! Catch." He tossed the silver tool across the room to her. It clattered to the floor halfway and skidded into her feet. "If you're stronger, free yourself—then you can free me."

Laina, whose wrists were still chained behind her back, threaded her legs through the circle of her arms so that her hands were in front of her, and picked up the Wartenberg wheel. Instead of trying to pry the ring from the wall, she tucked the handle into a single link of chain spread taut between her feet. With a groan, she twisted and lifted. The steel started to bend.

Nate stood up and approached the corner of his cell, pumping his arm in the air and mouthing *go, go, go*. Kyle still didn't understand Nate's role in this. Why had he lured them to Alex? Or maybe it had been a coincidence. He couldn't remember clearly. They'd been following Nate, and next thing he knew, he woke up in Nate's BDSM playroom in excruciating pain. It was all a blur, but he was troubled by a brief memory of Nate outside the cage, raising his voice to Alex and pointing at Laina. When had that happened?

With one last grunt of effort, Laina broke the link and tumbled into the wall behind her. She dropped the tool near her feet and unhooked the broken link. Although her hands were still manacled to each other, she was no longer bound to the wall. She bent to pick up the tool again, but Nate slapped the bars viciously and pointed to a wooden box at the far end of the room.

"I think he's trying to tell you to look in the box," Kyle said.

"What's in there?"

"Your guess is as good as mine. Like I said, I try to stay out of my brother's personal proclivities. BDSM is not my cup of tea."

Laina crossed to the box and propped open the lid. Her eyes widened at Nate as her lips spread into a smile. "I've never been so glad your brother was a sick bastard." She reached inside and pulled out a heavy, double-edged sword and an extra set of keys.

Nate clapped his hands and pointed excitedly at the lock on the cage door.

"You've got to be fucking kidding me," Laina said to him. "Do you think I'd free you after how you set us up?"

"What are you talking about?" Kyle asked.

"Your brother was working with Alex. He wanted to get rid of me. He couldn't stand the thought of our monogamy getting in the way of Hunt Club's profits." She shot Nate a nasty glare. "He cooperated with Alex and let him use his identity and image to lure us down here."

Nate couldn't speak, but the gesture he gave her with his right middle finger said everything.

Kyle looked at his brother and shook his head. He wasn't sure exactly what Laina meant by all that, but given Nate's reaction, it was clear he'd been in league with the psycho who'd locked them down here. "You fucking asshole. You just couldn't stand to see me happy."

Nate spread his hands and shrugged, then rubbed his fingers together. Money. It was always about money.

"We don't have much time." Laina approached Kyle with desperation in her eyes. She unlocked his cuffs and then handed him the keys so he could unlock hers.

"Thanks," she said. Sword in hand, she tugged him toward the stairs. "Come on."

"Wait, what do we do with him?" Kyle gestured toward his brother in the cage.

"We leave him right where he is. He'll be safe there until we can get help." Her words said *he'd* be safe where he was, but her expression suggested she thought *they'd* be safe from him as well. Kyle couldn't argue. He jogged after her, up the stairs to the door to the main part of the house. But when he reached the top, he found Laina with her fists pressed against a solid wall.

"I don't understand. Where's the door?" Kyle asked.

"There isn't one," Laina said. "Alex has sealed us in."

"Like hell he has." Kyle snatched the sword from her hands, raised it above his head, and stabbed the doorless wall.

THIRTY-ONE

"No!" Laina yelled, but she was too late. When Kyle stabbed the sword into the wall, a shower of sparks repelled the blade and knocked Kyle back. He tumbled down the stairs, narrowly avoiding the sharp edge of the weapon.

"Kyle! Are you all right?" She raced to his side.

"Fine," he said, scrambling to his feet. "What just happened?"

Laina shivered. "The chains were never meant to hold either of us, just distract us while the clock counted down. Alex sealed us in using magic. We won't be able to escape." *And no one can get in to save us*, she thought.

"Magic," Kyle repeated. He stared at the sword in his hands like he was going into shock.

"Sundown is coming." She paced the room. How would she save Kyle? She needed a plan.

"It can't be that late. We haven't been in here that long." Kyle tapped his watch. "Hmm. It's not working."

Laina paced faster. "Alex enchanted the room to distort our perception of time. I don't need a watch. The moon is rising." She met his eyes and tried to explain. "A werewolf senses the full moon as you might sense a train coming by the vibration of the track. Our hearts flutter, our fingers tingle and grow cold, the air ripples with energy. The hair on my arms is longer than it was this morning. I can smell the soap you used yesterday. I can smell that you need to pee."

"You can smell that?"

"Your blood is pulsing in your veins, a raging river of life. It makes my mouth water."

"What?"

She lowered her head and continued. "Everything about you is sharper, how slow you move"—her breath quickened—"how easy it would be to catch you if you ran. I don't want to chase you now, but I can feel my wolf, just under the surface, and she's tracking you with her nose to the ground. The closer she gets to taking over, the stronger I get."

Kyle backed against the wall, rubbing his chest with one hand. "Your eyes."

"It's coming." The change was close, very close. She had to do something to protect him from her. "I need the cage. You'll lock me in. It's our only hope." Laina grabbed the keys off the floor and tried to unlock it. Nate rattled the door when it didn't open right away. "Fuck! Alex sealed it with magic just like the door."

She dug her hands into her hair. *Think, Laina,* she said to herself. In her line of work, she solved complex problems before breakfast. All she needed was to focus. What could she use? Eyes darting around the room, she came up short. Her spine popped, and a ripple rolled through her body. "Kyle!" She whimpered. "It's happening. There's no time. Use the sword if you have to!"

As another wave of pain rolled through her body and she watched her fingers bend into claws, her mind finally kicked into gear. She was strong right now. Strong enough to bend metal. With a growl, she grabbed the bars to the cage and bent them apart. Nate joined in to help once he saw what she was doing. She slipped inside easily enough, circling Nate.

Nate wasted no time moving for the promise of freedom, only his portly form wedged to a stop halfway through. Kyle tugged at his arms to no avail.

Laina screamed as her ankles turned and her hips narrowed. She ignored Kyle's expression and pulled off her shirt and pants at record speed. "I can't hold it back much longer." Panting, she moved to the back of the cage, then lunged forward, plowing into Nate with her shoulder. He popped out the other side.

As her jaw lengthened, she easily bent the bars back into position. She'd barely accomplished her goal when she pitched forward, landing on the pads of her paws. Thick black fur spread up her arms. She had just enough time to register Kyle's horrified expression before the human mind that was Laina disappeared.

And then there was only the wolf.

THIRTY-TWO

Nothing could have prepared Kyle for what he saw happen inside the cage. The woman he thought he loved, the one he'd been obsessed with for months, shifted into a wolf in a grisly display of breaking bones and stretching muscle. Kyle's stomach twisted like a wrung towel, and he had to close his eyes to keep from becoming ill.

Nate slapped Kyle's cheek and shook him vigorously by the shoulders.

"I've seen enough. I can't watch this," Kyle said.

His brother flicked the side of his head.

"Owww." Kyle opened his eyes. Nate was holding out a cell phone. "What the fuck? Have you had this the entire time?"

With a flip of his middle finger, Nate went into a series of mouthed words and gestures that clearly indicated he'd had no plans of helping them as long as he was locked in the cage. He patted his throat and pointed at Kyle, then at the phone.

Kyle poked the text icon. Nate had, in fact, attempted to

text his personal security detail, but the text hadn't gone through. "For all I know, the magic that's keeping us in is blocking the signal. I'll try a call."

He didn't get a chance. Pain rolled through Kyle's body, and he pitched forward, catching himself on his knees. What the hell was wrong with him?

Whatever it was sent Laina into hysterics. Her wolf paced the cage, then started throwing itself against the bars. Another wave went through him, and she lowered her head, growling at the two of them.

Nate grabbed Kyle's shoulder and squeezed.

Ignoring the pain, Kyle thumbed through the contacts in Nate's phone. He stopped on the one person he hated to involve but trusted more than anyone else. It couldn't be helped. He pressed the call button.

"Kyle, where are you? Everyone is out looking for you!" Gerty's voice was shrill with panic.

"I'm trapped in Nate's basement. Gerty, everything is crazy. Laina's a werewolf. The room is magic and won't let us out. The door is gone. I don't think anyone can get to us. They took Nate's voice. I know I'm not making any sense, but you have to help me." He groaned as more pain barreled through him. "Send. Help."

"Kyle," Gerty said calmly, "are you safely away from Laina? It's a full moon."

"She's locked in a cage." The wolf threw herself against the bars again, the sound of bending metal making the hair on his arms stand on end.

"Do you remember the song I sang to you as a child?"

"What? Gerty…"

"Sing it, Kyle. Sing it now."

"We don't have time! *Ah!*" he screamed in agony. What

was happening to his fingers? "There's something wrong with me, Gerty! Everything hurts."

"Sing the song! *Now, Kyle!*"

"But—"

"Now!" she demanded.

Kyle panted against the pain but forced himself to sing.

"Deep in the woods
where the willows bloom
lives a fairy queen
and her handsome groom.
No children have they
but love them they do
Call to her child,
and she'll watch over you.
Fairy queen, fairy queen,
I call unto thee.
I am a child and
you are my queen."

A metallic screech filled the room as Laina's wolf worked herself between the bars. She was almost free.

"I love you, Gerty," Kyle said. He swallowed a lump in his throat, prepared for the end. "You were the mother I never had."

A flash of light beamed through the room, blinding him before forming into an elderly woman in a sparkling aqua pantsuit, carrying a silver wand. "I love you too, Kyle."

"Gerty?"

With a crash, Laina barreled through the cage and bound straight toward them, snarling with teeth bared. Kyle could accept being torn apart, but he'd never forgive himself if something happened to Gerty. He squared his shoulders, made eye contact with the wolf, and yelled the only words he could think to yell. "No! Laina, stop!"

The wolf skidded to a halt at his feet, head down and tail between her legs. Kyle remembered that from his lesson with Laina. Submissive posture.

"She knows you, Kyle," Gerty said. "Even in her animal form."

He held out his hand, let her take a good sniff. "Is this real? Have I hit my head or something?" Instinctively, he scratched Laina's wolf behind her ears. As soon as he touched her silky chocolate-colored fur, the pain in his body eased. He sighed in relief.

"I didn't want you to find out this way," Gerty said.

"You knew about Laina?"

"From the moment she stepped through my protective spell."

Mouth gaping, Kyle faced the woman who'd been nanny, housekeeper, and friend.

"I've always been more than your nanny and your housekeeper," she said. "I'm your fairy godmother, Kyle. Your father hired me to look after you two in case something like this were to happen."

Kyle shook his head. "My father expected my girlfriend would be a werewolf?"

"It wouldn't have surprised him, Kyle. Your mother was a shifter after all, and Nate's mother was half ogre." She lowered her voice in the endearing way she did when she was broaching a sensitive subject. "Your daddy loved anyone exotic, and between you and me, he couldn't keep it in his pants to save his life."

Nate gestured wildly.

"What's wrong with him?" Gerty asked.

"The thing that locked us up in here zapped his vocal cords."

"Hmm. Don't make me regret this, Nate."

With a wave of her wand, Gerty muttered a string of syllables, then pointed the tip at Nate's throat. A shower of sparks cascaded over his Adam's apple.

"—get us the hell out of here!" Nate finished.

"You always were the direct one. Now, I imagine Laina wants to help her brother against that thing they call Alex. We must bring her to her siblings."

"Wait, Gerty. I have so many questions," Kyle pleaded.

She placed her hands on his cheeks, her gray brows lifting. "I know, Kyle. I've waited so long to be able to tell you the truth. Just wait a little longer. There is too much at stake." She threaded her fingers into his and hooked her arm into Nate's. "You'll have to carry her."

"Who? The wolf?"

"We have to be touching, or I can't transport us all."

Kyle looked into the golden eyes of the enormous dark beast before him. The woman he loved was in there; he was sure of it.

Kyle took a deep breath. "Laina, up." He patted his chest. Without hesitation, she leaped into his arms. His knees almost buckled, but he caught her. Gerty didn't waste the opportunity.

"Stars above and depths below, take us where we need to go." With a swirl of her silver wand, Gerty sent a shower of sparks toward the ceiling. The magic plumed out like a sparkling umbrella, encasing them in white-hot fire.

Kyle had the distinct impression of weightlessness, followed by tumbling. In the time it took to blink, the sparks rained down and disappeared in the grass and twigs now under his feet. The wolf's face brushed against his cheek as she pushed off his shoulders and took off running at full speed through the thick band of trees.

"Where are we?"

"Laina's brother Silas is no fool. He lured Alex behind Hunt Club. He must have figured out what I was. They're in the clearing behind the house."

"Alex will kill her entire family," Kyle said. "We've got to help them."

"This way," Gerty said, heading in the direction Laina had gone.

But Nate objected. "What do we know about these wolves anyway? I got no skin in this game. I'm not going to risk my neck to save three freaks I barely know."

Kyle turned to face Nate. "Then find your way back home or wait here. Either way, you're on your own." He jogged to catch up to Gerty.

It wasn't long before the growls and snaps of a full-fledged dog fight reached Kyle's ears. He ran faster, breaking from the trees into a clearing filled with fur, teeth, and claws. He found Laina quickly enough, her mink-colored fur shining silkily in the moonlight. He assumed the larger black wolf next to her was her brother Silas. His fur was darker and duller, and his jade eyes carried the wary look of a leader. The third wolf fighting side by side with them had a dark stripe that ran along his back from his ears to his tail, with a lighter, tawny underside that made him seem patched together.

Despite the odds being in their favor, the red wolf, whom he assumed was Alex, was winning the fight. He was faster, unnaturally so, and Silas and Jason sported bloody fur where Alex had struck successfully. When Jason turned, one entire leg was matted with blood, a pronounced limp putting him at a disadvantage. Silas's wolf wore a nasty gash across his shoulder.

Laina had arrived just in time. She reared up. Alex went for her throat.

"Gerty, do something!" Kyle said.

Gerty raised her wand but paused as if she were caught in an invisible tractor beam.

"Don't you dare," said a woman's voice from behind them.

Kyle whirled. "What are you doing here?"

The amulet around Nickie's neck pulsed faintly against her pale skin, framed by the red-and-black-sequined dress she wore. Designed to represent a twisting dragon with a ruby eye, the metal the amulet was constructed from resembled pewter, but Kyle sensed it was something else. Something magical. The energy radiating from it hit him in the face like the warmth of a small sun.

"You should go," Nickie said. "I don't want to hurt any of you, but I will if you get in our way."

"So, let Gerty go," Kyle demanded. His stomach cramped, and his spine popped with the return of the pain he'd felt moments ago. Fuck, he needed to get to Laina.

"I can't. She'll interfere. It's imperative that Alex succeeds in overpowering Silas on his own. If Gerty ends the duel, the pack will not recognize his authority. He is the one true ruler of all wolves. You must understand this." Her voice had taken on a slight foreign accent.

"What does any of this have to do with you?" Kyle asked. "Why do you care about Alex?"

"Why do you care about Laina?"

"Because I love—" Kyle froze, thinking back to the conversation between Alex and Laina in Nate's basement. "You're the dragon fae princess."

"My name is Nickelova Rallinth, heir to the Siberian dragon fae dynasty."

"But I thought you were scorned. I thought you hated Alex!"

"A lie my parents told to save face. They couldn't admit that their oh-so-perfect daughter freely gave the amulet to a wolf. They never understood our love. Never understood that Alex was born to rule, and I was born to be by his side. He's stronger than you, any of you."

"Let her go, Nickie." Kyle buckled under another wave of pain.

Nickie shook her head. "No."

A small tree, four inches in diameter, barreled out of nowhere and connected with the side of Nickelova's head, knocking her to the grass. Nate tossed the branch aside. "Stupid broad. Nobody hurts our Gert and gets away with it."

"Nate! Thank God," Kyle said.

Nate grabbed Kyle by the shoulders and shook. "Did Tanaka slip something in our drinks, or did we fall down the rabbit hole?"

"Unfortunately, this is all real."

"For the record, I never meant to hurt you. I thought Alex was going to offer her a job, lure her away. I had no idea he wanted to kill her. Fuck, who woulda thought he was some kind of supernatural creature?"

Beside them, Nickelova groaned and rubbed the back of her head. "You want to make it up to me, brother? Help Gerty kick this chick's ass."

"Leave it to me," Nate said.

Kyle turned his attention back to the wolves, brawling in the nearby field. Fuck, Alex had the upper hand once again. As another wave of pain rolled through him, Kyle assessed the scene. Jason lay on his side, incapacitated. Silas limped, front leg tucked close to his sternum. Laina and Alex were entangled in a brawl that seemed destined to end in the larger red wolf's favor.

Kyle's entire body trembled with rage. Sweat broke out across his skin. He had to get to Laina, had to protect her, had to...he had to. "Ahh!" His legs buckled under him, and he pitched forward, claws sprouting from his knuckles, the hair on his arms transforming to gray fur. He tried to scream, but all that came out was a howl.

"Kyle, oh my God. Oh my God!" Nate cried.

Kyle charged toward the wolves with his fiercest growl, his thoughts suddenly simple as black-and-white. He must kill. He must save his mate.

THIRTY-THREE

As the first rays of sunlight broke the horizon, Laina's human brain became aware of a few things. Kyle was naked in the grass beside her, gray fur erupting and receding over his spine, and his limbs twisted in a half-shifted state. Shit. Slowly, the memories came back to her. Alex had been about to kill her when Kyle had shifted into a glorious gray wolf and tore into Alex's side. Kyle was a werewolf, and he'd saved her life. All of their lives. Jason was injured, his leg hanging at a grotesque angle as his skeleton began its slow shift back to human. And Silas... He was still trying to fight, inserting himself between Kyle and Alex where he could, but the grass was stained red from their blood. Kyle's blood. Most of it was his.

Without guidance or practice, Kyle couldn't hold on to his wolf. His upper body had already transformed, and goddess, he was injured—shredded was a better word—with so many scratches and bites, he looked like a bloody piece of meat. Using bare human fists, he punched the half-shifted Alex in the face, powered by will alone. Silas, as the eldest, was the last to start his shift, but finally, he could not deny the sun. His black wolf's bones started to bend and break. The distraction allowed Alex to gain the advantage.

"No!" Laina yelled. It came out as a growl. Her wolf form battled her human one for control. Flashes of lucid thought drove her forward, but her breaking bones betrayed her. The pain was excruciating. She yelled for Gerty, but the fairy had problems of her own.

Gerty and Nickelova were battling to the death, resorting to physical blows as fatigue set in and their magic grew weak. A shower of sparks flew from the rolling mass of shredded sequins, fists, and teeth. The spell carved a path above Laina's head toward Hunt Club. She couldn't tell if the source was Gerty or Nickie, but she heard glass shatter in the distance.

As Alex raised his open jaws above Kyle's head, Laina cried out. Her wolf's paw shot forward, dragging her toward him as patches of human skin erupted like boils through her fur. Although the process of shifting was inhibiting her, she dreaded its completion and actively worked to hold her animal form. She needed the wolf. She needed to be strong to save Kyle.

Suddenly, a blur of tawny brown rushed past her. Milo! One hundred sixty pounds of mastiff plowed the red wolf off his owner and straddled Kyle's bloody body. In her half-shifted state, she could see the purple aura surrounding the dog, the same aura she'd seen over Kyle's residence. Milo was enchanted!

Alex swiped a paw toward the mastiff, only to have his massive claws bounce off Milo's protective barrier. Alex growled in frustration. This was Laina's chance! On half-shifted limbs and breaking bones, she army-crawled toward him, each inch more excruciating than the last.

Closer. Closer. Alex spasmed in the bloody grass. She raised her head and, with a growl, sank her teeth into Alex's belly, a belly quickly shifting from wolf to human. Her wolf teeth tore through liver and spleen, human blood flowing over her tongue.

His human eyes met hers, even as his blood dripped from her now-human lips. It was a fatal bite, and he knew it as well as she did. His dark eyes flashed. He coughed, and a drop of blood stained his bottom lip.

An unseen force tossed her aside. Nickelova stood over Alex, dress torn. She peered at Laina, one of her eyes swollen shut. Deep scratches marred the flesh around her neck, and Laina flashed on hazy memories of Nate and Gerty trying to rip the dragon fae amulet off her.

Laina tipped onto her side, her fingers elongating in the bright glow of the rising sun. She had nothing left. If Nickelova attacked, she'd be dead.

But the dragon fae had problems of her own. Her knees wobbled as she scooped Alex's shivering body into her arms. She stared down at Laina and bared her teeth. The shear hate in the other woman's eyes goose-pimpled her flesh. "This isn't over," she said through her teeth. The amulet pulsed, and she was gone.

Laina spat the taste of Alex's blood from her mouth. "Kyle? Kyle!" Milo stepped aside as Laina crawled toward him. She patted the mastiff's neck. "Good boy, Milo. You did a good job."

Kyle was completely shifted back to human now, and he wasn't moving. Swallowing her fear, she knelt beside him and felt for a pulse. There was so much blood, so many wounds.

"We have to get him help." Gerty limped toward her. The old woman was missing one shoe, her gray hair completely loose from her chignon, and several large rips decorated the leg of her pantsuit.

"Are you well enough to gather the wounded together? I can only transport us if we are all touching."

"Transport us? How will you transport us?"

"Fairy magic, dear."

"You can do that?" She didn't know much about fairies and was still getting used to the idea of Gerty being one. Her wolf memories flashed back to her.

"Laina," Silas called. He was crouched naked by Jason, one arm hanging at an odd angle at his side. Even from a distance, Laina could see bone protruding above Silas's elbow, and in front of him, Jason wasn't moving at all. Scooping Kyle into her arms, she stood, her thighs straining with the effort of carrying him to Jason's side.

"One more, Laina," Gerty said, pointing to a dark mass across the clearing.

"Who is that?"

"Nate."

Laina shook her head. "He did this to us. He was working with Alex."

"He saved your furry neck! Tried to tear the amulet right off Nickelova and, if I might add, delivered a few impressive blows before she knocked him out. I've never seen a man take so much magical abuse and continue breathing."

"But I thought—"

"Alex may have bamboozled him into being his tool, but Nate did the right thing in the end. He needs help. I can get us to Bojingles Fae Hospital, but I have very little energy left. I can't do it twice."

Laina hobbled over to Nate, desperately wanting to ask where Bojingles Fae Hospital was. She'd never heard of it.

There was no way she was going to be able to lift Nate—the man weighed 300 pounds if he weighed an ounce—so she hooked her hands beneath his rounded shoulders and dragged him to the others. If the process hurt him in any way, it was not enough to rouse him. Laina knew he was alive only because his chest rose and fell at regular intervals.

"Very good." Gerty pressed a hand to her belly as if holding herself together. "Now link arms and pray this old tree has another ring in her trunk."

With a wave of her silver wand, Gerty gave Laina her first taste of fairy magic.

THIRTY-FOUR

Perched on the edge of the chair beside Kyle's hospital bed, Laina focused on the weave of the white blanket that covered him. The craftsmanship was exquisite, as if woven from spider's silk by the spider herself. Then again, maybe it was. One of many marvels of the Bojingles Fae Hospital.

The doctor, a blue man not more than two feet tall, had told her that if Kyle's supernatural side hadn't activated, he'd likely be dead. But because he had shifted, they could treat him with fire lily juice, a therapy that might kill a human. He'd heal quickly, although not as quickly as a full-blooded werewolf. Jason, whose injuries were almost as serious as Kyle's, had already woken up.

Kyle had lost so much blood. His skin was pale to the point of harboring a subtle gray tinge. As she stared at him, memorizing his profile and the line of his body under the spider web blanket, she was surprisingly numb on the inside. On an intellectual level, she understood he had shifted. He was a werewolf, like her. But the risk of losing him was too raw a wound for her to set aside her worry. If he'd died, it would have been similar in magnitude to losing her parents. To protect herself, she slipped into doctor mode, observing the situation from a distance with an icy, cold detachment, a stranger in her own body.

"How's he doing?" Silas asked, entering the room.

"Not well enough. They tell me he's healing, but I can't let myself believe it until he wakes up."

"Gerty saved our lives, bringing us here."

Laina focused on her brother. "What is she? I mean, I know she's fae, but—"

"She's Kyle's fairy godmother, a woodland fae. All woodland fae must return to their trees at regular intervals. Arthur didn't have knee surgery. He's been rejuvenating in his host tree. From what I understand, Kyle's father offered to buy and protect the land where her and her husband's host trees grow in exchange for her protection of his boys. Apparently the property is still owned by Kyle's family."

Laina remembered the story Kyle had told her about his father's death. "The cabin in Red Grove. Kyle and Nate wondered why their father went there to die. That explains it."

"Last night, when things were at their worst, it was Gerty who freed Milo to come help us. The dog was a gift from her to the senior Kingsley, enchanted for his protection. He never went anywhere without the dog because he knew Milo could protect him from a supernatural threat."

Laina marveled at the luck that Kyle had kept Milo, then deflated when she realized that if he hadn't, they would have never met, and Kyle wouldn't have needed the mastiff. She frowned at the implications, not prepared to go there. "What happened to Kyle's real mother?"

"No one seems to know. I'm a detective, but I couldn't find a thing on her. If Gerty knows, she's an excellent liar."

Silas scratched behind his ear. "What are you going to do about this, Laina?"

"What do you mean?"

"I know you love him, and it is painfully clear he loves you. But you are a werewolf princess targeted for assassination by a rogue wolf with a dragon fae girlfriend, a dragon fae strong enough to slip through a woodland fae's protection spell and live next to her undetected for two months."

Laina said nothing but hung her head and stared into her lap. "He's a wolf too. A wolf without a pack."

Silas frowned. "He is, and I hope you know that I will support your choice on this. He saved our lives by shifting when he did. You know, I want you to be happy."

"But?"

"Alex's magic, along with intense emotions, triggered Kyle's first shift. I can connect him with someone in Fireborn to mentor him if he shifts again. But I did some research into dormants, and as a half-breed, he may not. It's possible he could go back to his human life."

"And that's why you won't let us be together?" she snapped, sending death rays in his direction. She was so sick of Silas and pack politics keeping them apart.

Silas stroked one bushy brow with his thumb. "I'll support whatever you want to do, Laina. I swear I will. But you must know, his status as a werewolf isn't the issue here. You can't walk away from your role in the pack, even if you leave the pack. If Kyle is a part of your life, he needs to know that danger will be part of that equation. Alex *will* target him. He'll use him as a pawn."

"Alex is probably dead. I tore his liver in two."

"Nickelova will heal him. He'll want revenge. He'll want my head. And he knows who Kyle is now. Alex will use him to manipulate you at the first opportunity to circumvent

Gerty's defenses. And thanks to Nickelova, he now knows more about those defenses than ever before."

Laina rubbed her eyes. "Nothing you're saying is making sense. If Alex knows who Kyle is, which we both know he does, and he knows how we feel about each other already, then abandoning Kyle now won't change anything. Do you really think Alex will leave him alone after what happened last night?"

"A madman's thinking is hardly prone to logic, but it seems that Alex's goal is revenge on our pack and the Lycanthropic Society. He can't go in two different directions at once. Kyle has a much better chance of survival if Alex is distracted with you and you are somewhere else. If Alex thinks your relationship has run its course, he won't split his efforts to pursue Kyle. He'll be too busy focusing his revenge on the three of us and Fireborn Pack."

Everything Silas said was true. Laina slumped in her chair. On some level, she'd known this day would come. Her pack needed her, and it was well past time for her to return to her old life, both for their sakes and to salvage her business. She did love Kyle, but her being here was always supposed to be temporary. Gerty and Milo could protect him here. Alex, when he recovered, *if* he recovered, would strike again, but now that the protective wards were in place at Four Paws and Rivergate, they'd be ready for him. It was time to go back to her real life and to allow Kyle to have his. Her desire to keep him in her life was selfish. He deserved better. He deserved to be safe.

"Maybe someday, when Alex is truly dead—"

Laina groaned and waved a hand dismissively. "Someone else will take his place. There will always be some crazy, power-hungry creep with our family in its crosshairs, as long as you are alpha and leader of the Lycan-thropic Society."

Silas shrugged. "Maybe. Maybe not. Again, I'll back you up, whatever you want to do here, but I just—"

"You wanted me to be aware of the danger I'm putting him in if we stay together."

Silas nodded.

The pain that radiated from Laina's heart was unbearable. "Excuse me." She stood and strode from the room, plucking a Kleenex from the box at the nurses station as fresh tears poured from her eyes. She headed for the privacy of the bathroom.

"Laina?" Jason snagged her elbow, pulling her into an alcove of vending machines.

Laina stopped crying long enough to grab Jason's upper arms and scan his dark T-shirt and jeans for any signs of the devastation his body had once endured. "Goddess, you're as good as new."

"Fire lily juice. Who knew?"

"Apparently, our pack needs to improve relations with the fae." She dabbed her eyes.

"Why are you crying?"

"Oh"—she pinched the bridge of her nose—"just real-izing that I should have listened to you. Kyle is lying in that bed because..." She drifted off, the tears flowing anew.

Jason pulled her into his arms. "I get it, all right? I slept with Nickelova. I'm the reason Alex was able to find us to begin with. There's plenty of guilt to go around."

"What?" Laina pushed him back by the shoulders. "Who told you that?"

"I did," Silas said, coming into the alcove behind her. He slipped a silver coin into the coffee machine and pressed the button for black. Laina took a moment to appreciate that the offerings in the vending machines behind him included sardines and chrysanthemum flowers but not a single bag of Doritos. "Nickelova was probably searching all the supernatural safe houses in the country when she came across Jason. She would have sensed he was a wolf immediately, but she'd never met him in person. Once he got naked, the phoenix tattoo gave him away. Monty would have sniffed her out in an instant. So she took the job at Hunt Club, knowing Gerty's magic would mask her own."

"But why didn't Gerty sense what she was?"

"When Nickie was hired, they invited her in, allowing her to circumvent Gerty's wards. Then it was just a matter of finding a way to lure you out of hiding. When Monty sent you to Hunt Club, he handed you over to the enemy. Only, Alex was still on the outside, and Nickelova knew Gerty would sense him if he got too close to where she worked in the east wing. Together, they figured out a way to use Nate to lure all of us out." His bushy eyebrows sagged, and he fished the coffee from the machine. After one sip, his face twisted, and he frowned into the oddly colored brew. "Acorn coffee. I should have known."

Jason rested his hands on his hips. "It's my fault. I wish I'd never met Nickelova."

"No." Silas shook his head. "This is Alex's fault. He's a psychopath with a brainwashed, dragon-powered sidekick, who will stop at nothing to have his revenge. We didn't make him what he is. He did that to himself."

"I don't want to do this anymore," Jason said, his eyes finding Laina's. A tortured expression marred his face. "I just want to go home."

"Me too," Laina said.

With a shrug, Silas tossed the full coffee into the garbage

and gathered them both into a group hug. "Good news. River-gate Manor is fully protected and open for business. And I still have Grateful working on Four Paws too, Laina. You'll be able to go back in a matter of days. Cameron has agreed to let us stay at the manor, together, until we end this thing with Alex."

"You mean until we find him and kill him."

"There's no other way."

Laina glanced back toward Kyle's room. She could safely return to Four Paws. The idea should have thrilled her. Instead, her heart felt unexpectedly heavy. Goddess, she would miss him.

Jason grimaced, his eyes darting between Silas and Laina. "You're not thinking of leaving Kyle, are you? He's your wolf's vice! It'll kill you."

"It won't kill her." Silas slashed a hand through the air. "But it will likely save him."

Laina closed her eyes and drew a deep breath through her nose. Kyle wouldn't even be in that bed if it weren't for her. "I have to give him a chance at a life without all this violence. If I leave now, he might be able to go back to how things were before."

Jason's brow wrinkled in sympathy. He knew. Of anyone, he knew how this felt. She was splintering into a million pieces. She was dropping into an eternal, dark abyss. Nothing would be the same after Kyle. Nothing. The only thing strong enough to break the bond she had with Kyle was the bond itself. She loved him enough to leave him.

"I'm sorry, La." He pulled her into a hug and kissed the top of her head.

"I know," she said softly.

"Do you want to leave him a note for when he wakes

up?" Silas's tone was soft and kind. "Or we could wait, but—"

"It would only make it harder," she finished for him. "No, I think the less that is said, the better. Besides, I'd never find the words."

Silas wrapped an arm around her shoulders. Without another syllable, they left for home.

THIRTY-FIVE

Kyle stared at the spoon in front of his lips but refused to eat. Some part of him understood he was acting like a child, but he didn't care. His body might have healed over the last weeks, but his heart was irreparably broken.

"Milo," he called, patting the bed beside him. The mastiff crawled onto the mattress and snuggled in close, resting his head on Kyle's chest and whining softly. "You miss her too, huh, boy?"

"Not this again," Gerty said, plunging the spoon back into the bowl of enchanted oatmeal she'd made for her patient. "It's time for you to move on."

"But how could she just *leave* like that?"

"What other choice did she have? Her people need her. She had to go home. Your business needs you. You need to stay here. What type of relationship would be possible under those conditions?

"We could have worked something out if she'd given us a chance."

"It was for the best, Kyle. She's a werewolf princess with

a price on her head. You're a hybrid entrepreneur. She understood there was no future for the two of you that didn't involve putting you in mortal danger. You should be thankful she was brave enough to do the right thing and end it when she did." Gerty sighed.

"That's the real reason why she left, isn't it? To keep me safe. Just like she took that bullet for me."

"I'm fairly sure that bullet was meant for her, but yes, I believe your safety had much to do with her wise decision to leave. And the fact that if she stayed with you, her presence would likely draw out your wolf. As it is, with the right potion, I can make your animal go dormant again. You won't have to shift. You can live as a human." He thought about the pain it had caused him to turn into a wolf. Pain and losing himself to his animal brain. The loss of control was almost as bad as feeling his bones break. The thought of shifting again didn't excite him, but it wouldn't have been enough to keep him away from Laina, if she hadn't left him. "Now, come. You must eat. You're wasting away."

He shook his head. "I'm tired. Why don't you take the rest of the day off?" He curled on his side away from her and closed his eyes.

Gerty made a disapproving grunt and left the room in a huff. Several minutes later, footsteps entered the room again. "I told you I'm not hungry."

"Move over," Nate said. "My back is still killing me."

Although Milo protested, Kyle managed to scoot the mastiff over and make room for Nate's considerable girth. "You feelin' better?"

"Yeah. Practically good as new. Can't you tell?" Nate held up his right arm, still in a cast, and flopped back on the pillow.

"How 'bout you?"

"Gerty says the scars on my face won't ever go away." Kyle pointed to a bite mark that ran from his left cheekbone to his jaw and continued under his chin. He didn't remember the moment the bite happened or precisely when he'd passed out from either pain or blood loss, but after weeks of magical treatments, the shiny silver scars had proved there to stay.

A rumble of laughter bubbled from Nate's chest. "Don't worry, kid. You're still prettier than me."

"She left me, Nate."

His brother sighed deeply. "I heard. I had to threaten Gerty with breaking her wand, but she told me. Obviously, she feels this is the best way to protect you. I mean, the chick took a bullet for you. Why? I will never understand. Personally, I'd find that level of commitment suffocating. Not you. You seemed to enjoy monogamy. Bleck."

Kyle rolled over to get a better look at his brother. "Of course I enjoyed it. I had real intimacy, Nate, for the first time in my life. She loved me for me—not for what I had, not for who I was, for me. I'll never find that again."

"Most people never find that at all," Nate said toward the ceiling. There was a long stretch of silence. "What do you plan to do now with all your free time?"

Kyle furrowed his brow. "Free time? You mean while I recover?"

"No, I mean now that you can't work at Hunt Club. The board is asking for your resignation. You effectively quit your job before this all went down, and the general consensus is that Hunt Club can get along without you."

"They can?" Kyle knew damn well that he'd been an integral part of leading the company and not just because he had a pretty face. But what was Nate up to?

"Yes. And actually, I was thinking that since you're not

exactly useful to us anymore, maybe you should take some time off at full pay and go to New Hampshire to manage the cabin Dad left us and the property with Gerty's trees."

"Yeah? You think I should?"

"And maybe, while you're at it, you should stop at this address." He pulled a piece of sparkly blue paper from his pocket and handed it to Kyle. "I had to pay a pretty penny to the nurse at Tinker Bell Memorial Hospital for that one."

"Tinker Bell Memorial?"

"Hell if I know the real name of the place. I'm just glad to be somewhere they don't sprinkle rose pollen on everything. I was still hopped-up on fairy dust when Gerty brought us home. Anyhow, that address was expensive, so it would be great if you, you know, checked it out."

"Whose address is this?"

"Whose do you think?" The corners of Nate's wide mouth spread almost to his ears.

"I can't just show up on her doorstep. She left me. What if she doesn't want to see me?"

"You know what the problem with you is? You've always been the pretty one. You've never had a girl tell you no, so you don't understand that sometimes you gotta, you know, sell the goods. Chicks tell me no all the time. But I get more fox than a chicken coop because I'm persistent."

"What are you trying to say?"

"I'm saying, you go after her, shit-for-brains. And considering she's a werewolf, I wouldn't do it gently. Be the alpha. Take her back." Nate crossed his arms over his chest and closed his eyes.

Kyle turned the sparkly paper between his fingers. It took him less than a minute to make up his mind. Bounding from the bed, he snatched a suitcase from his closet, opened drawers and shoved clothes into it as fast as he could move. He pulled on his shoes as he stumbled with it toward the door.

"Don't you dare leave this dog here. I'm not taking care of it," Nate said, pointing at Milo.

"Milo, come." Kyle slapped his thigh. The mastiff jumped from the bed, tail wagging, and pattered after him. Man and dog slipped into the world like fallen sycamore seeds spinning on the wind, searching for a welcoming place to lay down roots.

THIRTY-SIX

"You're going to look like a snow queen," Becca said.

Laina's human friend and assistant finished zipping the tight waist of her fur-trimmed dress. The first snow of the year had blanketed Rivergate Manor in a thick layer of white that morning, hiding every imperfection in the garden that would serve as her aisle and altar. She supposed Becca was right; the white fur cuffs and hem of her dress, along with the diamond tiara that held her veil, fit the winter wonderland royalty motif. But even Becca had no idea that the chill in the air penetrated straight through Laina's skin, all the way to her heart.

"Thank you for doing this," Laina said.

"Are you kidding? I wouldn't miss it for the world. Since I found out you were a wolf, I've been dying to see this place. I'm so happy for you. All the time you were gone, I prayed they'd catch that asshole and you'd be able to come home. I never thought you'd find a husband too."

Laina gave Becca a small smile and nodded toward the door. "It's time."

Her human friend led the way to Rivergate's courtyard,

the snow-covered garden overflowing with flowers brought out minutes before. They'd only last for the ceremony in this chill, but they were beautiful. Over Becca's shoulder, Laina saw Cameron in the traditional belted wool robe of her people. He wore deep blue, Rivergate pack's signature color, the insignia of three parallel lines on the back to match his tattoo. She knew the ancient garb was probably scratchy and uncomfortable, but it was necessary for the ceremony. Both her dress and his tunic had one detachable sleeve that would be removed so that once they were married, the *Preotka*, or priestess, could carve Cameron's Rivergate tattoo under her phoenix tattoo and vice versa, forever uniting their packs through marriage. Children of their union would be able to choose which of the original packs to belong to upon their first shift.

The music started, and Becca strode down the short aisle, an icy breeze stirring her hair. Laina picked up the pillow holding two enormous fangs, one from the original ancestor of Fireborn pack, the other from the original ancestor of the Rivergate pack. Resting it on her upturned palms, she carried it to the altar and set it down beside Preotka Artemis, who was dressed in her crimson ceremonial robes.

When the music stopped, Preotka Artemis raised her hands. "Welcome, wolves, to the binding of Cameron James of Rivergate lineage and Laina Flynn of Fireborn pack. It is my honor to—"

The door at the back of the gardens slammed shut, and a large man with a very large dog stood at the top of the aisle. "Stop this, Laina," Kyle demanded, staring her right in the eye. "You will not marry him."

Inside her head, Laina's wolf whimpered, not out of fear but out of the desire to submit to Kyle's demands, to go back to that place where she felt warm and safe in his arms. "What are you doing here, Kyle?" She meant to sound firm, but the words came out like wisps of smoke.

"I'm here for you. You can't marry this guy." He stepped forward, Milo heeling perfectly at his side without a lead.

"Why?"

"Because you love me. You're mine. You promised yourself to me."

"Kyle..." Laina couldn't find any words. Her entire being was nothing but emotion. She wanted so badly. Wanted him. Ached to run into his arms.

"How is he here?" Preotka Artemis asked softly, referring to Rivergate's enchantment.

"I don't know," Laina whispered. Her eyes darted to Cameron, whose expression was curiously blank.

Kyle held out his hand, only a few feet between them now. "Come with me. I know this isn't what you want."

Her eyes burned, and she blinked repeatedly. "I can't, Kyle. It isn't...allowed." Her eyes darted around the garden. "Cameron, I.."

But Cameron wasn't paying any attention to her. Instead, he was looking quite dreamily at Kyle.

Kyle held out his arms and turned in a circle, the light catching on the scar on his face. Alex had put that there. It was a scar Kyle had earned defending her, a brutal-looking memento of the sacrifice he'd made for her.

"Let me introduce myself. I'm Kyle Kingsley. My mother was a wolf, and I'm a human hybrid. I fought Alex Ravien Bloodright and lived to tell the tale."

There was a collective gasp from the crowd.

"If anyone challenges my right to marry this woman— should it be her will to have me—please stand and allow me the opportunity to change your mind." He made a beckoning motion with his hands.

No one stood. There were a few muffled whispers, but no one dared challenge the imposing presence among them. Laina's heart galloped faster in her chest. Her wolf panted excitedly in her head.

"Goddess, Laina, that man has a set of brass balls," Cameron whispered. "If you don't run into his arms right now, I swear I will."

Heart thumping, she started for Kyle, when Silas cleared his throat.

"Ah, the brother alpha," Kyle said. "I remember saving your furry ass as well. Why are you looking at him, Laina? You're as much alpha on the inside as he'll ever be, and you know it."

Silence. Dozens of grim faces stared at him with dagger-filled eyes. A growl came from deep within the crowd.

Silas's lips pursed. "You don't understand how it is, Kyle."

"I understand that you'd be dead and most, if not all, of these fine people would be bowing down to Alex if it weren't for Laina and me. You can't deny that."

"I don't," Silas said through his teeth. The murmurs among the crowd grew louder.

Cameron shook his head and stepped down from the marital platform.

"What are you doing?" Laina asked.

"Helping you," Cameron said. "I'm your friend. I won't let you fall on your sword. If you're going to sacrifice yourself for the pack, I won't be the means. I couldn't live with myself." He strolled calmly down the aisle and disappeared through the glass doors.

Preotka Artemis sighed. "There is no law against binding a wolf and a hybrid. He brings himself willingly to your door. The goddess will allow you to open it if you choose."

Laina looked again to Silas.

Her alpha brother scratched the back of his head and scanned the staring faces of the crowd. After a long moment, Laina saw something come over him, a resolve, a softening of the shoulders. When he looked at her again, it wasn't as her alpha; it was as her brother. "Kyle's right. You've always found a way to do what you wanted to do. Your pack needs a brave and daring leader, a princess who knows her mind, not a mindless robot. As your alpha, I order you to choose for yourself, follow your heart, and do the thing that will bring you happiness." Silas rubbed his chin. "He's worthy of you."

Kyle's gaze turned back to Laina. "Not a single objection." He took another step toward her and held out his hand.

"It isn't safe for you to be with me."

"It isn't safe for anyone if I'm not with you," he whispered.

At war with herself, she thought about being strong, about protecting him, about doing the right thing for her pack. None of it mattered. None of it mattered if she couldn't have Kyle.

Slowly, she slipped her fingers into his. And he promptly yanked her off her feet and threw her over his shoulder to the loud murmurs of the crowd. "Nice meeting you all. Hope to see you again real soon." Kyle saluted as he carried her from the gardens, Laina bouncing on his shoulder.

Panting, Milo looked up at her from Kyle's side. She

didn't protest. Kyle could have carried her back to Sable Creek for all she cared. Instead, she watched the marble floor morph into the velvety blue of the north parlor. Kyle shut the door behind them and set her down on a chaise in front of a crackling fireplace. He sat down next to her, crossing his leg at the ankle and staring into the flames.

He said nothing, but as the silence raged on, Laina thought she knew what he was waiting for. "I'm sorry I left you. I wanted to keep you safe and give you room to do your work. I didn't want to ruin your life."

"Oh Laina, you didn't ruin me. You saved me. I was a puppet. Do you think I enjoyed being trotted out at the company's whim on the arm of some beautiful stranger hell-bent on advancing her career at my expense? No. I was numb, not happy."

"But your company..."

Kyle leaned on his elbows. "As it turns out, I've been let go from my position at Hunt Club."

"What?"

"Nate reassigned me as groundskeeper of our Red Grove property."

As if to back up his favorite human, Milo moved between them, nudging Laina's hand with his sloppy wet nose.

"You're moving here? Permanently?"

Kyle nodded. "I'll be living in our father's cabin where Gerty's and Arthur's trees are for the time being, but I am free to live wherever I want as long as I can maintain the grounds. I have a feeling, given the circumstances, I could convince Gerty to provide us with a protection spell anywhere we wanted if I asked."

There was no stopping the tears now. Laina let them flow down her face with abandon.

"Are you crying because you don't like the idea?" Kyle asked hoarsely.

She shook her head. "No. I'm crying because I have everything, everything I ever wanted. Only, what now?" She glanced toward the door.

"You're wondering why I brought you in here instead of marrying you on the spot?" He raised an eyebrow.

"Well, yes. After that speech…"

"Oh fuck yes, I want to marry you. But hell if I'm going to do it on that altar, with you in that dress, and the groom's spot still warm from another man's feet."

Breathless, she took his hands. "But you will marry me, in our own ceremony in our own time, and, um, will you join Fireborn pack?"

A slow smile spread across his cheeks. "I think I'd better. That other man—"

"Cameron—"

"He's all wrong for you." Kyle's gaze darkened. "You're mine, Laina, and I'm yours." He gathered her hands in his. "Let's make it official."

She released a deep exhale. "I should go tell the guests."

She started to rise, but he reached out, taking her face in his hands. And then he kissed her, long and deep, as if there wasn't a 160-pound mastiff watching, as if Alex was already dead, as if the entire world had melted away and left only them in a cocoon of their happiness. She thought back to what Jason once told her. Love might not be enough to change the world. He was right about that. But maybe, at least for today, it was enough to change her desire to live in it.

THIRTY-SEVEN

Days later, Laina woke to the blissful sound of birds singing, the chatter of foraging animals, and a warm stream of sunlight through a frosty window that baked her naked body. She rolled over, right on top of Kyle, who woke enough to wrap one arm around her waist before closing his eyes again.

"Haven't you had enough, woman?"

"Never."

"Seriously. Give the hybrid a break. Kyle. Need. Sleep. And maybe food."

"There's a combo grocery store and bait shop in Red Grove. Or we can drive into Carlton City for pancakes at Valentine's."

"Valentine's. The site of our almost first date. Awesome burger and chocolate cake, by the way."

"I'm aware."

"I'm in." He rubbed his sleepy eyes.

"And maybe, between the syrup and the bacon, we can decide if we want our wedding reception there."

That popped open his eyes and made him smile like

he'd won the lottery. "I like the sound of that. So you're still marrying me, eh? Despite my meager accommodations?"

She held up her left hand, allowing the sun to catch on the two-carat diamond he'd put on her finger the night before. "Your accommodations are nothing short of magical." In fact, the cabin had turned out to be safer than expected. On top of an enchantment by Gerty to keep all evil supernatural creatures out, they were practically neighbors to Silas's favorite witch, Grateful Knight, who, it turned out, had helped Kyle get into Rivergate Manor. Kyle said she was a sucker when it came to love. Silas seemed to think that her presence would keep Laina safe. She wasn't sure about that but was happy Silas approved of her new residence. Plus, it was close enough to Carlton City that she could commute to her animal clinic every day.

"I thought we could be married here in the spring, outside, between Gerty's and Arthur's trees. Is that too soon?" Kyle stroked her hair back from her face.

"I've always wanted a spring wedding." She traced his pectoral muscle with her finger. "You'll have to get our phoenix symbol tattooed on your shoulder."

"I've always wanted a tattoo. It seems we'll both have what we want." He flipped her over, positioning his hips between her thighs and entering her with a satisfied moan.

"I thought you were tired." She moved her hands to the small of his back.

"I guess you bring out the animal in me." His eyes flashed golden, and she grinned, her inner wolf sensing his. "I love you, Laina."

"I love you too. There's more to it than that, though. There's something you should know." She glanced away, unsure if this was the time to tell him about her wolf's obsession with him.

"Tell me."

"You're my wolf's vice, Kyle. You're her addiction. I felt it the moment I first saw you, and every time we're together, it grows stronger. Even when we shift, she's going to be obsessed with you."

He bit his bottom lip and grinned as he rocked into her, making her gasp.

"I'm more than willing to serve."

"What happened to 'you're mine'? I rather liked when you took what you wanted. Your possessive streak turns me the fuck on."

He drew back and thrust into her hard, his lips a breath away from hers. "You are mine. But I meant what I said before. You can be the alpha any time you choose. I think, Laina, you're my vice too. If this isn't obsession..."

She dug her fingers into his hair as he increased his pace. "Then it's settled. We're addicted to each other. It's a good thing there's an unending supply of us."

He kissed her wickedly. Laina hung her head off the edge of the bed and gave herself over to her love, her vice, and now her fiancé as he proved once again how very addictive he could be.

https://geni.us/FatedBondsBonus

Thank you for reading Fated Bonds, book 1 in the Wolves of Fireborn Pack trilogy. Want to make a little magic for the author? If you enjoyed this title, please leave a review wherever you buy books!

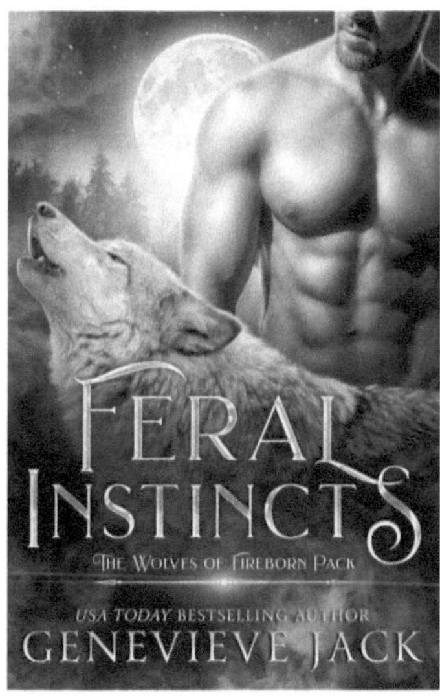

https://www.genevievejack.com/books/the-wolves-of-fireborn-pack/feral-instincts/

A WOLF DENIED CAN TURN FERAL.

Of all the Fireborn pack royalty, werewolf Jason Flynn is the most virile, his raging appetite for the opposite sex well known among his pack mates. What they don't know is that his lifestyle is a salve for the loss he endured when his potential fated mate was murdered by a rogue pack member. But when his playboy lifestyle becomes a risk to the pack, Jason is resolved to change his ways. Until a curse by an ex lover sends his libido into overdrive.

Selene Andrews is an acolyte to Preotka Artemis, Fireborn pack's high priestess. Adopted as a homeless teen, her only desire is to serve the pack as Artemis's successor. To advance, she must prove her mastery of the ritual magic required of a werewolf priestess.

When Artemis assigns Selene to help Jason break his curse, neither of them understands the danger. Jason's beast is feral with instinctive needs that acolyte Selene struggles to resist despite her vow of celibacy. Curing him will mean working through Jason's tortured past and facing her own. Only together can they truly heal... if they're both willing to to take a chance on each other.

Read more in Feral Instincts, Book 2 in the Wolves of Fireborn Pack.

MEET GENEVIEVE JACK

USA Today bestselling and multi-award winning author Genevieve Jack writes wild, witty, and wicked-hot paranormal romance and romantic fantasy. She believes there's magic in every breath we take and probably something supernatural living in most dark basements. You can summon her with coffee, wine, and books, but she sticks around for dogs and chocolate. Her novels feature badass heroines, fiercely loyal heroes, and fantasy elements that will fill you with wonder. Learn more at GenevieveJack.com.

Do you know Jack? Keep in touch to stay in the know about new releases, sales, and giveaways.

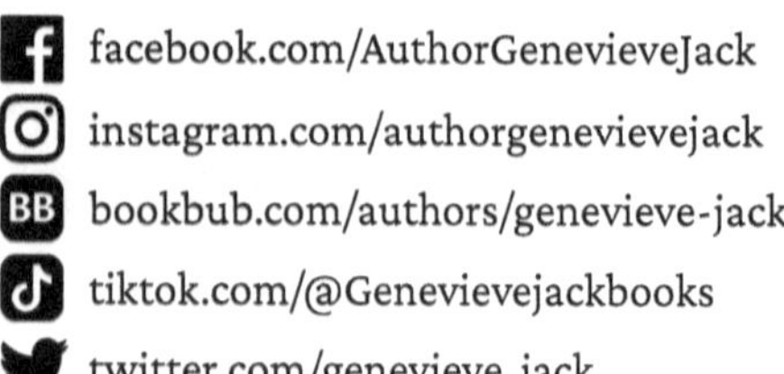
facebook.com/AuthorGenevieveJack
instagram.com/authorgenevievejack
bookbub.com/authors/genevieve-jack
tiktok.com/@Genevievejackbooks
twitter.com/genevieve_jack

MORE FROM GENEVIEVE JACK!

His Dark Charms Duet

Lucky Me

Lucky Us

The Treasure of Paragon

The Dragon of New Orleans, Book 1

Windy City Dragon, Book 2,

Manhattan Dragon, Book 3

The Dragon of Sedona, Book 4

The Dragon of Cecil Court, Book 5

Highland Dragon, Book 6

Hidden Dragon, Book 7

The Dragons of Paragon, Book 8

The Last Dragon, Book 9

The Angel of Paragon, Book 10

The Three Sisters Trilogy

The Tanglewood Witches

Tanglewood Magic

Tanglewood Legacy

Knight Games

The Ghost and The Graveyard, Book 1

Kick the Candle, Book 2

Queen of the Hill, Book 3

Mother May I, Book 4

Logan (companion novel)

The Wolves of Fireborn Pack Trilogy

Fated Bonds

Feral Instincts

Forever Mated